THE POISONED PARTRIDGE

Jacqueline Beard

The Constance Maxwell Dream Walker Mysteries are published by Dornica Press

The author can be contacted on her website
https://jacquelinebeardwriter.com/

While there, why not sign up for her newsletter and receive a FREE novella.

ISBN: 1-83-829558-5

ISBN: 978-1-83-829558-5

First Printing 2022

Dornica Press

The Constance Maxwell Dreamwalker Mysteries

The Cornish Widow
The Croydon Enigma
The Poisoned Partridge

Also, by this author:

Lawrence Harpham Murder Mysteries:

The Fressingfield Witch
The Ripper Deception
The Scole Confession
The Felsham Affair
The Moving Stone
The Maleficent Maid

Short Stories featuring Lawrence Harpham:

The Montpellier Mystery
A Peculiar Puzzle (newsletter only)

Box Set (Kindle only) containing
The Fressingfield Witch, The Ripper Deception & The
Scole Confession

Novels:

Vote for Murder

The Poisoned Partridge

CHAPTER ONE

At Peace in Gorran Haven

Monday, October 3, 1932

I lean against the harbour wall in Gorran Haven, fighting the urge to throw myself into the sea. It is nearly nine o'clock in the evening, and tomorrow I will return to Pebble Cottage to resume my life of imprisonment with Mrs Ponsonby. Not that I have been at liberty here, as she is still fussing over me like the proverbial mother hen, but there is something peaceful about Gorran. I have felt calmer and less anxious since our arrival four weeks ago.

Oriel House is a wide, double-fronted fisherman's cottage, carefully chosen for its proximity to the beach. Mrs Ponsonby, in a rare moment of consideration, sought a property within easy walking distance of the sea to help with my recovery. Gorran Haven was not the first location on her list or even in the top three. Mevagissey, Polperro and Fowey were too steep in her opinion, and I couldn't persuade her to take a cottage in

1

Bosula where I could have seen my friend Mary. Fortunately, Isla Tremayne knew someone with a suitable place to rent, and before I knew it, we had decamped from Pebble Cottage and were en route to Gorran. The nightmares stopped soon after we arrived, and I knew she had made the right choice.

The most peculiar dreams had plagued me since falling ill back in the summer. Something happened in my sleep, but I cannot remember what. One day, when I didn't appear at the breakfast table, Elys came to my room to see what was wrong. She couldn't rouse me and took immediate action when she saw a trail of blood running from my nose onto my bedclothes. They rushed me straight to Plymouth hospital, where I remained unconscious for several weeks. And when I awoke, Mrs Ponsonby insisted on my removal to the same convalescent home in Newquay that Dolly used two years before. Back then, the house was called Sunnyside, and I remember seeing lots of grim-faced nurses and docile patients. It had not improved since being renamed The Pines, a peculiar choice as there wasn't a conifer in sight. I swear they chose the first name they could think of to shake off the poor reputation it had previously enjoyed. I was so ill when I first arrived that I didn't care about the shabby surroundings and half-hearted staff. And I couldn't interact with them much anyway, as Mrs Ponsonby was there from dawn to dusk, and when she wasn't there, Elys was. But after two weeks in Plymouth and another three in The Pines, I felt well enough to beg them to come home. And after consulting with Kit Maltravers, Mrs Ponsonby agreed.

Then the nightmares began almost every night. I couldn't bear them in my head or face my fears with dignity. Every terrible dream preceded a shrieking, screaming torrent of emotions as I thrashed from side to side, sweating and crying for a mother I had never known. Dr Maltravers prescribed sleeping pills, and although they gave a brief respite from time to time, I still suffered dreadfully, too afraid to sleep and permanently exhausted from broken nights and a fractured memory. The nightmares went on for weeks, but when Mrs

Ponsonby pulled a camp bed into my room one night and said she would sleep with me in future, I realised enough was enough and asked Elys for her advice. And, wise beyond her years, Elys said she thought a change would be as good as a rest and would have a word with Mrs P. She did, and that is why I am currently clinging to the harbour wall, feeling as if I am saying goodbye to an old friend.

Gorran has been good to me. I have wandered down to the beach every day, stick in hand and not taking any chances with my recovery. I have made friends with an old fisherman who sits outside sewing his nets by the wooden shack facing the sea. He tells me tales of the shipwrecks on the Dodman and the large cross erected as a holy navigation aid. Old Barney has lived in Gorran all his life, as his father did before him. Marriage never tempted him, and he says he is wedded to the sea. Barney sails whenever he can, although he is seventy if he is a day. But his life of quiet industry and his love of nature leave me less fearful for the future. I may never marry or have a family, but I will always yearn for the sea and the great outdoors, especially now I have Teddy.

Teddington Douglass is the reason I haven't thrown myself from Gorran Haven's harbour wall, not that it would do any good as I am too close to shore, and someone is bound to rescue me. The good-natured cocker spaniel I inherited from Maud Douglass has changed my life and given me a responsibility that matters more than I do. I had only been home for a few days when Maud visited me out of the blue, having written to Peter Tremayne. She had found his address among Jim's personal documents on the third page of a letter, the previous two of which were missing. Seeing my name, Maud sent an urgent telegram asking for my address. Peter naturally replied by return, advising her of my poor state of health, to which she wrote back immediately, saying the situation was desperate. It was. Jim had gone missing, and nobody knew where he was. Even the police couldn't help. He had vanished as if he had never existed. Reluctantly, Peter gave my address to Maud, and she arrived early one morning accompanied by Isla Tremayne, who had met her at the station. She had warned Mrs Ponsonby, who gave her consent to our meeting, on the strict condition that it did not go past ten minutes.

Maud Douglass was beside herself with grief and worry. And I wanted to help her so badly, but I could barely remember a thing. Jim and I had played amateur detectives with a poisoning case in Croydon, but whether our investigations were fruitful was another matter. I didn't know where he was, and I couldn't say for sure when I had last seen and spoken with him. I could only remember his dear face and wondered what our relationship had been that my heart hurt so badly at the thought of never seeing him again. The Croydon constabulary declared Jim a missing person, and his mother, distraught at the loss of her son, was heading to Alnwick the following week to stay with her old school friend but didn't know what to do with Jim's dog.

The moment she mentioned Teddy, I burst into tears, heaving great racking sobs at the memory of Jim petting his beloved animal, and I knew Teddy would save me. I begged Mrs Ponsonby to let me have him, and she agreed without argument, offering to collect him off the train if Mrs Douglass loaded him up at the other end. And that's what happened. Less than a week later, Teddy came down in the mail carriage and arrived at Pebble Cottage in the afternoon. Mr Moggins, household cat and master of all he surveyed, was unamused. Fortunately, Mrs Ponsonby had already booked Oriel House, and Teddy and I have become firm friends while staying in beautiful Gorran.

I drop my cane, slide down the wall and slump in an unladylike heap against the harbour, watching owls swoop low in the distance. The thought of returning to Porth Tregoryan weighs heavily on my mind. I can't face the nightmares again, and somehow, they belong there, haunting me in my home like spiteful wraiths. Oriel House has given me eight hours of sleep a night, lying in bed with Teddy curled into my knees while

Mrs Ponsonby turns a blind eye to his presence, even though she promised the owner he would stay downstairs. Scratching Teddy's head, I see his soft, soulful eyes and return his gaze, acknowledging our shared sadness at Jim's absence and wondering if we will ever see him again. I put my head in my hands and squeeze my eyes shut, trying in vain to remember our last conversation. Was it over the telephone? Perhaps, but that is only a guess, a fleeting pop of memory that lingers for a second and then floats out of sight. I have other daydreams where I feel aloof and detached from my body – almost as if I were flying. I mentioned them to Peter when he visited me at The Pines, and he responded with a puzzled expression and an odd remark about the benefits of memory loss. There is nothing remotely helpful about the white blocks occupying the space where my recollections ought to be. But for some unaccountable reason, Peter is relieved and has told me not to be silly, and that dreams are dreams and nothing more. Still, now, and then, I feel a strange tugging in my head that I cannot adequately explain, and part of me wants to run across the cliffs as if I had two working legs. Sadly, I do not, and after another ten minutes of contemplation, I force myself to my feet and trudge towards the shore, Teddy walking obediently at my feet.

We pass the old shack, and I wave to a man who isn't there, thinking fondly of Barney and how much I will miss him. Then, picking my way across the sand, I turn onto Church Street and walk down the narrow road to Oriel House. I enter for the last time, cast a rare smile at Mrs Ponsonby, who is reading a book, and make my way upstairs. I sit at my dressing table, remove my writing pad, and fill my ink pen. Mary Newson has written to me every week. She offered to visit, but Mrs Ponsonby wouldn't hear of it. I am much better now, and my hair is growing over the scar from the surgery on my head. So, if Mary can't visit me here, she must come to Pebble Cottage. I start my letter and extend an invitation to that effect, not knowing or caring if Mrs Ponsonby minds. After addressing the envelope, I return downstairs to put it on the side for one of us to post on our way back tomorrow. I am just preparing to go back up when Elys appears clutching a mug of cocoa.

"Go on," she says, thrusting it in my direction. "You must be cold."

"A little," I admit.

"Why so late?"

"I couldn't tear myself away. I will miss this place."

"We've had a good time," she says generously. We dragged poor Elys here very much against her will. She would have preferred to stay with Jory and make her wedding plans, but the thought of spending four weeks alone with Mrs Ponsonby was more than I could bear, and I am ashamed to say that I indulged in a heinous orgy of emotional blackmail to persuade her to join us. It worked, and she came, but she has paid her penance and thoroughly deserves to be reunited with her betrothed when we return tomorrow evening.

"Will you be alright?" asks Elys, seeing a tear that has slipped unnoticed from my eye. I brush it away.

"I'm sorry. I didn't mean to…"

She doesn't let me finish the sentence and draws me into her before hugging me tightly. "It will get better, I promise," she says.

"It's this space, this darkness. The things I can't remember are important, but I don't know why."

"Better not to think about it," she says.

"That's what Kit told me. He said my memory might never return. But I don't think I can go on with this dreadful void in my head. It's killing me."

"No, it isn't. You've made remarkable progress," says Elys. "It was touch and go for a while, Connie. We feared you would die. You're over the worst of it, and if losing part of your memory is the price you must pay, then so be it. A bleed on the brain is serious. You could have lost your ability to talk, think, or move around – honestly, Connie. Please see the good in your situation. If you think yourself well, you will become well."

Elys sounds just like Kit Maltravers. She has quoted him

almost word for word. A spike of anger flashes inside, but I swallow it down. Elys is right. I am looking on the dark side when I should be grateful that most of my faculties are in working order. I squeeze her hand.

"Noted," I say and head for my bedroom.

CHAPTER TWO

Going Home

Tuesday, October 4, 1932

We arrive at Pebble Cottage late in the afternoon to the sight of Isla Tremayne emerging from our front door, closely followed by Peter.

"Why are they in our cottage?" I ask, confused by their presence.

"Isla offered to straighten things up for our return," said Mrs Ponsonby, waving graciously to her friend with all the grandeur of King George.

"I hope she has set the fire," said Elys, not relishing the thought of that on top of the unpacking.

"She won't do it herself," said Mrs Ponsonby, "but I expect she's brought her housekeeper."

As it happened, she had not. The Tremayne household was in chaos due to a nasty bout of gastric flu, which had laid the servants low. But despite their problems, Isla and Peter had turned out to help, as promised. And not only had Peter set the fire and put the shopping away in the larder, but Isla had baked a cake and prepared a high tea for our return. She was about to leave when we arrived, and Mrs Ponsonby naturally asked her to join us. While Elys took a plate of sandwiches upstairs and started her chores, we sat down to tea in the parlour.

Mrs Ponsonby begins a lengthy monologue about our time in Gorran Haven while Isla nods politely, and Peter and I wolf down the cake. And as soon as we finish, Peter tips me the wink, and I ask Mrs Ponsonby if she minds if we go for a walk. Peter fetches my coat, and as I adjust my hat, I see a note on the dresser in Jory's messy hand. "Dolly says Mr Fox telephoned the hotel, asking for you. Please return his call."

I stare at the note, trying to decipher its meaning, and must have pulled a puzzled face as Peter notices and asks what I am reading. I hand him the message, and he screws it up and puts it in his pocket. "It must be a mistake," he says. "Come on."

"I'm sure it isn't," I reply, whistling for Teddy. "Mr Fox is Jim's neighbour. I wonder if they've found him. What else can Fox want with me?"

Peter holds out his arm, and I take it. We walk towards the beach in silence, Teddy running ahead, then Peter asks, "How much do you remember about your time in Croydon?"

I close my eyes and think. "I worked as Mr Fox's typist," I say. "His handwriting is awful, and he's an odd little man, but his wife is pleasant."

"Do you remember what you typed?"

"Notes about his dreams," I say. "He studied astral travel." I stop talking as I process the information I have just recounted as if it were yesterday. These memories have lurked out of reach up to now.

"I think he wanted to teach me how to dream walk," I say, vaguely recollecting time spent lying down in his study.

"And did you?" asks Peter abruptly.

"Don't be silly," I say. "It isn't real."

Peter stops walking and searches my face. "No, it isn't," he agrees. "And I'm sure Mrs Douglass would have contacted you by now if they'd found Jim. I wouldn't bother calling Mr Fox back. As you say, he is an unusual man, and there's no need to continue your association."

"It's rude to ignore him."

"Not really. You've been unwell, Connie. I'm sure he will understand. Anyway, Jory hasn't written the telephone number down."

"I hadn't thought of that. And it won't be in my room. All my important papers are missing."

"Which ones?"

"I'm not sure. I can't remember what I had. But I'm certain Jim wrote to me at least once or twice, yet I searched my room three times before we left for Gorran, and I can't find his letters anywhere."

"I'm sure they'll turn up," says Peter as we step onto the sand.

We walk towards my cave. The tide is high, and the sea wind is blustery. I drop Peter's arm and pull up my coat collar, trying to keep warm. The temperature has dropped several degrees since yesterday.

"Shall we go inside?" I ask, unsure whether Peter wants to spend time in a cold, dark cave.

"Of course," he says, grinning broadly.

And the moment I go inside, I can see why he is so pleased with himself. My solitary chair has multiplied into two, both containing comfortable cushions and a blanket draped over the back. Peter has replaced the worn crate with a solidly built trunk stacked high with old library books.

"Peter. I don't know what to say. How kind."

"It was my pleasure," he says, smiling benevolently.

"But what's happened to my old books?" I ask, sifting through the new collection.

Peter's smile falls from his face. "They were getting tatty."

"I know. I came here once, and the books were all over the floor. They were a bit dogeared, but not ruined. Don't think I'm being ungrateful, but I would love to have them back."

Peter sighs. "I'm afraid that won't be possible."

"Why ever not?"

"Sit down, Connie," he says, gesturing towards the chairs. "And put a blanket on. Let's not take any chances with your health. Now, look at your chair."

"Oh, that's not my chair at all."

"It's as close a match as I could get. I hoped I wouldn't have to tell you this, and I should have known better than to think you wouldn't remember your old books. But while you were away, someone destroyed the entire contents of your cave. Dolly uses it occasionally and came down one day to find the remains of your furniture and a few soggy books in the sea. She called me, and we did our best, but it was all too damaged to save."

"Not again. And why would anyone do such a thing?" I ask, my voice shaking with anger. "I must have made an enemy. This isn't the first time."

"I'm sure you haven't. Some people are destructive by nature. They see something nice and resent it because it doesn't belong to them. I've witnessed this behaviour many times in the library – people tearing pages out of books for no obvious reason or scribbling on them. They do it because they can. You mustn't worry, Connie. Your cave is perfectly safe, and I'm sure it won't happen again."

"It isn't," I say as a flash of memory paints the bottom of my stick red. I stare at it, trying to remember when it happened and why. "I found blood on the bottom of my stick after one of my visits to the cave, and I think it happened when the books got damaged."

"You probably picked it up somewhere along the sand," says Peter. "Perhaps from an injured animal or a dying bird."

"Perhaps," I say uncertainly. But something nags at the back of my head, a feeling of apprehension and danger.

Peter stares at me, eyes round with concern. "You would tell me if something was wrong?" I ask spontaneously. I don't know

11

why I ask, but it feels like a question that needs answering.

Peter pauses. "Nothing is wrong," he says.

I lean back in my chair and stare towards the sea, listening to the soporific waves rolling across the sand. A feeling of belonging has replaced my unease.

"Have you missed the old place?" asks Peter, sensing my mood.

I nod. "Gorran Haven is idyllic," I say. "And I will go there again one day. But I have lived here for so long that it has a place in my heart nowhere else can fill."

"Good girl," says Peter, with a crooked smile.

"How about you?" I ask. "Are you still living the thespian dream?"

Peter looks away, and a scowl slips across his face. "I've left the drama group."

"But why? You loved it."

"I've got better things to do."

"No, you haven't. What's going on?"

"I don't want to talk about it," says Peter curtly.

"You're jolly well going to. We're friends. Besides, you won't let me keep secrets, and I won't allow it from you."

"Don't be pushy," says Peter.

"It's better out than in," I say. "You'll feel much better once you've said it."

"You won't let go of this, will you?"

"No," I reply firmly.

"It's Frank," he says, and I feel a lurch of unease at the look on his face. Frank and Peter have been constant companions for the best part of last year, and though I have known Peter forever, I'm not quite sure what makes him tick. By which I mean, I'm aware he likes Frank, but how much and in what way, he's never said, and I am far too polite to ask. I fear I have forced Peter into revealing something he would rather keep private.

"You don't have to tell me," I mumble, blushing lobster red.

"It's not what you think," he replies with a wry smile.

"Then what happened?"

"I thought Frank was my friend, but that snake in the grass auditioned for my part."

"Your part?"

"The one I wanted. It was only a one-act play with a small cast, but Noel Coward is my hero, and that part should have been mine."

"What happened?"

"I caught a cold while you were away, didn't go to the drama meeting that week, and missed the audition announcement. Frank knew how much I wanted the role, but he didn't tell me and auditioned himself instead. And he got it. We are barely speaking, and I can't bring myself to watch him prancing along the stage at rehearsals."

"Can't you get another part?"

"There are only three actors, and the other two are female."

"You should go anyway and rise above it. After all, Frank might have got the part through fair means had you both auditioned."

"Never," says Peter, visibly seething.

We remain in the cave for a while longer, but talk of Frank has soured our time together, and I am relieved when Peter suggests we return to Pebble Cottage.

CHAPTER THREE

Amnesia

Friday, October 7, 1932

Three days later, I am moping around the house, feeling a little healthier in body but subsumed with an overwhelming sense of grief. Kit Maltravers is a frequent visitor, ministering to my medical needs with kindness and concern. A year ago, I would have been giddy with excitement at seeing so much of the handsome doctor, but Jim's loss has tempered my feelings and changed them from longing to gratitude. Soon after breakfast, Kit arrived and flew through the usual medical checks in Mrs Ponsonby's presence. But then, to her disgust, he asked her to leave the room so he could speak to me in private.

"You can speak freely about Constance in my presence," she had said, drawing herself to her full height and fixing him with a steely gaze. "She doesn't mind."

"But I do," Kit had said firmly. "I need a few private moments with my patient if you would be so kind."

Mrs Ponsonby had glowered, and I feared she would argue

14

the toss, but after a moment of palpable tension, she had left the dining room, closing the door with a firmness it didn't require. I am now alone with Kit and feeling somewhat puzzled.

Kit, who had been standing during the encounter with Mrs P, takes a seat opposite me and clears his throat. "What is wrong, Connie?" he asks.

"Nothing," I say, feeling awkward in his presence for the first time since he began treating me.

"Something is," he replies, searching my face.

I can't meet his gaze. It is too intimate, and the heat rises in my body, forcing itself upwards until a heavy blush settles across my cheeks. I am burning with shame and embarrassment.

"I'm sorry, Connie," he says, immediately noting my discomfort. "Here, take this." He pours a glass of water from the jug in the middle of the table and passes it to me. I seize it and take a sip. The flushing retreats as his distraction technique works, but I am still inwardly burning with humiliation.

He tries again. "You are recovering well," he says. "But I've known you for several years now, and your spirits are low. I'm pleased you took a break, and I can see you've made splendid physical progress, but you won't get better while you are miserable. I don't want to pry, but if you think a tonic or restorative might help, I can prescribe something."

"But will it help my memory return?" I ask.

"No. That will only happen over time, or not at all, as the case may be."

"I remembered something yesterday," I say.

"Well, that's excellent." Dr Kit beams as if I was a pupil who had just won a prize.

"It's frustrating," I say. "I barely remember anything, but when one memory returns, I feel others bobbing in my head, just out of reach. I know they are there, but I can't get to them. And I really must know."

"Your recovery is the only thing you should be concerned with," says Dr Kit, patting my hand.

I wish he hadn't. A flash of pleasure shoots through me,

15

followed by a wave of disgust at my body's disloyalty to Jim.

"You don't understand," I say.

"Then, tell me."

"My friend is missing," I say. "No one can find him, and I can't help thinking that there's something in my head that could help if I could only remember."

"Were you near him when he disappeared?" asks Kit.

"No. I couldn't have been. I fell ill in bed at home."

"Of course, you did," he murmurs. "Which rather suggests that you are worrying about nothing."

"But he wrote to me, and I can't find his letters anywhere."

"Are you sure?"

"About what?"

"That he wrote. If your memories are foggy, then how could you know?"

I ponder his words. "I remember reading them," I say lamely.

"What did he write?"

"I don't know." My voice quivers, then breaks as I disgrace myself by bursting into tears.

"There, there," says Dr Kit, patting my hand again. He reaches into his pocket and offers his handkerchief. I take it and try to hide the tears still streaming down my face. I try to speak, but my throat is raw with unspoken grief, and all I can do is sob.

Dr Kit says nothing but strokes the back of my hand with his thumb. Even though my loss of control and profound sadness has thrust me into this undignified outpouring, I still find time to wonder how Charlotte Napier would feel if she could see us now. Probably pity, and that thought saves me. The notion of her pious face had she witnessed me breaking down in front of her fiancé is enough to quell my tears. I wipe my face and look up.

"Do you remember anything about the night you fell ill?" asks Kit.

I shake my head. "Nothing," I whisper. I can't remember going to bed that night. Swathes of my recent life are missing."

"Do you remember your childhood?"

"Some of it."

"Do you remember the summer ball?"

I snatch my hand away from his, ashamed at the torrent of memories that return unbidden. "Yes. But only now you've mentioned it. I haven't thought about the ball in a long while. It was a horrible night. Did they find the ring?"

"Yes. Can't you remember?"

I screw my eyes tightly shut. "Yes," I say. "I'm allowed back in the library."

"Quite right," says Kit. "With an apology and your good name fully restored. Generally speaking, medically caused amnesia is slow to resolve, if it happens at all. Yet, with the right prompts, you've said that your recall returns, implying that there may be another underlying reason for your memory problems. And don't forget, you already have a history of childhood amnesia."

I nod. Kit has always been interested in psychology and has tried to help me remember my early childhood, to no avail.

"What do you mean?" I ask.

"I wonder if you are suffering from dissociative amnesia. Something more than the bleed on your brain."

"Such as?"

"A profound shock or an emotional trauma."

I shake my head. "I don't know. And how will I ever find out if I can't remember?"

"Do you want to?"

I think about the grey holes in my consciousness and the pops of energy flitting like fireflies inside my head, each a potential source of helpful information but firmly out of reach. I am curious, and I need to know.

"Yes. I want to."

"I've trained in a technique called hypnosis," says Kit. "Are you familiar with the concept?"

I nod. "But I thought it was for entertainment."

Kit smiles. "Not at all. The British Medical Association

17

accepted the therapeutic use of hypnosis last century."

"How does it work?"

"By guiding the patient into a trance-like state through peacefulness and relaxation."

I see a candle in my mind's eye – my hand, a moth, a row of pulsing words. I stare at Kit, my mouth hanging open.

"What's wrong?" he asks.

"I might have already done it," I say, trying to make sense of the disparate images.

"Someone hypnotised you?"

"I don't know. Perhaps. I can't quite get there..." My words trail away as yet another potential memory dissolves before I can capture it.

"I would like you to spend the next few days considering the prospect of hypnosis. It would not be without risk if a trauma triggered your memory loss. And you might try helping yourself in the meantime. Speak to your friends and family. Get them to talk about recent past events. Then, when it's quiet and you feel settled and relaxed, let those conversations drift through your mind. Solidify your recall and make it tangible. If that works, then so much the better. I'll visit again next week, and if you want my help to recover your memory, we can start with a little hypnosis. How does that sound?"

"Like a ray of hope," I say, a frisson of positivity breaking through the gloom.

"Good," says Dr Kit. "Now, don't get up. I'll see myself out."

He snaps his bag shut, stands, and leaves the room. I hear him say goodbye to Mrs Ponsonby and I am not in the least bit surprised when she makes straight for the dining room to grill me about our conversation.

"What did he want, dear?" she asks.

"Just a chat," I mumble.

"What about?"

"My amnesia."

"Can he help?"

"I doubt it," I say, feeling my newfound hope slide away

under the weight of her expectations.

She studies my eyes, and I realise they are probably still red from crying. I look away, but not before I see her eyes widen with concern. Mrs Ponsonby doesn't know how I feel about Jim. She is unaware of much that happened during my time in Croydon. But for Maud Douglass' visit, she wouldn't know he even existed. So, I cannot share my grief with her or my confusion about the extent of my relationship with Jim. Not that I would anyway. She is hardly a mother figure.

"Are you going out for a walk today, dear?" she asks.

I shake my head. I haven't returned to the cave since I went with Peter.

"Or perhaps the library?"

"No. I don't feel like it." Reading is another thing that I left behind in Gorran. Since my return, I haven't picked up a book, and I haven't visited the library since my illness started.

"Then why don't we go out together? I need to do some shopping in Newquay. We could go for tea and cakes."

My spirits sink further still at the thought of getting ready to go out, let alone spending time with Mrs Ponsonby.

"I don't think so," I say.

"And don't forget. Elys has a birthday next week. Wouldn't you like to choose a gift?"

I groan. She has got me there. Though I know Mrs Ponsonby will put my name to any purchase she makes, Elys has been good to me, and I owe her.

"Very well," I say. "Let's go after lunch."

"We'll go now," says Mrs Ponsonby firmly.

CHAPTER FOUR

A New Friend

I gaze towards the sea as the omnibus stutters towards Newquay, wondering if we will get there in one piece. Mrs Ponsonby purses her lips and clings to the seat in front as if her life depends on it. We've only been aboard for five minutes, but half the passengers are grimacing in undisguised concern while the others look bemused. Mrs Ponsonby had already remarked on the driver's age while we were waiting at the bus stop, loudly proclaiming that he looked as if he should still be in school. I ignored her concerns, but she might be right. He is driving too fast and with gay abandon as if he hadn't a care in the world. He will if the bus topples over, not that it would be the worst thing that has happened to me recently. I'd be more worried if I could work up the enthusiasm for it, but if the bus falls off the cliff, it will simply be a poor end to an awful year.

"I'm going to complain," hisses Mrs Ponsonby.

I shrug, but the woman opposite gives a ringing endorsement. "You should, dear," she says. "I feel quite sea-sick with all the turbulence. It's too much."

"Don't worry. I shall," Mrs Ponsonby replies, her face a

mask of gritted teeth and ill-concealed temper.

"I expect he's new," I say. "Everyone must learn."

"Not with real people on a coast road," says a man two seats behind us. His knuckles are white where he has grasped a metal pole. His remark provokes another diatribe which continues until the bus is abuzz with complaints, while the driver is blissfully unaware.

Against the odds, we make it to Newquay, and there is a scramble to leave the vehicle as soon as it stops. I don't participate.

Mrs Ponsonby stands, remembers who she is travelling with and retakes her seat, shooting daggers toward the driver.

"Don't say anything," I plead.

"Of course, I will. He's a danger to the public."

"Please don't make a scene. I couldn't bear it."

"Very well, Connie. But I will write to the omnibus company. They should strike him off."

"Off what?" I wonder. He is not a member of the medical profession, but I don't argue with Mrs P. She is not happy, and anything could happen when we leave. I wait until the last person has departed before getting to my feet. Mrs Ponsonby follows behind, and I look firmly ahead, so she doesn't embarrass me with an ill-timed glare.

"Charming," says the bus driver as I navigate the steps leaving me in no doubt that Mrs Ponsonby couldn't resist registering visual disapproval.

"Connie, wait," barks Mrs Ponsonby, and I cast my eyes heavenwards, wondering why she thinks it's necessary to slow me down when I lack the basic equipment to go sprinting ahead. But all becomes clear when I turn around. Mrs Ponsonby has dropped her handbag, and the contents have spilt onto the pavement.

"Let me help," I say, stooping to grab some coins.

"Stand up, Connie. I can manage."

I do as she says, but not before retrieving a battered compact that rolled under a bush. I pass it to her. "Yours, I presume?"

"As you know perfectly well," she says, snatching it away.

"I don't, actually."

"I've had it long enough."

"Well, excuse me for losing my memory."

Mrs Ponsonby sighs. "Connie, dear. This is not a good start. I'm sorry. I shouldn't be cross with you."

"Don't worry," I say. "I was grumpy too." I cannot bring myself to apologise to Mrs P, but this is a reasonable compromise.

"Good," she says. "Let's start again. Now, any ideas what Elys might like for her birthday?"

"Something she can use when she gets married?"

"Hardly. Elys deserves a personal gift, not something for her bottom drawer. We will get her a wedding present nearer the time."

"How about a sweater, then? Mr Moggins snagged her best jumper last week."

"An excellent idea. That will do very well. We can go to Madame Hawkes on Bank Street. That's hardly any distance to walk, and Eva's creamery is on the next road. It's such a lovely day today. We could sit outside."

I examine the sky, wondering whether it's worth the risk. There's nothing nicer than sitting outdoors, but we'd be pushing our luck to expect the weather to stay clement in October. Yet the wispy clouds show no sign of grey, and I nod my approval.

"That's settled," says Mrs Ponsonby, linking her arm through mine. I almost stop walking at the shock of it. This gesture of camaraderie is not only unusual but unheard of. I may be missing a substantial amount of memory, but I know we don't have a close relationship. Perhaps she is showing extreme relief that I survived my brain bleed. If so, I will have to relapse again to avoid encouraging it. I cannot pull away without appearing rude, so I walk awkwardly, arm in arm, leaning on my stick and feeling unbalanced.

Fortunately, Madame Hawkes' establishment is only a few minutes away, and I eye the front door with relief. Mrs

Ponsonby unhooks her arm while I stare up at the monogrammed roundel above. This, together with the shop front and furnishings, oozes quality. I haven't been inside for a long time, which is hardly surprising as I barely travel alone, although Mrs Ponsonby has reluctantly tried to give me a little more freedom since I decamped to Croydon without telling her.

"This way, Connie," she says as if I couldn't work it out myself. I follow her and find myself in a small shop that smells of sawdust for some inexplicable reason.

"Can I help?" A willowy shopgirl pounces on us the moment we pass through the door.

"We're looking for a gift," says Mrs Ponsonby.

"For this young lady?" asks the girl, smiling at me.

"No. It's a surprise for my servant," says Mrs Ponsonby. I grimace. Elys knows her place but wouldn't enjoy that term if she was within hearing distance.

"Oh," says the shop girl disappointedly. "I was going to show you these," she says, pointing to a set of stacked jerseys beneath a half manikin. "But if it's for your hired help, this is more appropriate."

Mrs Ponsonby scowls. "I prefer these," she says, moving towards the former, more expensive selection.

I can't help smirking at the disgusted expression on the shop girl's face, and I award a silent brownie point to Mrs Ponsonby for loudly proclaiming Elys' value. Mrs Ponsonby may be many things, but she is no snob.

"What do you think, Connie?" she asks, pointing to a scarlet, short-sleeved cable jumper.

"I think Elys would prefer long sleeves," I say. "She's been noticing the cold recently."

"A good point," says Mrs Ponsonby. We narrow it down to a choice of two designs and eventually settle on a teal jumper with a bow neckline which will look exquisite on Elys. The shop girl wraps it in paper and fastens it with string, then thrusts it towards Mrs Ponsonby as if she can't wait for us to leave. Mrs Ponsonby pays, then wrinkles her nose in concern. She tucks the parcel under her arm and is still examining the contents of her purse when we go outside.

"What's wrong?" I ask.

"Nothing," she says, snapping her purse shut.

"Are you sure?"

"Probably."

I ignore the enigmatic remark, and we make our way to Eva's creamery, where I accompany Mrs Ponsonby to the counter to place our order. We choose a pot of Darjeeling and a slice of Victoria sponge, then ask the waitress if there are any set tables in the courtyard garden. She tells us there are and asks us to take a seat while she makes our tea.

We open the inner door and find ourselves in a small walled garden with four neatly set tables containing cutlery and a vase of artificial flowers. A smartly dressed soldier wearing an officer's insignia already occupies one of the smaller tables and smiles as we enter. Mrs Ponsonby nods, then beckons me to sit.

I slide into my chair, lay my stick beneath the table, and then take stock of my surroundings. Though rather more enclosed than I would prefer, the walled garden benefits from being a superb windbreak. Sorely tempted to remove my coat, I wait instead to see how I will feel when the warmth of the walk has worn off. Meanwhile, I admire the delicate walls of ivy and clever positioning of mirrors while trying not to be distracted by Mrs Ponsonby, who is rooting around in her bag again.

"No, it's not right," she mutters.

"What isn't?"

"There should be more money." Mrs Ponsonby opens her purse and thrusts it towards me.

"Are you sure?" I ask.

"Yes." She taps her forehead and then gasps. "I'm missing a ten-shilling note as well as some coins."

"That's an awful lot of money," I say.

"Indeed. But where can it have gone?"

"You dropped your bag, didn't you? Did your purse fly open?"

"Oh, dear. It must have. Well, that's it. I can kiss goodbye to the money."

"Not necessarily. Your compact rolled under the bush. I just happened to notice it. I do wish I'd looked a bit harder."

"Which one?"

"Immediately left of the bus stop. Within a foot of where you dropped the bag. It might still be there, you know. There's next to no wind today."

Mrs Ponsonby looks up. "You're right. There isn't. It's worth a quick look. Do you mind?"

"Not at all," I say, thinking how nice it will be to sit alone and gather my thoughts.

"I'll be back in a jiffy."

I smile as she leaves and lean back in my chair, contemplating the brick wall. But the garden is neither serene nor comfortable. I suddenly feel acutely aware that only two of us are in the small, enclosed space within touching distance and too British to exchange small talk. I look up, down, to the floor, the wall and back up again, wishing that I had a book on my person. But I have nothing with me to detract from the awkwardness of being this close to a stranger. Then I remember that's not entirely true. I rummage in my bag, find a tiny notebook, and pencil, and idly scribble my name and address to look as if I am doing something important. I do not fool my disloyal brain, which continues to sabotage my efforts to stay calm. The soldier, who benefits from a newspaper, looks up and flashes a weak smile which I do my best to return without looking half-witted. He nods and resumes reading. I flush and look away. My discomfort begins to echo the embarrassment of my earlier encounter with Kit, and I thank my lucky stars that if I flush beetroot red, I won't have to see the soldier ever again. I am so conscious of the situation I start worrying that I might articulate my thoughts. It wouldn't be the first time. I have whispered played out conversations while travelling in the cart with Elys, unaware that I was speaking aloud. I am sitting with my elbow on the table, and my fingers pressed firmly to my lips just in case my thoughts accidentally emerge, when the waitress bustles through carrying our food. I have never been so glad to see anyone.

"Thank you so much," I say in an unnaturally excitable slew of words. The waitress is taken aback by the strength of my gratitude and quickly sidles out. I am alone again, and I distract myself by pouring the tea and dropping a sugar cube in the China cup. It plops down, displacing the hot beverage and shoots boiling tea on my hand. Naturally, I drop the spoon.

Oh, dear God, how much worse can this get?

The soldier puts his newspaper down and starts laughing.

"Do you need a hand?" he offers.

I contemplate refusing, but the ice-breaker remark is just what I need. "I think I can manage," I say, "though goodness knows what will happen if I try to cut the cake."

"Sebastian Letwin," says the soldier, offering his hand.

I move to stand, but he shakes his head. "Please don't get up on my account," he says.

"Connie, that is to say, Constance Maxwell," I reply.

"Oh, are you related to the Hampshire Maxwells?"

"Not that I know of," I reply, cutting him short. The subject of my parentage is a source of continual irritation. I could be related to the North Wootton marching band for all I know. I pick up my pencil and start writing a list of reasons why Mrs Ponsonby annoys me, her refusal to tell me about my background being foremost.

He glances away, shakes his newspaper as if to resume reading, then reconsiders, folds it, and stows it purposefully under his chair.

"Do you come from Newquay?" he asks.

"I live in Porth Tregoryan," I reply.

"Oh, near the hotel?"

"Yes. Do you know it?"

"I've never been inside, but I've passed it more than once since returning to Blighty."

I sigh. I don't know why he has engaged me in conversation,

but I am disinclined to chat. I am alone with a stranger, and the absurdity of this situation after Mrs Ponsonby has kept me a virtual prisoner all these years has just dawned on me. I cannot believe she has walked away and left me. I'll never understand why Mrs Ponsonby feels the need to give me round the clock supervision. Still, she must be preoccupied with something else to make such a fundamental error of judgement in leaving me alone. She's bound to be cross if she comes back and finds me deep in conversation with a man I don't know, and I momentarily consider the best course of action. I should cross my arms, turn away and employ the correct body language to let him know I am not interested. But that would be a wasted opportunity. Instead, I lean forward and speak.

"What regiment do you belong to?"

"The Duke of Cornwall's light infantry," he replies. "Second Battalion, to be exact."

"How interesting," I say. "Where are you based?"

"Bodmin," he says. "But not for long, I hope."

"Don't you like it?"

"Not particularly. It's tough when a chap is apart from his regiment."

"Oh. Where are they?"

"In Gibraltar. I was too until I took a bullet in the leg during training manoeuvres."

I glance towards his foot and notice he has propped a wooden cane topped with a silver lion against the table. I can't help but smile – a kindred spirit.

"You too," he says, nodding towards my stick. "Though I'm sure you didn't take a bullet in the shin."

"No. Mine was a childhood accident," I say, hoping he doesn't quiz me further. I'm not sensitive about my injury – I just don't know how it happened.

"Will you get better?"

I shake my head. "No, but I can walk short distances if I don't overdo it. Things could be much worse. Are you on the mend?"

Sebastian nods. "I hope to be on board a ship to Gibraltar in eight weeks if my progress continues."

"What's Gibraltar like?"

"Warm," he says.

"My friend Mary's been there. She's a painter."

"Stunning views, cobalt skies. It's an artist's dream."

I sigh. "I would love to travel."

"Then do so."

"It's not that simple."

I expect him to respond by listing the many ways I could make it happen, but he doesn't reply. He steeples his hands and leans forwards. "You have sad eyes."

I don't know about sad, but my eyes snap open as I listen to his words. A thousand thoughts flit through my brain. Is he making advances? Can he read minds? Have I smudged my make-up, or is my natural tendency to frown suggesting dampened spirits? Worst of all, am I wearing Jim's loss like a black veil of misery? Surely not. I may never see him again, in which case incorporeal widow's weeds will swathe my face for eternity. "How do you know?" I blurt out, immediately regretting my hasty words.

Sebastian raises a half-smile and looks past me, his grey eyes misty and distant.

"You too?" I ask.

He nods imperceptibly.

"Who did you lose?"

"You first," he says.

"A friend."

"Just a friend?"

"Jim and I weren't, at least I don't think we had an understanding."

"You mean you don't know?" Sebastian's mouth twitches as if he is stifling a smile.

"I lost my memory."

"Good Lord. When? How?"

"A few months ago, I think. An aneurysm. I don't know what

caused it."

"Will your memory ever return?"

"It has a little. The rest may come in time or not, as the case may be."

"I'm sorry about your friend. May he rest in peace."

I chew my lips as I ponder how to explain the situation. "Jim is missing," I say.

"Not dead?"

"I don't know."

"How awful for you. No wonder you carry the weight of the world on your shoulders."

"I didn't know I did. Perhaps I need a good night's sleep," I say curtly. I haven't bothered with cosmetics recently, and now there's even less point if I look this miserable to a stranger. I'm wearing one of the dresses Elys made last year, together with my best shoes and freshly bought stockings. If I still look like a walking Greek tragedy, why bother trying?

"I'm sorry. I've offended you. Forgive me."

"It's not you," I say, chewing the pencil's tip. "Things haven't gone well recently, but it's time I pulled myself together. I won't be one of life's victims."

"That's the spirit. Good for you."

I smile and prepare myself to ask about his loss. But as I open my mouth to speak, the door slams open, and Mrs Ponsonby charges through. "Connie," she says, staring at me as if she can't believe the evidence of her own eyes.

"Yes," I reply, bemused.

"Oh, my dear. I abandoned you – just left you alone. What on earth was I thinking? Who knows what might have happened?"

Part of me withers and dies at her toe-curlingly embarrassing display of emotion.

"I'm twenty-six years old and quite capable of looking after myself. You must not worry," I say in a loud voice, as much for Sebastian Letwin's benefit as to console Mrs Ponsonby. She treats me like a child, and it's the last thing I want even a casual acquaintance to witness.

"I know," she soothes. "But we don't want to take unnecessary chances, now do we?"

"Did you find your money?"

Mrs Ponsonby beams while waving her purse in the air. "I may be missing a coin or two, but you were quite right. The ten-shilling note was under the bush together with my handkerchief.

Sebastian watches then opens and shuts his mouth. I suspect he is trying to decide whether to introduce himself to Mrs Ponsonby, and I pointedly turn away. It feels rude, but I can't trust Mrs Ponsonby to treat me like a grown woman, and I've suffered enough embarrassment today. Besides, Sebastian has intruded on private matters. He may be perceptive, but that doesn't give him the right to grill me about things he doesn't understand and that I don't properly remember. It is better to terminate our acquaintance here and now.

"Do you want another cup of tea?" Mrs Ponsonby opens the teapot and stirs the dark brew.

"It's probably stewed by now."

"Well, I'll have a cup with my cake." She takes a sip and pulls a face.

"It's cold. Never mind."

I spear a forkful of cake and eat it distractedly, watching while Sebastian reopens the newspaper and pretends to read, continually looking in our direction. His surreptitious glances do not go unnoticed.

Mrs Ponsonby lowers her cup, takes a serviette, and wraps her piece of sponge before thrusting it into her handbag. "I'll eat this at home with a hot drink," she says, snapping it closed. "Come on, Connie."

"But I haven't finished."

"Bring it with you, dear. Come now – quick, smart."

I barely have time to grab my stick, much less finish my cake, before she pulls my arm as we head towards the door. I turn and flash a brief smile towards Sebastian, but Mrs Ponsonby has beaten me to it with a narrow-eyed scowl. We head through the coffee shop as quickly as my limp allows before finding ourselves in the street. "We didn't leave a tip," I say.

"I didn't like the look of that young man," says Mrs Ponsonby.

"Why? He seems perfectly pleasant."

"He was looking at you, Connie. Leering at you. You are at that age where men might try to take advantage."

"I wish they would," I say.

Mrs Ponsonby steps back as if someone has hurled a mackerel in her face. She stares at me in abject horror. "That life is not for you."

"Why ever not?"

"I couldn't trust anyone to take proper care of you."

"I'm not an invalid."

"I know. But you don't understand."

"Then tell me."

"One day."

"So, you keep promising. But one day never comes."

Mrs Ponsonby closes her eyes with a sigh. "Oh, Connie," she says. But I don't hear her. I am already doing my invalid version of stalking ahead in disgust.

CHAPTER FIVE

Poor Dolly

Saturday, October 8, 1932

I am still cross with Mrs Ponsonby the following day and decide to take breakfast in the kitchen, so I don't have to tolerate her presence. Elys is rolling out pastry when I open the door. She sees Teddy following behind me and raises an eyebrow.

"Mr Moggins is in the pantry."

"Teddy won't hurt him, I promise."

"I know. But Moggins won't like it. This is his domain."

I look at Teddy and consider leaving him in the hallway, but he gazes at me through trusting eyes, and I can't do it. He has already lost one master, and I can't bring myself to inflict even the smallest disappointment on the loyal little spaniel.

Elys sighs. "I'll open the back door. It's chilly out there, but I'm sure master Edward will want to go outside. He can come and go as he pleases, and Mr Moggins won't mind as much. Elys' pet management plan works like a dream. Teddy eagerly disappears for a snuffle around the garden, and within moments, Moggins jumps on my lap.

I tickle his ears and contemplate asking Elys for something

to eat.

"Why are you here?" asks Elys directly.

I sigh, wondering where to start.

"You've fallen out with Mrs P again, haven't you?"

"Not exactly."

"What a shame. She was happy you agreed to go to Newquay with her. She's fond of you, Connie."

"What did she say?"

"Nothing much, but she gave the impression that things didn't go well. Why not?"

"The usual. Mrs Ponsonby watches me like a hawk and won't tell me anything."

Elys sighs. "I don't know how you will manage when I'm gone."

"Gone?" I am so shocked that I inadvertently scrape my chair back, sending Mr Moggins flying. He falls to the floor and then stalks off in disgust. "Where are you going?"

"I'm getting married, silly."

"I know, but I thought you would still look after us."

"I will do for a while. But I'll have my own house to run, and children will follow in time."

I stare at the table, aghast, wondering at my stupidity. Elys has been engaged for almost a year, but the implications never dawned on me. "I will miss you so much," I say, close to tears. Elys and her wise words have kept me sane, and I cannot imagine the house without her.

"I won't be far away," she says.

"You will if Mrs Ponsonby sells the house," I reply.

"She's not going to," says Elys.

"How do you know?"

"She told me yesterday. She can't face it while she's fighting..." Elys flushes red and stops mid-sentence.

"Fighting? Fighting what?"

"While you're fighting the after-effects of the aneurysm," says Elys, regaining her composure.

"Oh. Well, that's a worry lifted. I wish Mrs Ponsonby had

told me. I knew she had put the move on hold, but I thought we would go eventually."

"I can't speak for the future," says Elys. "But you can scrub it from your list of worries for the time being."

"That's a relief," I say, and suddenly the day seems brighter.

"Why don't you join Mrs Ponsonby?" Elys suggests. "I'll be taking her a cup of tea in a moment. She's alone in the parlour, and she'd enjoy the company."

"No thanks," I say. "I've got other plans."

"Like moping around your room again? Or staring at four walls? Perhaps you could waste half an hour waiting for the daisies to grow on the lawn."

"That's harsh. I've been ill."

"You're a lot better than you were."

"There's more to it than that."

"Such as?"

I consider telling Elys about Jim, but I don't know what to say or what she already knows. I curse my faulty memory and wish it was all there or entirely gone. This horrible middle ground where I remember some things and not others is disconcerting, but I decide to test the waters with a single word.

"Jim," I say.

"What about him?"

"Do you know who I mean?"

"Your friend, I presume?"

"What did I tell you about Jim?"

"Very little, only that you'd met him while you were away. I don't know where you went or under what circumstance, and you kept it very close to your chest."

"How did Jim come up in conversation?"

"Is he important to you, Connie?" Elys looks straight into my eyes while wearing a puzzled expression on her freckled face.

"Yes. I think so. It saddens me, and I can't bear that he's still missing. Did you know that they can't find him?"

"Of course. Jim's mother came here. I was amazed that Mrs

34

Ponsonby allowed it, and if it weren't for Isla Tremayne, she wouldn't have. What is Jim to you?"

"More than just a friend, but I can't remember how much more."

"I'm sorry. I didn't realise. Jim wrote to you, Connie. I brought you the letter."

"Of course. Did I tell you much about him when you gave it to me?"

"No. You couldn't get me out of your room quickly enough. I suppose you wanted to open your mail as fast as possible. I should have guessed there was more to it than a simple friendship."

Elys wraps her carefully rolled pastry around a chunk of salmon, brushes it with milk and slams it in the oven. Then, she pours boiled water into a pair of mugs and joins me at the round table in the corner of the room.

"Here," she says, handing me a cup of tea. "So, Jim is the reason you have been so low."

I nod. "That and not being able to recover my memory. If I could only remember where Jim was and what he was doing."

"You might never have known."

I pause. Elys is right. Not finding Jim has consumed me with guilt, but perhaps my worries are ill-placed.

"How can they be sure he hasn't taken off for his own reasons?"

"He isn't like that. And he would never have left Teddy or his mother."

"Perhaps. How well did you know Jim?"

"Not greatly."

"And what did he do?"

"Jim was a policeman."

"Are they looking for him?"

"Of course, but they can't find him, or so his mother said."

"Have you spoken to her recently?"

"Not since she came here."

"Then how will you know if he turns up?"

"I won't, will I? And that's half the problem. Thank goodness I have Teddy. At least Jim will try to find his dog if he returns. But with Mrs Ponsonby's aversion to newspapers and my virtual imprisonment here, I don't know what progress they've made. Oh, my God. He could be dead, and I wouldn't know."

I put my head in my hands, sickened that apathy has left me incurious about this matter so close to my heart. Choking back tears, I see Jim's body broken and still in my mind's eye. A two-second flash of recall brings a stark image of a clifftop, snatched away as the memory fades and I am left slumped over the table sobbing like a child. Elys leans over and hugs me, stroking my hair as I give in to despair.

"Oh, Elys."

"Just cry it out."

It must be five minutes or more before I am sufficiently composed to lift my head. Elys squeezes my shoulder and returns to her seat. "I'll find out what's going on," she says.

"How?"

"I'll order some old newspapers. It's bound to have been reported, with Jim being a policeman."

"Mrs Ponsonby will be furious."

"She doesn't need to know, although it wouldn't do you any harm to confide in her, Connie. I'm sure she would understand."

"Relationships aren't for people like me," I say, remembering yesterday's conversation.

Elys stares quizzically, but I don't embellish.

"Mrs Ponsonby would hate to think you were so unhappy."

"I can't tell her. I won't."

Something dark tugs at the back of my mind. A feeling of terror, a sinister malevolence. A thing I cannot and must not reveal to Mrs Ponsonby. What? Why?

"Connie?" Elys has noticed my mood change, and I suddenly feel a burning need to remove myself from the conversation. "I'm going out," I say, feeling the pull of the hotel library for the first time in ages.

I whistle, and Teddy comes running.

"Are you alright?"

"I will be." I collect Teddy's leash from the kitchen cupboard, then walk through the hallway and remove my coat and hat from the stand. I glance towards the parlour. Mrs Ponsonby is sitting quietly, staring at the contents of a brown bottle she is holding in a trembling hand. I stop in the doorway, surprised at this show of vulnerability from my formidable captor and feel an unfamiliar pang of conscience that I haven't taken breakfast with her. But I have my own cares, and I don't detract from my purpose. Instead, I leave the house and make my way to the hotel, feeling strangely nervous.

#

I open the hotel door to see Dolly standing in her usual place behind the reception desk. She stares into the distance with a frown on her face while drumming her fingers on the wooden top. Her uniform is unusually dishevelled, and she's loosely pinned her hair in a failing top knot. She looks up and stops tapping as I approach, and I see, to my horror, flaking nail polish and a broken thumbnail.

I refrain from asking what is wrong and instead greet her enthusiastically. "Dolly, how are you?" I say with forced cheerfulness.

"Connie. How nice to see you." Her tone is stiff and formal. She is perfectly polite but lacking in warmth.

"Are you well?"

"Yes. I am perfectly healthy. You?"

I fiddle with my bracelet as I try to navigate this new, frosty landscape. "I'm well but still under lock and key."

Dolly forces a smile. "That explains why you haven't been in this week."

The penny drops. My self-indulgent despair has been all-consuming, and I didn't give a thought to Dolly, who was having difficulties at the hotel before I left for Gorran. And I cannot expect her to sympathise with my loss as she doesn't know anything about it. She must think I don't care.

"Tough times?" I ask.

"Awful." Dolly's face crumples, and she turns away.

"Oh, Dolly. What can I do?"

She doesn't answer, and I don't press her. Her shoulders shake, and it's all she can do to hold herself together. She gulps and sniffs a little.

I give her a moment, then ask, "Is there somewhere we can talk?"

"Not here," she mutters, still facing away.

"Where?"

"Don't bother, Connie. I'll be fine."

"Well, you're not. And I want to help."

"You can't. Nobody can."

"I'm not leaving until you tell me what's wrong."

Dolly turns around and brushes tears from her cheek. "Just go, Connie. Before someone comes."

"When are you off duty?"

"After lunch."

"Come to the cave. I'll be there at two."

"I don't know. I don't want to talk about it."

"Meet me at the cave, or I'll come to your room."

Dolly tuts but nods her head. "Whatever you say, if it means you'll leave me in peace."

"Good. I'll see you later."

#

I arrive before Dolly and settle down under a blanket while looking out to sea. I can't yet bring myself to open the trunk where Peter's spare library books have replaced the former inhabitants. But it makes a good footrest and is so comfortable that I am in danger of falling asleep.

The cave hasn't changed since I came with Peter on Tuesday. But when I consider the destruction wrought while I was away, I am riven with an involuntary shiver of fear. I still don't know why someone targeted the cave or whether they intended to frighten me. Perhaps I shouldn't come here alone, but Mrs

Ponsonby knows where I go, and she has never tried to stop me. Considering her overprotective nature, she must deem it safe. And if she thinks so, then I must too. But perhaps Mrs Ponsonby is unaware of this latest act of vandalism, and I'm not going to enlighten her.

I glance at the watch that Mrs Ponsonby gave me for Christmas. It keeps time quite well if a little fast. But at ten past two, I can hardly blame my timepiece for Dolly's absence. She is late by anyone's standards. I give her five minutes more and pass the time picking tiny stones from the cave floor and throwing them at the white rock near the entrance. The longer I wait, the more my aim improves through concentration and worry. But I meant what I said. If Dolly doesn't come to me, I will go to her, and I'm sure she would prefer the former course of action. At sixteen minutes past two, I stand up and fold the blanket, grab my stick and stomp crossly to the front of the cave. But as I prepare to leave, Dolly comes flying down the beach full pelt and almost careers into me.

"Ah. Better late than never," I say.

"Don't, Connie." Dolly's eyes are full of tears. She waits for a moment before entering, swiftly looking over her shoulder as if something is in hot pursuit.

"Sit down," I say, gesturing towards the second chair. Dolly reaches for the blanket with trembling hands and pulls it to her chin.

"What kept you?"

"An unhappy customer if you must know. She found a frog in her room, so she says. A frog, I ask you? In a seafront hotel in the middle of October. Where did it come from? Her overactive imagination, I suspect. And I wanted to say that, but of course, I didn't. So, I've just spent ten minutes apologising for something that probably never happened."

I reach below my chair and unpack the bag I brought with me earlier, removing two tin cups and the thermos flask Cora gave me last year. And as I pour two steaming cups of coffee, a slew of memories return, all involving Coralie Pennington.

Happy times in Newlyn, games of whist at home in Pebble Cottage, friendly chats, womanly advice. Where is Coralie? Why does nobody mention her? Then another memory hits with a hammer blow – Coralie, dressed in a purple robe while passing a glass of wine to a fat man with wobbling jowls. Fear slithers across my skin like a fast-growing tendril as a paralysing terror strikes.

Dolly looks up. "What's wrong? Are you ill?"

I gasp, desperate for air. I'm panting, but my lungs are empty. I have forgotten how to breathe.

"Connie. What is it?" Dolly gets up and kneels in front of me. I want to ask her for help. I move my mouth, but nothing happens. I am drowning and desperate for air. The edges of my world start to go black, and then I suddenly feel a flash of pain across my cheek. I raise my hand, taking a deep and satisfying breath as I clutch my painful face.

"I'm sorry I slapped you. I didn't know what else to do." Dolly stares anxiously at me as I recover my composure with big gulping breaths. "Don't say anything. Stay calm until you get the colour back in your face."

My breathing returns to normal. "Thank you," I say. "I don't know what happened."

"You turned blue," says Dolly. Her hands are still shaking, even worse than before.

"I couldn't catch my breath."

"I know. But why?"

"A memory," I say. "An awful, terrible memory."

"What was it?"

"Who was it, is the question?" I say. "And I don't know. But I should. His face was terrifyingly familiar."

"He?"

"I can't think about it," I say, feeling the pulse in my neck quickening. "Please, let's talk about something else."

"If, you're sure. I ought to call Dr Kit."

"No, Dolly. Just change the subject. What happened to you?"

"It seems trivial now," says Dolly, picking up her coffee.

40

She takes a sip, flinches, and puts it back down.
I blow mine and wait for her to continue.
"Mr Brookbank has promoted Roxy Templeton to the Assistant Manager position."
"What about Georgio?"
"He's gone back to Sicily."
"And Roberto?"
"He's about as happy as I am. Mr Brookbank overlooked him for the position."
"I wonder why he gave it to the rottweiler?"
"He's left his wife."
"No." The unexpected news has wiped all dark thoughts from my mind. I hate myself for it, but this piece of salacious gossip has set my heart racing in a good way. "You're not suggesting...?"
"I'm not, but the rumour mill in the kitchen is working overtime."
"Surely, it won't make any difference to you?"
This time, Dolly takes another sip of her coffee without burning her lips.
"The last six months have been awful," she says, shaking her head sadly. "Roxy Templeton has responsibility for the rota, and I get all the worst shifts. She never rosters me with anyone I like, and you know how hard she's worked to turn the staff against me. I've never felt so friendless and alone. Roxy wants me out, Connie, and she's doing everything to make it happen, short of firing me."
"To what end? Good help is hard to come by?"
"I don't know. Brookbank has stood by me up to a point, but she's wearing him down."
"But Newquay is full of hotels. You'd get another job in a heartbeat."
"That's out of the question." Dolly sharply rebuts my suggestion with a thin-lipped scowl.
"Why? One hotel is much the same as another."
"I must work here in this hotel," says Dolly slowly,

emphasising each word. "This hotel and no other."

"I don't understand."

"Of course, you don't. And that's one of the reasons I didn't want to speak to you about it. And I can't make you understand because I'm not sure myself. But take it from me, changing hotels is not an option. Now, do you understand why Roxy Templeton is such a problem?"

"Can't you speak to her?"

"And say what? There aren't any bridges to build. I've done nothing, said nothing. She simply doesn't like me."

A sudden suspicion enters my mind. "Did Roxy do this?" I ask, waving my arm around the cave.

"Oh, so you've heard."

"Peter told me."

"I don't know. It crossed my mind. I wouldn't put it past her."

"Does she know you come here?"

Dolly shakes her head. "I shouldn't have thought so. I always wait until the coast is clear."

"Then I've made an enemy."

"No. It's just one of those silly things."

I shake my head. "Peter said that, and I might have believed him if it hadn't happened before."

"Before?" Dolly raises an unplucked eyebrow.

"Yes. Last year. The same sort of damage. Oh, and I found a bracelet."

"What did it look like?"

I cast deep into my brain, hoping I didn't lose the information in the grey fog of memory loss. But it is there, easily retrievable, and reasonably clear. "Unpolished brass with an etched symbol."

"Describe the symbol."

"Sorry, I can't. But I've kept it, and I'll look it out if you are interested."

"Do that," says Dolly. "One of the girls lost one last year, and it might belong to her."

42

"One of the staff?"

"No. A local girl," says Dolly, vaguely. "Bring it to the hotel tomorrow if you don't mind. We might as well get it back to its rightful owner."

"Are you feeling better?" I ask. Dolly's skin is flushed now, replacing the earlier grey tinge.

"Are you?"

"Yes," I lie. I am calm now, but I must unpack the recently emerged torrent of memories and re-acquaint myself with them.

"Shall we return?" I ask.

"Not together," says Dolly.

"Why ever not? Everyone knows we are friends."

"Roxy Templeton dislikes you almost as much as me."

"There's safety in numbers," I venture.

"Better to be safe," says Dolly, replacing the blanket on the back of the chair.

I stand and take her hand, wondering at the change in her. Dolly was so different last year – one of the nicest, calmest, and most loyal people I have ever met. Now she is frightened and as prickly as a cactus.

"As long as nothing else is wrong," I say.

Dolly stares back, and fear flickers momentarily in her eyes. "It's the waiting," she says. "The lull before the storm. When it's done, it's done. But this infernal waiting…" And with that, she is gone, striding up the beach in a pair of low-heeled Mary Janes, with her coat collar shrugged up, head bowed. Dolly's departure heralds a brooding silence in the cave. Someone unknown has violated my sanctuary, and now it is marred by mystery. Few of Dolly's words make sense. Why must she stay at the hotel? What does she expect to happen? I recline in my chair, intending to mull it over. But as I lean back, my scalp tingles with a familiar sensation, and I leap to my feet, my senses alert to an unknown danger. I grab my stick, lurching up the beach, deportment forgotten and balance askance. And though tired and breathless, I don't stop until I am safely inside Pebble Cottage with the door firmly locked.

CHAPTER SIX

An Unusual Poisoning

Sunday, October 9, 1932

I sprawl across the settee with Teddy snuggled into my chest, about to drop off when the doorbell rings. I languidly raise my head and wait for someone to answer it, but thirty seconds later, it rings again. I push myself up, craning my neck to see where Mrs Ponsonby has gone. She must be in the back garden as she would usually have rushed in by now to interrogate the hapless caller. I sigh and gently push Teddy to the floor. Elys takes Sundays off, and we must manage alone, which today includes heating a pheasant pie and opening the door to unwelcome guests. I lower my feet, fumble for my stick, and proceed towards the hallway, wrenching the door open, half expecting it to be Peter or Isla Tremayne. After all, who else would visit on a Sunday morning? But it is neither. Standing on the other side of the door is a tall lieutenant in a smart red uniform carrying a stick.

"Lieutenant Letwin," I say smugly, pleased that I have remembered his name. "What are you doing here? How did you find us?"

"Call me Sebastian," he says, removing his peaked hat, which he tucks beneath his arm. "And I came to return this. You left it behind at the tea shop."

Sebastian passes me the notebook I had been carrying the day we met. I flick it open and flush bright red at the sight of my name and address, followed by a few choice phrases describing the worst of Mrs Ponsonby's habits. At the bottom of the page, I have written in underlined capitals, *tell me where I came from, you old battle-axe.* I stand guppy-like, mortified at the childish literary outburst.

"It's not what it looks like," I say, unable to stop the lie.

"Please don't try to explain. It's none of my business. I'm just doing my good deed for today by returning your jotter."

"That's kind," I say, casting a nervous eye behind me. I dread to think what Mrs P would say if she saw the young soldier. She would march him back to Bodmin, I suspect.

"Well, thank you," I say, closing the door a fraction, hoping that he will get the hint.

"You're busy, I suppose," he says.

"I'm afraid so." *Me – busy – as if.*

"That's a shame. I would love to take a walk, and it's always more pleasant in company."

Temptation spreads its tendrils. "I can't go very far."

"Neither can I," says Sebastian, brandishing his cane.

"Mrs Ponsonby wouldn't approve."

"She doesn't need to know."

I consider his proposal for a second, which is all it takes to decide that I will confound Mrs Ponsonby with my unexpected absence. She won't worry but will assume that I've gone to the cave, and I will have the pleasure of knowing that I'm being contrary.

"I'll meet you opposite the hotel in five minutes."

Sebastian salutes me, winks and walks off. I watch him limp

away. His leg might be damaged, but he is moving at a lick of pace, and it will be challenging to keep up. But fresh air and exercise are good for me, and I have spent far too long feeling sorry for myself. I don my coat and hat, but an unexpected pang of guilt nests momentarily in my heart. I grab a pencil and scribble a quick note. "I'm at the cave. Connie."

I leave Pebble Cottage and find Sebastian perched on the flat rock by the side of the hotel.

"Shall we take a turn along the beach?" he asks.

I shake my head. Though only a remote possibility, the thought of Mrs Ponsonby intruding is more than I can stomach.

"Or a stroll along the cliffs. I appreciate we can't go far."

"Sorry, I can't." Sebastian has clearly misunderstood the extent of my abilities. Steep climbs are quite beyond me, and as I glance towards the towering cliffs with Newquay snug in the distance, dark thoughts settle like clouds in my head. "Not cliffs," I say. "Let's go inland. There's a convenient bench about half a mile from here. I can get that far, even on a bad day."

Sebastian smiles. "Good for you."

We set off together, Sebastian with his cane in his right hand while my stick stays firmly in my left. We are twins, opposite but the same, one damaged, one soon to be repaired. But having been injured, he understands my difficulties and periodically stops to check my progress with a subtle look or carefully worded sentence. He is mindful of my feelings, and I respond by being stronger, trying harder and not giving in to my ever-present hip pain. At first, we walk in silence, then Sebastian asks if I got wet in yesterday's downpour. I tell him I didn't go outside, and the conversation peters away. He tries again.

"Have you any plans for the rest of the day?"

I laugh a hollow laugh, but I don't try to explain that I rarely go anywhere or see anyone, not since Croydon. But the conversation is floundering, so I give something back.

"I thought you'd have returned to Bodmin by now?"

"I did. But I'm on light duties, and there's little for me to do. I knew I must return your notebook at some point, and today was as good a day as any."

"You shouldn't have gone out of your way."

"But I did, and I'm here now. Look, we've made it. I presume this is your bench?"

I nod and take a welcome seat as the light breeze ruffles my shawl.

"Are you cold?"

"Not at all."

"I could give you, my jacket?"

I smile. "I would look a little odd wearing a uniform, and you would be down to shirtsleeves in the middle of October. It's kind of you to offer and just the sort of thing Jim would do. Would have done." I correct myself and gaze towards my feet, partly in sadness but also at my ingratitude. I'm sure Sebastian didn't come here to talk about my missing friend. But I am wrong.

"It must be difficult for you," he says. "I understand how you feel. And I'm sure you have many people to talk to, but if not, feel free to confide in me."

"It's easier not to with the memory loss and all that. I'd like to know more about you, though."

"There's not much to tell."

"You said you'd lost someone too. Was it recently?"

"Last year," he says.

"What was her name?"

Sebastian raises his eyebrows. "You misunderstand," he says. "It was a friend – a chap I went to school with at Charterhouse. Then we both joined the army. I've known him for most of my life."

"Oh, dear. That is unfortunate. Was it an accident?"

"No, Connie. Someone poisoned the poor chap to death."

"Poisoned!" I exclaim. "No. Not again."

Sebastian regards me as if I am not quite the full ticket. "I'm sorry. Have you encountered something similar before?"

"I have," I say, "but please go on. I was rude to interrupt you. What happened to your friend?"

"He ingested strychnine," says Sebastian grimly. "Hugh died in agony. He must have suffered terribly."

"Poor man," I say. "Were you there?"

"No. I was abroad. One of the Sandhurst chaps told me."

"Your friends?"

"Yes. Hugh and I were in the same intake. Four of us palled around together, Hugh and I, Tony Harding, and Drake Mallard. The four musketeers, we called ourselves. Well, there's only three of us now."

"Was it deliberate?"

Sebastian nods. "Yes. Somebody put poison in his dinner."

I gasp aloud. "Why, that's almost exactly what happened in Croydon. But that time, it was arsenic."

"I remember the case," says Sebastian. "They didn't find the culprit."

"I know who it is," I say confidently.

"Do you?" Sebastian looks doubtful.

"Yes. No. I feel I should know, but I can't quite grasp it. Damn, damn, damn." I slap the bench so firmly that my palm stings.

Sebastian shifts uncomfortably. "It must be frustrating," he says. "But are you sure? As far as I know, the Croydon murders remain unsolved."

"I'm not sure about anything," I say. "But I get moments of clarity, and I honestly thought I knew for a brief second. I couldn't have, I suppose."

"What can you remember?" asks Sebastian.

"Some of my childhood memories are missing," I say. "But I don't want to talk about that. My adult memories are starting to return, though not with any consistency. It's just the last week or so before my accident that I can't get back at all."

"You will," says Sebastian.

"I hope so. Anyway, enough about me. Did they find out who poisoned your friend?"

"No, though God knows there were enough clues. Too many, in fact, which led the investigators a merry dance. But no one was ever arrested, and I doubt they will be now."

"So, the case will remain unsolved? And another murderer will get away with it, just like Annie."

"Annie?"

"Annie Hearn. She killed her friend."

"Forgive me, but she did not. I remember the case. It was only a short time ago. They let her free."

"I know. But the jurors were wrong."

"How do you know?"

"I saw her diary. And her sister's too."

"How could you have?"

I close my eyes and try to recall, and the memory zips back with barely any effort. I am standing and looking down at pages of Annie's scrawl. Except that it isn't Annie's. The diary belongs to her sister, Bessie, who wrote of her shock at finding out that Annie was a killer. But how do I know this? When was I in Annie's house? An army of ants crawls up my spine as I feel an intense tugging at the back of my head. My eyes are stuck shut, I can't see Sebastian, I can't move, and I am sinking into the bench as if it was cardboard. I'm falling, tumbling backwards through the earth when I suddenly feel a strong hand clutching my arm, gripping me tightly as if to arrest my fall.

"Are you alright, Connie?"

My eyes snap open, and I am back. I glance at Sebastian's concerned face. "Yes," I say in a shaky voice. I don't know what just happened, but it evoked a familiar feeling, not unpleasant in itself, but with the threat of danger looming ahead.

"You were very pale, and I think you must have fainted. It's my fault for taking you out when you are still unwell."

"I enjoyed the walk," I say, not wanting Sebastian to take the blame for my frailty.

"Even so."

"How much do you know about your friend's murder?" I ask, changing the subject.

"Not a great deal. I wasn't there. Why?"

"Because although I'm currently sketchy on detail, this is the third time in as many years that I've come across an unsolved crime. Somehow, they find me as if drawn by magnets. He is behind it."

"He, who?"

I see a podgy finger with a well-manicured nail as it thrusts towards a forehead. It doesn't touch, but leaves a mark. An indelible black fingerprint that lingers a long time after. I shake my head, and the memory vanishes. I don't know what it means, but I know it's related to the poisonings.

"Never mind," I say. "But the fact is that I have some experience of these matters. If the police can't help, then perhaps we can take a look together?"

"I'm sorry," says Sebastian. "I have no appetite for amateur sleuthing. Besides, I must return to Gibraltar."

"Don't you want to know what happened to your friend?"

"Of course, but I am not the right man to intervene. And, with the greatest respect, how can you help?"

I follow his gaze to my stick. "We've just walked over half a mile," I say crisply. "And not all investigations rely on the physical. Intellect is equally important."

"Talking of walking, shall we take a stroll back? Are you feeling strong enough?"

I nod, rise, take my stick, and begin the slight climb back towards Porth Tregoryan.

We exchange small talk, but I'm not really listening. I don't fully understand the reason for it, but Sebastian's friend's poisoning has taken on labyrinthine importance. I feel a burning need to find out more, and something deep inside me knows I am fated to do so. Without Jim, I am floundering in a pit of misery. Something, anything to take my mind off my depression, can only help. But Sebastian is right. I can't do this alone, and I don't have much to go on."

"Remind me of Hugh's full name," I say.

"Connie, you're fishing."

"I'm interested."

"You can read all about it in the newspapers."

I inwardly sigh, too embarrassed to explain about the newspaper ban in our household.

"Have this if it's so important," says Sebastian, reaching into his pocket. He withdraws a notebook and removes a folded clipping from the centre. "Drake sent this when Hugh died. That was the first I knew."

I unfold it and find myself looking at a press report. "Are you sure?" I ask.

Sebastian nods, his mouth set in a thin line. I am not the most percipient person, but even I can tell that he is finding it hard to continue the discussion. He evidently feels a profound loss for his friend, even if it doesn't extend to finding out more.

"Are you sure you don't want to help?"

Sebastian sighs. "Why are you doing this, Connie?"

"To keep my mind from my own problems. Is that selfish?"

A smile breaks across his rugged face. "No, it isn't. I understand. Look, I'll think about it. I haven't got long left in Blighty and only a handful of free days, but I'll see what I can do. Wait a moment." He stops and fumbles for his notebook, then scribbles an almost unreadable address while balancing his cane between his arm and torso. "There," he says, passing me the page. "And I've got your address. We can correspond if you like."

I nod. "I would."

"And perhaps I can come and see you again in a few weeks?"

"Yes. Please do."

We are almost at Pebble Cottage, yet not quite within sight. "I'd better take the last few steps alone," I say.

Sebastian dons his hat and smiles. "Well, thank you for a pleasant walk," he replies, holding a hand up in farewell.

I turn and plod back to Pebble Cottage, tired but feeling lighter than I have in a while. Though perfectly pleasant and blessed with good looks, Sebastian does not romantically appeal to me. Not like Jim. But he is an engaging companion, and, in my grief, I have allowed myself to become lonely. A new friend will be good for me, and I am pleased that he wants to see me again. I turn around for one last wave, then go inside.

#

I wait until bedtime before reading the news article about Hugh Chevis and his wife, Frances. His murder disturbed an otherwise ordinary evening meal at their bungalow in Aldershot when their butler served a brace of partridges, one of which contained poison. Chevis died, and his father received several unpleasant telegrams from the murderer who signed himself J Hartigan. The spitefully worded telegrams were intended to wound, and they did. But although I find the names of the principal actors in the poisoning, the article provides little context and no clues. I dutifully write all I have learned into the notebook that Sebastian returned, using a page for each name so that I can keep track of what they did and where they went. Then, I settle down to sleep, tossing from one side to the other, tired but unable to drop off. I should have known better than to fill my mind with facts and stories at bedtime. Wild theories jostle for position in my brain, and I realise I must take steps to tire myself out if I am to sleep. I rise and move towards my bedroom window, leaving my stick behind. I take a few wobbly paces, then reach for the bedstead, a few more, and then clutch the ledge. I open the window. The howling wind snatches the latch from my hand, slamming the window into the side of the wall. I lean out to grab it and haul it in, terrified that the glass will shatter, and Mrs Ponsonby will hear. The window shuts, excluding the wind, and I secure it. Then still unable to tear myself away from the outside world, I lean over the sill with my chin on my hands and watch the waves glinting beneath the moonlight.

The waves glide in and out, in and out, and I find myself swaying in time with the swell. The moonlight dappled water sparkles in the night sky, luring me like sirens into the black night. I lean forwards, nose against the glass for a closer look, but the pane seamlessly fizzles away into the night, and I am falling forwards. I land, not on my face, but on my feet, not outside Pebble Cottage, but on the beach. Although I wear no shoes, I do not feel the sand beneath my toes, and I am not afraid because I've been here before. I joyfully run up the beach with my arms outstretched, feeling boundlessly energetic. Then, I rise up the cliffs, climbing ever higher until I am on the top, looking down as free as a lark.

I remember this feeling. I have always dream walked along the Cornish cliffs. Why did I ever stop? How did I forget I could do this? The freedom of running unimpeded, unfettered compensates miraculously for the drudgery of an invalid's life. Yet I stopped trying and gave it all up. The joy dissolves as I stand on the cliffs, contemplating my memory gaps. And my thoughts return to those things that kept me awake. All at once, I am spinning out of control, whipped into a black vortex spiralling through space and time. It stops, and I open my eyes and peer into my new surroundings. It is light, and I am in a room with people and feeling exposed. Though experience tells me they cannot see me, I dare not risk it, and I drop to my haunches beside a high-backed chair and wait.

CHAPTER SEVEN

There's Something in my Partridge

Sunday, June 21, 1931

I must be in a dining room large enough to contain two easy chairs, one of which provides comforting, if non-essential, cover. My vantage point allows me direct sight over a large, mahogany dining table set for two. I see a handsome, smartly dressed man at the far end of the table wearing a uniform with shoulder insignia not dissimilar to Sebastian's. I must be in the presence of an officer, possibly a lieutenant. He regards his dining companion through kindly eyes set below an unfurrowed brow, and I assume she responds favourably to his film star good looks as she gazes up and his smile broadens. I cannot see her face, for she is sitting with her back to me, and I have only a side view of her slim frame. But it is enough to appreciate her exquisite pastel chiffon dress with clusters of beads sewn strategically to accentuate her best features. I am no judge of fashion, but unquestionably, this woman has access to considerable funds.

My arrival coincides with dinner, and a stiff-backed manservant arrives, also uniformed. "Thank you, Boulger," says the lieutenant as his batman places two plates of food at either end of the table. He nods, then leaves, hastening to the door that he closes behind him.

The pair eat in silence, the woman pausing only to say, "These slip soles are delicious."

The man enthusiastically agrees, taking mouthful after mouthful, then lays his cutlery on the plate.

"Mrs Yeomans has excelled herself," he says.

"She's a treasure," the woman replies.

"What did you make of Philip?" asks the officer. "He seemed a little peaky. Said he may not make the military tattoo tonight."

"I'm sure he will. I suppose I had better change."

"You look lovely as you are."

"But it's hardly suitable."

"I don't know," says the lieutenant admiringly. "It's a balmy afternoon. You won't be cold."

"I think I'll wear the red-feathered gown," replies the woman, as she scrapes her chair away and walks towards the window. She passes me but doesn't feel or sense my presence, and I take the opportunity to scrutinise her face.

The woman is comely enough, but not the beauty I thought she would be. Her freckle-free fair skin exudes health, and her cheeks are round, but her thin-lined lips set naturally into a frown. Her eyes are her best feature and sparkle inquisitively beneath well-plucked brows. But for her dress, she could be a shopgirl, until she smiles and then her features match the splendour of her clothes, and she comes alive, vivacious, and enigmatic.

"What a beautiful evening," she says, clutching the windowsill and staring out across the garden. "I wish we were going dancing. If only we were still in London."

"I know the tattoo lacks glamour," says the man, "but you'll enjoy it, old girl."

"I miss London."

"Give Hampshire a chance. You haven't had time to get to know anyone yet."

"So, you say, but the countryside is so dull."

"Come here." The man stands, approaches his wife, and spins her around. She smiles coquettishly, and he plants a lingering kiss on her lips.

"Boulger will be back at any moment," she says.

"Damned staff." The lieutenant drops another kiss on her forehead and retakes his seat. And just in time. The door opens, and the batman reappears, carrying a large tray bearing a silver domed platter and a couple of side dishes of vegetables. He places them on the sideboard, almost knocking into a photograph of Chevis and three companions, one now familiar, and then he turns around.

"Shall I carve?" he asks.

"No, I will," says the woman.

"Thank you, ma'am. Do you need anything else, sir?"

"No, off you go," says the lieutenant.

The woman waits until the batman leaves the room before making her way to the sideboard, where she arms herself with a carving knife and fork.

"What have we got?" asks the man.

She removes the lid.

"Hmm, partridge," he says appreciatively.

I gasp, and it as well that they cannot hear me. I was so distracted by being here, wherever here was, that I hadn't considered who I was watching. But the brace of partridges beneath the lid leaves me in no doubt. Somehow, I have drifted back in time, and unless I am much mistaken, I am about to watch Lieutenant Hugh Chevis die.

#

Thoughts of his likely demise send my head spinning, and the need to close my eyes and return to my room comes on urgently. I instinctively know that I should, but I don't want to. I need to witness this moment and glean every possible clue. I am in a privileged position, one that no policeman will ever know. And if I concentrate hard, I can ride out the urge to step back into the vortex and go home. Another, more sensible voice joins the one clamouring for me to stay. It reminds me of my illness, suggesting that something triggered it, something like this. I listen but disregard my better self, knowing I must fight to remain in this time and place long enough to see Lieutenant Chevis eat the partridge. Then I will let nature take its course, both for him and me. I block the internal dialogue by focusing on his face. He is leaning back in his chair, watching while his wife dexterously carves the birds. She has done this before and separates them neatly into three pieces, one bird on each plate. Then, she surrounds the partridge with new potatoes, peas and gravy, and a dollop of bread sauce.

She passes the plate to her husband before resuming her seat. He waits until she has settled before picking up his cutlery, carves a piece of breast, spears a potato, and puts it in his mouth. I watch with bated breath as his expression changes from one of eagerness to one of disgust. He retches but swallows the contents of his mouth before using the side of his fork to take a second tiny piece of partridge. He tries again, holding it to his nose uncertainly, then timidly places it on his tongue. This time he spits it back onto his plate with no attempt at disguise.

"That tastes foul," he says. "What has that bloody woman done to my dinner? It's vile. How is yours?"

"Perfectly alright," says the woman, daintily mopping her mouth with a napkin. "Taste it."

"I'd rather you tried mine," he says. "To prove that I'm not going mad." He forks another tiny piece and passes it across the table. Frances Chevis takes it and touches it to her tongue.

"Oh, my dear. That's no good at all. It tastes fusty."

"For God's sake. Now we'll go hungry. There isn't time for another meal before the bloody tattoo starts." Hugh Chevis

57

reaches for a brass bell, which he rings angrily, and within moments, the batman appears.

"Take this away and burn it," he hisses. "Don't let it anywhere near the dogs."

"May I ask what's wrong with it?" enquires the batman in a mellow Irish brogue.

"God only knows," says Chevis. "It's gone off, I suppose. It's put me right off eating."

"You must," says Frances. "Or you'll be grumpy all evening. Tell Cook to make up a cheese salad."

"Very well," says Boulger, clearing the plates away and stacking them on the tray.

"And mind what I said about burning them."

"Yes, sir."

"I don't know what's got into that woman," says Chevis. "I'd get another cook if they weren't so hard to come by."

"She's very reliable, darling," says Mrs Chevis.

"My mouth tastes disgusting." Hugh Chevis stands and rummages in the sideboard, where he retrieves two glasses and a bottle of sherry. He fills them to the brim, hands one to Frances and knocks the other back. Then he returns to his seat and wipes droplets from his moustache with the back of his hand.

I wait and watch, remembering a similar moment when Violet Sidney died in Birdhurst Rise. Once again, my recall comes easily, and I realise tiny triggers return vast swathes of memory. When I return to my own place and time, I will start asking questions and root out the truth. There is more to come. I know it.

But the here and now brings nothing more interesting than the conveyance of the promised cheese salad by the ever-patient batman, who must now surely be due for a rest. He departs, and Mrs Chevis tucks in with the enthusiasm of a woman with a half-empty stomach. Hugh Chevis, on the other hand, pokes his fork around the plate in a desultory manner, settling for a radish which he crunches half-heartedly.

"It's no good. I can't get this blasted taste from my mouth. It's revolting."

Frances sighs and pushes her plate away. "Come into the drawing-room, dear," she says, leading the way.

I wait until Lieutenant Chevis rises and follow a few paces behind. He flings himself into a chair, and I loiter in the corner of the room.

"I'll just phone Ivy and check on the children," says Frances, departing.

I watch her retreating form, wondering if I should follow her. But my place is with Hugh. It's the least I can do for Sebastian.

He crosses his legs and then swaps over before hunching forward. And when he sits up again, his face is pallid, and beads of sweat mark his brow. It begins.

Frances Chevis returns, bearing a tray of coffee. "I just intercepted Boulger," she says cheerfully. "Do you want one?"

"Do I look as if I'm capable of drinking coffee or anything else?" he growls.

"Are you feeling ropey?"

"Awful," he says.

"What about the tattoo?"

"I can't face it."

Frances sips her coffee. "At least I won't need to change," she says.

Hugh Chevis leans forward and glares at her. He looks as if he is about to speak, but his face contorts in a spasm before he shuts his eyes, as if riding a wave of pain. Chevis pats his thighs. "I can't feel my legs," he says, his eyes wide with alarm.

"Are you sure?"

"Of course, I'm sure." He raises his upper leg with two hands and tries to control it. But when he releases his hands, the leg flops uselessly.

"I'd better send for the doctor."

And as Frances Chevis utters the words, my scalp tingles, and a pain shoots from temple to toe. I know I must go, and I don't hesitate. I close my eyes and give in, waiting for the whirlwind to take me. But my journey back is peaceful and controlled. I fall backwards into an endless feather bolster, down, down, down until my hand brushes the mattress. My eyes flutter open. It is dark, but I can just make out the familiar layout of my bedroom. Too tired to contemplate what I have seen; I lie back and fall into a dreamless sleep.

CHAPTER EIGHT

The Uncomfortable Truth

Monday, October 10, 1932

"Wake up, sleepyhead," says Elys, rousing me with a cup of coffee and a Welsh cake.

"What time is it?"

"Half-past nine. You should be up by now."

"Should I? What for?"

"Because it's unhealthy to wallow in bed all day."

"Nine-thirty hardly qualifies as all day."

"I've been up since five."

"Alright. What's this for?" I pick up the Welsh cake and inspect it, wondering what it is doing in my bedroom.

"It needs eating up," says Elys. "Go on. You might enjoy it. And you won't have time for breakfast."

"Why not?"

"Master Peter dropped by. He is working in the library today and asked me to say – these are his exact words, mind, so don't get upset with me – get over there sharpish, or I'll drag you out of bed."

"How dare he," I say, mock offended.

"He was expecting you to be up when he called."

"What does he want?"

"He didn't say. But you've barely seen him lately, so he'd probably like to know how you are."

Elys departs, and I polish off the tea and Welsh cake before dressing and hauling myself to the hotel. Though reluctant to socialise, I need to talk to someone about last night. Snippets of memory suggest that Peter knows about my extra-curricular travel. I vaguely recall him sitting near my bed when I returned from at least one waking dream. I am surprised he hasn't mentioned it, and now is the time to interrogate him.

Roxy Templeton is hovering by the hotel door when I arrive. She clutches a file and pen and is evidently waiting for someone important.

"You," she says disappointedly as I enter.

I take a furtive glance towards reception in case Dolly is there. I keep forgetting to bring the bracelet I promised to show her, and it's getting embarrassing. But it must be her day off, as I can't see her anywhere. I turn instead to Roxy.

"What a lovely day," I reply, beaming. I wait for a moment, determined to make her smile, or at least give me the courtesy of a response, but she does neither. Though some memories are slow to return, all the reasons for disliking Roxy have never disappeared. I don't trust her, and I'm sure she hid Charlotte Napier's ring, for which they blamed me and ostracised me from the hotel. Peter routinely defends her and says it could be one of many people, but I don't know any reason why anyone else would want to hurt me. Roxy, on the other hand, has never hidden her hostility.

Her determination to ignore me is like a red rag to a bull. "I said, isn't it a lovely day?" I repeat, moving towards her until my face is half an inch from hers, with a Cheshire cat smile so forced and wide that I must seem like I am about to eat her.

She sighs and lowers her clipboard. "I don't have time for small talk. We are waiting for a rather important guest."

"Who?" I ask, intrigued.

"Never you mind," she replies with a smirk, and I feel a burn of rage. I wait for a moment and consider my options. The old Connie would do something ill-considered and rash, but grief and illness have destroyed my impulsiveness and granted me patience. I take a seat a few yards away from Roxy, cross my legs and wait.

Roxy's eyes bore into me, and she twitches her head, signalling to Roberto across the room. He diligently collects cups from a coffee table, and though his head is down, I swear he is deliberately ignoring her. She scowls and steps towards me, then away again as the crunch of gravel by the front door heralds the arrival of a sleek black Bentley. The car has barely parked before a chauffeur leaps out and opens the rear door to a sharp-suited, middle-aged man carrying a black attaché case. The pair enter, and Roxy rushes to the door. "Oh, you must be Mr Pennington," she says, ticking his name off the register as if they housed VIPs every day. He is the only one in recent memory and probably the only name on her fabricated list.

"We are honoured to have you at The Porth Tregoryan Hotel. My name is Roxanne Templeton, and I am here to provide you with every comfort. Don't hesitate to let me know if you need anything at all, and it will be my absolute pleasure to help you."

My stomach turns at her unfettered obsequiousness. If she had a tail, she'd be wagging it and licking his face. Then, my brain catches up with her words, and I realise she has called him by the name of Pennington. Cora's husband was a politician. Could it be him? I can't ask Roxy, and as he's only a few yards away, I decide to act. I rise and approach the guest while Roxy stares at me in horror, her jaw-dropping to the floor.

"Excuse me. I hope you don't mind my asking, but you look familiar. Like someone my uncle pointed out once when he worked as a government official."

Roxy glowers at me, preparing to find a reason to move me along, but the man beams and offers his hand.

"My name is Robert Pennington," he says. "Vice President of the Board of Trade. Pleased to make your acquaintance."

I shake his hand firmly. "I thought so," I say. "It is an honour to meet you." If Roxy can fawn, then so can I. I smile and turn to move away, but he raises his hand.

"Who is your uncle?" he asks. I hesitate and think for a moment, reluctant to get stuck in a lie that I can't escape from. "I'm afraid I can't say," I reply, tapping the side of my nose with my finger.

"Oh, I see," he says, winking conspiratorially. "Good for you. Walls have ears, don't you know?"

I nod. "Please excuse me," I say. "I'm late for my appointment."

He smiles, and I walk away, feeling Roxy Templeton's eyes burning like daggers in my back. By the time I reach the library, I am in an excellent mood.

#

"About time," says Peter, tapping his watch as I enter the room. I smile in genuine delight at the sight of my friend, the familiar bookshelves, and comfortable armchairs. I haven't been here for an age, and it's been a mistake. My heart lightens at the thought of curling up with a good book, and I know that however much I miss Jim, I will be alright. I just need to resume my old habits and be kind to myself.

"Well, how are you, and where have you been?"

"Tolerable and wallowing in self-pity."

"With good reason," says Peter kindly, approaching me with a handful of books.

"It's quiet today," I say.

"I expect everyone is outside waiting for this mysterious visitor."

"Nothing mysterious about it. I've met the man, and you've already heard of him. He's a politician called Robert Pennington, Cora's ex-husband."

Peter steps back, looking like he'd just put his finger in a light socket. "What's he doing here?"

"I don't know. Whatever politicians do, he's dressed up to the nines, so it must be business rather than pleasure."

"I don't like the sound of it." Peter has slumped on the nearest seat, put the books to one side, and sits with his head in his hands.

"Why? Do you know him?"

"No. I've never met the man."

"Then what's the problem? It is because he was mean to Cora?"

"Do you remember when you saw her last?"

"Cora? Yes, but oddly enough, I can't remember being with her. I have a strong recollection of her wearing a purple robe. She must have been at a fancy-dress party. It was an odd-looking thing – gives me the shivers whenever I think of it."

Peter looks up and stares into my eyes. "Anything else?"

"Such as?"

"Nothing. It doesn't matter."

"You're acting peculiarly, Peter. Things are confusing enough. And I need to quiz you on my past. My memory has been returning beautifully, but only when someone gives me a morsel of information to start things rolling. So, you must tell me anything and everything about all the things we've done together. Even if you think I might already know. We can start with Cora if you like."

"I don't," says Peter, thrusting the books at me. "Have these. Elys says you're not reading anything. It's not like you, and I'm worried."

"Elys should mind her own business."

"She's trying to help. Take them back with you."

"I will."

"Now, tell me what you've been up to. Nothing much, I suppose?"

"Wrong, wrong, wrong," I say. "I've been rather busy. Mrs Ponsonby took me to Newquay on Friday."

"Well, I never. Is it a blue moon?"

"Very funny. She wanted me to help find a birthday present for Elys."

"Did you have a nice time?"

"Tolerably. But we ran into an army officer, and she didn't like it. You know how stupidly protective Mrs Ponsonby gets. But she must have been abnormally distracted because we went to tea, and she left me alone for at least twenty minutes."

"That doesn't sound like her at all. Frankly, I'm amazed. I suppose you took full advantage of the situation?"

"Naturally," I say. "I had a chat with the soldier. His name is Sebastian, and he's a lieutenant in the army, currently stationed at Bodmin, but off to Gibraltar as soon as he's better."

"What's wrong with him?"

"He was shot in the leg," I say dramatically. "And is now walking with a stick but healing nicely. And you'll never guess what I did yesterday?"

"Another shopping trip?"

"No. Sebastian came to see me."

"How did you get away with that?"

"Mrs Ponsonby didn't notice him. She must have been out the back. So, I slipped out and went for a walk."

"With a man, you hardly know?"

"It isn't like that," I say defensively. "Sebastian is a kindred spirit. He can't walk, and he's just lost someone dear to him. It helped to talk."

"You can always confide in me," says Peter sadly.

"I know. And I'm about to. Sebastian's loss results from a murder. What do you think of that?"

Peter's face falls. "Oh, dear. These things do follow you around."

"Don't they just. This is the third poisoning to come to my notice."

"You're right. Your memory is definitely returning."

I sit opposite Peter, stow my stick, and lean forward. "I went for a walk last night."

66

"In the dark?"

"Yes." I nod.

"Alone?"

"In a manner of speaking. But I ended up in company."

Peter squirms uncomfortably. "Where?"

"Where indeed, and more to the point, when?"

"Well?"

"Hampshire and sometime in the recent past."

"Oh."

"Is that all you have to say?"

"I'm sorry, Connie. I hoped it would all go away. Your dream walking is dangerous. It nearly killed you. Don't you remember?"

"I remember parts of my life, and that's why you must stop trying to protect me. You should have said something sooner. Is there anything else you're not telling me?"

Peter flushes and looks away.

"Peter?"

"I need to think," he says. "I don't know what to do."

"Oh, no, you don't," I say. I know that look from old. Peter is obfuscating, and I won't allow him to keep secrets.

"You don't appreciate the danger," he hisses.

"What danger?"

"To your health and sanity."

"You're being a little dramatic."

Peter gives me a withering 'if only you knew' expression and throws his head back while contemplating the ceiling.

"I'm going to solve the murder," I say.

"How?"

"I don't know yet, but I'll go to Hampshire and find someone to talk to. I've already witnessed the crime, and I know who was there when it happened."

"Is that where you went last night?"

I nod. "Yes."

"Did you see anyone else?"

"Only Mr and Mrs Chevis and the batman. Oh, and I

glimpsed the cook."

"And that was it?"

"Yes. Who did you expect me to see – Mrs Ponsonby?"

"If only," says Peter, clenching his teeth beneath a furrowed forehead and looking as if he carried the weight of the world on his shoulders.

"Stop worrying. I'll be fine, and I'll get better even quicker when I'm busy investigating this case. Otherwise, all I do is mooch around thinking of Jim."

"It's not a case. I read the papers even if you don't. The Chevis murder happened last year, and they've largely consigned it to history. You are wasting your time."

"I don't care. I need something to do."

"You can't go to Hampshire alone."

"Yes, I can."

"Come on, Connie. You know better than that."

"I'll get Mary to help again."

"I've already written, instructing her to refuse any such request."

I laugh. Peter is clearly blustering and doesn't even know Mary.

"I mean it, Connie."

"You don't have her address."

"Yes, I do."

"Have you been poking around my personal effects?"

Peter has the good grace to appear embarrassed. "I may have looked over a few items while house sitting."

"And you've really written to Mary?"

"I thought she should know about your illness. She replied, and we've exchanged a few letters since. I nicely suggested that it would be unwise for you to leave home while still recovering."

"Oh, Peter." I am half angry, half grateful for his intervention, but clearly, Peter has put Mary in a position where she is unlikely to help. "Sebastian might come," I say.

"Not if Mrs Ponsonby has anything to do with it."

"I won't tell her."

"Then I will. She was beside herself last time. And don't be naive, Connie. You will ruin your reputation by going away with a man you hardly know."

"Will you come with me?"

"Absolutely not."

"Then I'll take my chances alone. I am going, Peter, and nothing will stop me."

"You won't manage."

"I'll dream walk my way there. Sometimes I can do it at will. I've remembered that much. What's wrong, Peter?"

I stare at my old friend, wondering why his face is turning ashen. He looks sick to the gills, his high-boned, bloodless cheeks making him seem thinner than ever.

Peter turns to face me. "I haven't talked to you about astral travel because it is so damned dangerous. You have no idea, Connie. It's bad enough that you became so ill you nearly died, but you're not alone out there. Other people travel on the astral plane. People like Felix Crossley."

The name spills from his mouth like a slippery serpent as a shiver of fear streaks through my body. I remember a face, only a few yards from my own, a man with thickset jowls and reptilian eyes, and around his neck, he wore a unicursal hexagon. He is evil, pure evil and has touched two black souls in my presence – Annie Hearn and Grace Duff. Memories tumble thick and fast. And not only memories but joined up reasoning I didn't appreciate before. Felix Crossley takes innocent souls and makes them wicked. So far, only women, but who knows what he is capable of? I stare at Peter with my mouth hanging open.

"You remember," he says.

"Yes, I do now. Although there are still gaps. Oh, Peter. He is a terrible man with a dreadful, malign influence – a force for evil. You knew, of course."

"Yes. You told me, though I have never seen him. Connie, stay here. I need to make a call, but I'll be back shortly. Don't go anywhere."

I nod, knowing that I couldn't if I tried. Recalling Crossley has made me sick to my stomach, sapped my energy and laid me low. If only I could remember where I last saw him. It might be at Grace Duff's house. But why was I there? Is this the key to Jim's disappearance? I bury my head in my hands, searching through the greyness of my missing memories for that last piece of information that might lead me to Jim. I shake my head, but it doesn't help. Instead, I think of Crossley, examine every detail of his appearance, and remind myself of the many reasons to fear him, but parts of the puzzle still elude me. I cannot quite reach everything. I am still trying with gritted teeth when Peter appears.

"Are you alright?" he asks, eyeing me with concern.

"Fine. I'm not frightened, and Crossley won't stop me from going to Hampshire."

"Don't go alone," says Peter. "I will help you get there if you agree to something first."

"What?"

"See Mary in Bosula. You are not strong enough to travel alone, physically or astrally. If you spend a few weeks with her, I will help you solve this crime if you still want to. Hopefully, you won't once you're in company."

"Mrs Ponsonby won't let me go to Bosula."

"I'll ask Mother to intervene. Can I count on you?"

"Am I invited?"

"You will be?"

"Did you telephone Mary?"

"No, but I will. I'll ask you again. Will you go to Bosula?"

"I suppose so," I say.

CHAPTER NINE

Worple Road

Worple Road, Croydon

"Oh dear," says Hugh Calloway, placing the receiver back in the cradle.

"What's wrong, dear?"

"That was young Peter Tremayne. Our plan didn't work."

Bertha puts her sewing down and regards her husband. "Does Constance remember her time here?"

"I don't know. But her memory is rapidly returning. She travelled to Hampshire last night."

"Astrally?"

Fox nods, and Bertha hesitates, forming the words in her mind before opening her mouth. "Does she remember him?"

"Crossley? Yes. And it's only a matter of time before the inevitable happens."

Betha nods. She doesn't need her husband to utter his fears, knowing well enough what he means.

"They're near, aren't they? Even I can feel them."

"I'm glad you can't see them. They're fearsome, Bertha. The manifestations are growing larger and more threatening as Crossley's power increases."

"What does he want from you?"

"Constance, I suppose. And it won't be long before she remembers me. Peter is right to get her away. Crossley is still in London, and Constance wants to go off investigating in Hampshire. It is too close for comfort."

"What's Peter going to do about it?"

"Persuade her to go further south."

"That's a good plan."

"Isn't it? And our best chance of keeping them apart. For now, at least."

"I take it you're no further forward with Stella McGregor?"

"She's fully committed. But psychic defence training takes time, and they are weaker than Crossley. Still, they have a longstanding underground network – people around the country who have been in position for years. Stella could see this coming when Crossley overthrew Carmichael a decade ago. Of course, there are not enough of them, but it's a start."

"And she told you this?"

"She alluded to it. I am in her confidence, but Crossley has a network of loyal supporters too."

"It sounds dreadfully like a conflict."

"It is. I'm convinced that these manifestations are Crossley's calling card. His own inimitable declaration of intent. And I'm glad Peter called because I've wanted to speak to you for some time, Bertha. I would like you to go to your sisters in Halifax."

"Why?" Bertha tosses her sewing into a wicker basket, too alarmed to continue.

"Because it's too dangerous for you to stay. Crossley's creatures all but vanished while Connie was unwell. And as her health has improved, so they have reappeared. There is no doubting the connection between Connie and Crossley – their fates are inexorably linked. Her recent dream walking came as no surprise – I should have guessed. Last night, the garden was thick with Crossley's beasts – watching me and waiting. I have asked Peter not to contact me directly again."

"What should he do if he needs you?"

"Send a message addressed to Hilda via the announcements page of the Telegraph."

"Can you trust her?"

"Hilda? Yes. I think so."

"I don't want to leave you. And I can't neglect Maud Douglass, not while her son is still missing."

"Why not take her with you? She might appreciate a break."

"She might. And I'm sure Sheila won't mind another guest. But what about you? How will you cope?"

"I'll keep Hilda on, take a few weeks' leave from the civil service and become Oliver Fox full time for a while. Hilda can keep house while I work things out with Stella."

"Oh, Hugh. Must I go?"

"I'm afraid so. Things are moving at an alarming rate."

CHAPTER TEN

An Invitation

Thursday, October 13, 1932

I am sitting on my counterpane, trying to decide what to do. Peter has foiled my plans again, boxing me into a corner from which I cannot easily manoeuvre. I promised him I would go to Bosula, but I didn't say when because I wanted to write to Mary in my own time. Peter thinks he can dissuade me from solving Sebastian's crime, but he cannot. I am determined to see it through. When, is an entirely different matter. For Peter has taken it upon himself to write to Mary, who posted an invitation to visit Cormorant House by return. It arrived today, and now I am in a quandary. I would normally relish a visit to Bosula, but I'm meeting Sebastian tomorrow and having persuaded him to help with the investigation, I don't want to disappoint him. I am considering turning the invitation down when Elys enters my room.

"What are you doing skulking up here?" she asks with her

customary candour.

"Reading a letter."

"From whom?"

"Mary."

"Oh, yes. Is she well?"

"Very much so. And she's asked me to pay a visit."

"How lovely. When are you going?"

"I'm thinking of putting her off for a while."

"Why? You love it down there."

"I know, but..." I stop myself short, knowing I can't tell Elys about my urge to investigate the Hampshire poisonings. Not after the last time when we badly fell out after my moonlight flit. Elys did not appreciate the way I left telling no one, an ill-considered decision that still makes me blush when I think about it. Fortunately, Elys misunderstands my reluctance to continue.

"Oh. You're thinking about Mrs Ponsonby, aren't you?"

"Naturally," I murmur. I hadn't been, but she is right, of course. Mrs Ponsonby is hardly likely to let me go. Elys has inadvertently provided a potential flaw in Peter's plan.

"I could offer to escort you?" Elys suggests. "After all, Mrs Pennington is still in London."

"Good old Cora," I say, feeling a mix of affection combined with a sharp slice of trepidation. I don't know why Cora inspires such conflicting emotions. I wonder if we argued and wish I could remember.

"Well?"

"I wouldn't dream of putting you out. Not with your upcoming wedding plans. You've only just returned from Gorran."

"That's true," says Elys, looking relieved. "Not that it will be a big wedding. We've only modest plans."

"And I don't want to impede them," I say firmly. "If Mrs Ponsonby says no, then I will respect her wishes."

Elys narrows her eyes and views me suspiciously. "I never thought I'd hear those words coming from your lips."

"Well, it's only right."

"If you say so."

"I do. In fact, I'll ask her now," I say. "I may as well get the disappointment out of the way."

I leave Elys behind and make my way downstairs and into the parlour, where Mrs Ponsonby reads a book. She looks up and smiles weakly. I curl my hands over Mary's letter, which I've stowed in my cardigan pocket. But something about Mrs Ponsonby's pale demeanour is troubling. "Are you alright?" I ask. "You look tired."

"I didn't sleep very well," she says.

"What's wrong?"

"I'm a little under the weather, that's all. There's nothing to worry about."

"Can I fetch you anything?" The words tumble from my mouth, taking me by surprise. My genuine concern for Mrs Ponsonby is alien and new to me. Her reaction is stranger still. Her eyes well up with tears, and it takes a few moments of lip chewing to gulp down what looked embarrassingly like a potential sob.

"I'll come back another time," I say, feeling distinctly uncomfortable.

"Please stay and tell me what you want." Mrs Ponsonby is back in control again.

"I'm sure you'll say no, and I'm fully resigned to it, but here is a letter from Mary. She's invited me to visit this weekend."

Mrs Ponsonby reaches out, takes the letter and glances at it. She can barely have read a line before she hands it back to me.

"That's fine, dear," she says.

"I'm sorry?"

"Yes. You can go. I would come with you, but I'm not at my best as you've seen."

"You mean I can go alone?"

"No, Connie. Of course not."

"Then who with?" I speak the words slowly, dreading her reply.

"Peter Tremayne."

"Peter." I am astonished.

"Is that in order?"

"Well, yes. But how do you know he can get away? Mr Whitstable usually needs considerable notice of Peter's absence."

"It's all sorted out," says Mrs Ponsonby, weakly.

"I don't understand."

"Isla Tremayne popped by yesterday to have a chat about it. Mary and Peter have been in touch this past week, and it is all arranged. She's letting Peter borrow the car."

"And you don't mind?"

"It will do you good," says Mrs Ponsonby.

#

I am still reeling from Mrs Ponsonby's odd behaviour when I meet Sebastian on the beach later that day. It is only four days since his previous visit, but someone unexpectedly sent him to Newquay to pick up some provisions for the base. He has parked his Morris open cab lorry opposite the hotel. And when I say parked, I use the term loosely. It is skewwhiff and stands out like a sore thumb, not only from the parking but also because the lorry's contents smell distinctly fishy.

I don't ask what he's carrying, but I greet him with a big smile and suggest we head straight for the cave. Mrs Ponsonby appears too unwell to come out spying, but there's no point in taking chances. I gesture towards the cave, and we walk together, legs and sticks, in unison. We stow our various walking implements when we arrive, sit, and place a blanket across our knees.

"Will this do?" I ask uncertainly.

"Very well," grins Sebastian. "It's different, that's for sure. Still, I wasn't sure you'd be able to meet me at all when I posted the letter through your door this morning, so anything is better than a no show."

"You shouldn't do that," I say. "Mrs Ponsonby could have

got hold of it."

"Does she read your mail?"

"Not as far as I know, but she might have asked awkward questions."

"Never mind. We're here now."

"Would you like a coffee?" I ask, producing my trusted thermos.

"Or a brandy?" asks Sebastian, removing a hip flask.

"You win," I say. The cave has blocked the worst of the wind, but a nip of alcohol will go a long way to keeping out the remaining cold.

Sebastian pours half an inch of the amber liquid into my coffee cup. "Steady on," I say. "How are you, anyway?"

"Bored," says Sebastian. "Bodmin barracks is no life for an army officer who should be abroad doing other things. I'm turning into everyone's gopher. Even the lower ranks."

I raise an eyebrow, wondering whether I would qualify as an upper or lower rank in his eyes, but I don't remark on it. "Any word on your travel date yet?" I ask.

He shakes his head. "No. It depends on what the doctor says. I'll slip him a few shillings if I need to."

"I doubt he's that easily bought."

"You'd be surprised. There's so little going on that we'll stop at nothing to relieve the boredom. I never thought I'd be as keen to collect ropes from the chandlery."

"Ah, that explains the smell."

"On me?"

"No, silly. From the truck. It's rather offensive."

"Can't be helped," he says cheerfully. "And it got me away from the barracks for a day. But for that, I'd be tidying the quartermaster's stores for the umpteenth time. Anyway, enough about me. Have you done anything since we last met?"

I hesitate. I have kept my mind firmly on mundane matters today, but I am still profoundly disturbed by my returning memories of Crossley. Peter has told me the bare minimum, and I am still trying to work out how my dream walking and the jowly occultist interconnect. I suspect it is not a subject fit for a new acquaintance, though I would like to use my encounter with Chevis to my advantage. "I've been researching," I say, crossing my fingers behind my back. Well, I suppose astral travel is a kind of research.

"Have you?"

"Yes. I thought I would look into your friend's murder more closely."

"Did you read the article?"

"I did. I've noted the relevant points and sketched the bungalow."

"How? I don't believe that information is in the public domain."

"I told you. I have experience with this sort of thing."

"Really." Sebastian looks doubtful, and I rack my brain for something gleaned during my dream walk to convince him. I think of the handsome young officer and his vivacious wife, but my perception of their personality traits won't cut the mustard. Then visions of the batman Boulger stacking silverware on the sideboard prompts another memory.

"Your friend kept a photograph in pride of place in his dining room," I say. "And I recognised one of the young men. It was you."

"I know that picture," says Sebastian, smiling fondly. "There were four of us. I think I mentioned it before. "Hugh, myself, Tony and Drake Mallard. Hang on. How do you know it was on Hugh's sideboard?"

"I couldn't possibly say," I reply, tapping the side of my nose.

"Seriously. I haven't seen Chevis for a while, but I visited his old barracks, and he kept it on his dresser, so I don't doubt you are right. But that kind of detail didn't make the newspapers."

"I have my methods," I say, hoping he doesn't press me. While it's helpful to demonstrate my investigating credentials, I can't say much more without giving the game away. Fortunately, he takes me at my word.

"Well, I'll be," he says. "Look, I will help out if you like."
"It won't be for a while," I say. "I'm taking a trip to Bosula."
"Where?"
"An artist colony in the south of Cornwall."
"How very exotic. I didn't know you could paint."
"I can't. It is not one of my talents. But my friend Mary is a gifted artist and exhibits in London. And being bohemian and the child of artists, Mary naturally lives with other fellow painters."
"I'm not sure I'd consider that natural."
"Don't you live in a barracks with other men?"
"Touché. Good comparison, although I expect your artist friends spend less time in uniform than I do. Now, is Bosula anywhere near Mousehole?"
"Just up the coast. Why?"
"My friend Tony Harding is staying there with his folks. A spot of leave, in between tours, you know. He should still be there." Sebastian looks at his watch as if to confirm his recollection, and I can't help grinning at his earnest face.
"What a coincidence. If I ran into him, I'd know three-quarters of your gang of four. And considering I'd never heard of any of you before last week, it's quite remarkable."
"That's stretching it, Connie," says Sebastian, frowning.
I bite my lip. Once again, I've overreached. Clearly, I couldn't have met Chevis in real life – he's been dead for a year. "How silly of me," I say. "I didn't mean that I'd actually met him, only that I feel I know him better, having heard your story."
"Fair enough," says Sebastian. He reaches for his hip flask and gestures toward me. I shake my head. I am already feeling pleasantly relaxed, and any more brandy could be disastrous. Sebastian pours a modest slug into his cup and knocks it straight back.
"Will you be in Bosula for long?"
"I don't know. A couple of weeks, possibly."
"I might tap up Tony for a weekend visit. We could meet up

if you like?"

I consider his suggestion. Peter will be there, and I'm not sure he will approve. Still, if I don't mention it beforehand, he'll have no choice but to go along with it.

"Why not?" I say, smiling.

CHAPTER ELEVEN

Back in Bosula

Sunday, October 16, 1932

I am sitting in the dining room at Cormorant House, feeling like I have never been away. It's raining outside, and thunderous clouds roll across the skies, black and wicked as if heralding earthly doom. But I don't care. Logs crackle on the blazing fire, and the room is abuzz with noise. All but Stephan St John have returned from their summer vacations and are glad to be back together, close like family, the petty squabbles, and niggles from living together in abeyance for now. I wasn't sure how Peter would fit into the bohemian painter's world, but he took to it like a duck to water. We have been here a little over twenty-four hours, and he has already made friends with people I haven't spoken to yet. And he's clearly bonded with Mary during my months of illness, taking several furtive walks already, no doubt to discuss my fragile health. But I don't feel weak, especially not here. I am strong in body and spirit – indomitable. Crossley and his wicked ways seem a world apart from the cheerful commune in which we will dwell for the next few weeks, and I can't help feeling grateful to Peter for insisting that I come here.

Boo Lyons waves across the room, and I return a smile. I haven't seen her at close quarters yet. Boo spent yesterday painting fishing boats in Fowey, by which I mean pictures on canvas, not repainting the actual vessels. The fruit of her labours is currently hanging in the main storeroom until it dries before being packaged and sent to the art dealer who commissioned it. She has another to do next weekend, this time in Penzance. I watch as she greets Mary, hovering by the doorway, and notice Peter chatting to Carrington Blake. Peter is getting on with him better than I did, presumably because he hasn't soaked him in red wine. For a moment, I feel a pang of jealousy. Mary is my friend, and this should be my domain, but Peter is making the most of it and revelling in the atmosphere when he should be looking after me. Not that I need his help. I don't, and I am not unhappy sitting outside the throng indulging in some people-watching. But Mrs Ponsonby allowed my visit on the strict understanding that Peter supervised, and he wouldn't know if I had run off to Timbuctoo for all the attention he's currently paying me.

I lean back into my seat, stretch, yawn, and sigh my cares away as Boo finishes her conversation and makes her way over to me. "Care for a mint?" she asks, offering a glass dish of humbugs. I take one for now and another for later, then attempt to engage in small talk while sucking my mint without over salivating.

"How have you been?" I ask.

"Very well, which is more than I can say for you. How are you feeling, my dear? Oh – I can see where they operated," she continues, leaning forward and stroking my hair back with no consideration for my privacy. "You poor thing. Tell me all about it." Boo takes my hands in hers, kicks off her shoes, and curls her legs onto the couch. Under any other circumstances, her intrusion into my personal space would make me uncomfortable. Still, for all her arched eyebrows and cold, angular appearance, Boo is very tactile, and I have grown accustomed to it.

I talk about my accident until I run out of things to say and have barely time to draw breath before she gasps and touches my cheek. "But you're still missing memories?"

I shake my head. "I'm afraid so."

"Do you remember us?"

"Yes, I do. As far as I know, anyway."

"Even Laura?"

"Laura Newson? How could I forget her hospitality? And her lovely grounds, for that matter. Oh, I do hope we will get to see her."

"That's on the cards for tomorrow if Mary's plans stay the same. Now, a quick memory test. What's the name of Laura's butler?"

I look heavenwards and search my memory. "Jonathan," I say, not entirely knowing where the answer came from but certain it is correct.

"Well done," says Boo admiringly. "Well, if you can remember those things, what can't you remember?"

I raise an eyebrow, and she giggles.

"Silly me. How can you know what you don't know?"

"It's not a completely worthless question," I say. "My biggest memory loss covers the days immediately before my accident. And there are fuzzy spaces specific to certain people, like my friend Jim Douglass and Coralie Pennington."

"You don't remember Coralie? She's not the type of woman easily forgotten. Coralie left a considerable impression here, especially with Stephan St John."

"I know."

"You remember that much, then?"

"Yes, but I don't know how. Were Cora and I good friends?"

"Very much so. And it obvious because she's picky about who gets to shorten her name. But yes, you seemed close. More like sisters than two women a generation apart. What a pity you can't remember."

"I can, but my memories of Cora are like a spider's web with more holes than threads."

"Will it always be that way?"

"Not if I can help it. Being here can only help." I am about to explain why that should be when Mary approaches, along with Peter and Carrington Blake. They take their seats, with Peter slumping into the couch beside me and giving my shoulder a friendly pat.

"Where have you been?" I ask, mindful of his recent neglect.

"Across the room, chatting to Carr."

"Carr?" For a moment, I don't know what he means. Then the penny drops. "Oh," I say, glancing at Carrington and hoping he can't read minds. Mine is currently contemplating how someone christened him with that mouthful of a name, then settled on the crude and uninspiring shortening. I stifle a smirk. "I mean before then."

Peter and Carrington exchange glances. "We took a stroll along the cliff road," says Peter. "I wanted to see the harbour. We didn't get a chance yesterday."

"Really," I say, wondering why he didn't ask me. I can't walk far, but I could have managed half a mile on the flat. Peter says nothing, and it seems that the thought hadn't crossed his mind.

"Never mind that," says Boo. "I'm more interested in what we will do after dinner." She looks at Mary conspiratorially, and Mary chews her lip.

"I'm not sure whether it's appropriate," says Mary, trying to avoid my eyes.

"What?" I ask.

"Yes, what?" echoes Peter.

"Well, it's Carrie, you see. Carrie Yeats. She lost her husband last year under odd circumstances. Supposedly a heart attack, but there was some doubt. Anyway, long story short, she's invited a medium to dinner. They're holding a seance in the study once we've eaten, and Carrie says the more, the merrier. They need at least six people, and the men won't play, of course, present company excepted."

"Present company included," says Carrington. "You can count me out."

"What about you, Peter?" asks Mary.

"That depends," he replies, looking at me. I can tell from his pained expression that he expects me to decline, but I am intrigued by Carrie's story. "I would like to join in," I say.

Peter scowls. "Then I will, too," he says.

Carrington laughs. "I am surprised at you giving credence to their silly parlour games. You should meet us in the library for a game of billiards instead."

Peter looks almost relieved as he apologises to Carrington. "I must look after Connie," he says. "She is still far from well."

"Nonsense," I say, but Carrington ignores me.

"Of course, old man. You must do the right thing."

I grind my teeth in silent condemnation at Peter's ingenuity. He may well have reservations about seances and other esoteric matters, but I know as well as he does that his ungainliness and lack of coordination make him an unsuitable billiard opponent. He would not give a good account of himself in front of Carrington, who he obviously admires, and looking after me is a handy excuse. I wouldn't mind if he was honest about it, but he makes me sound like an invalid.

"You might be the only man," Boo warns.

"So be it," says Peter.

"Look, there she is," whispers Mary, pointing across the room. I follow her finger towards the door as a tanned woman with dark hair swept into a turban follows behind Carrie Yeats and Gay Curnow. In her late fifties, the woman is long-legged and willowy with a knee-length black lace gown over which she has draped a cape. She carries a dark suitcase in her hand. Mary and Boo exchange glances and Boo licks her lips before flashing a cat-like smile. "This should be interesting," she says.

#

We assemble in the library at eight o'clock prompt. My second glass of wine at dinner has left me feeling wobbly, and I shuffle quietly into my seat, trying to regain my composure before the seance begins. Boo and Mary take their seats opposite while Peter stares out of the window, bristling with quiet annoyance. He spent most of dinner trying to dissuade me from joining in and is evidently uncomfortable with the whole idea. He says it is silly to court danger in this way and seems dismissive on the one hand while fearful on the other. I suppose it must be because of my encounters with Felix Crossley, but that is an entirely different matter. I've always considered seances nothing more than entertainment, but astral travel is a fact of my life. I wish it wasn't and as my memory returns, I grow more fearful of it. But my recent unexpected projection at the Chevis bungalow was not unpleasant, and I wasn't frightened at all. So, those dark memories, some of which still elude me, might remain in the past.

I am optimistic about future travel, and though I have solemnly promised Peter not to instigate it, we are both resigned to the fact that dream walking is often beyond my control. Nevertheless, I do not believe tonight's plans have any bearing on the likelihood of being called to the astral plane. Peter is worrying unnecessarily, and it will all be over in an hour. I flash him a comforting smile as he joins us at the table. He shakes his head, sits, and reaches for my hand. I respond by giving his hand a squeeze. Peter has been a good friend to me, and his actions are all born of genuine concern.

"Have you done this before?" asks Boo enthusiastically.

"No," I say, shaking my head. "I don't quite know what to expect."

"It doesn't always work," says Mary. "But have a care. It can be quite distressing when it does."

Boo pats her on the shoulder. Mary visibly shudders, not at Boo's touch but because something has disturbed her. Boo catches my puzzled frown. "Mary's younger brother came through last time," she whispers.

"Really? How often do you do this?"

"Now and then, usually when someone has a loss. It's quite

therapeutic, you know." Boo examines her fingernail and pulls at a jagged tear. "Bother," she says.

"What did your brother say?" I regret the words as soon as they leave my lips. Contrary to Boo's suggestion of comfort, Mary looks pained by the memory.

"He warned of a loss," she says.

"Before or after Crawford's accident?"

"Before. Laura was here, too. We thought nothing of it at the time. In fact, I didn't remember until Carrie proposed this latest seance."

"I expect it's nothing more than a coincidence," says Peter. "It just seems like a portent, in hindsight."

"You might be right," says Mary. "I would like to think so. I'm not comfortable with the idea of the afterlife. We should make the most of the one we've got."

I can't help but admire Mary. She has lost her father and both brothers, yet she keeps a cheerful disposition in the face of adversity. "I'm surprised you want to do this under the circumstances," I say.

"Carrie is still grieving for her husband," says Mary. "If it helps her, then it is worthwhile."

We sit in silence for a moment while Boo examines the delicate face of her watch. "What's keeping them?" she asks.

But before anyone can answer, we hear a noise on the stairs, and three women appear in the doorway.

"Sorry," says Carrie Yeats as she enters. "Trouble with the cats." She doesn't embellish but ushers the other women into the room. "Have you met Muriel?" she asks, gesturing to the medium.

"Briefly," says Mary.

"Oh, yes," says Boo. "Though you didn't sit for us last time, did you?"

"No. That was Cassandra. Unfortunately, she is unavailable." There is something unusual about the medium's voice. For all her cut-glass elegance, I hear the faintest trace of an accent I cannot recognise – something exotic, I think.

"Where shall we sit?" asks Carrie Yeates in uncertain tones. She puts on a brave face, seemingly enthusiastic, but her voice is husky with emotion.

"I will sit at the head," says Muriel.

Carrie and Gay take their seats to her side, and we wait expectantly for instructions.

"Draw the curtains, please." Muriel looks straight at Peter, who jumps up and cedes to her command while I surreptitiously examine her features. Muriel's turban hat frames her face, hiding her hair and emphasising her square jaw. It does her no fashion favours. "Dim the lights while you are up." Muriel's vocabulary does not contain the word, please, but Peter doesn't seem to mind and lowers the lighting until the room is almost dark.

We wait in silence while Muriel snaps open her bag and removes two candles which she lights and places in the centre of the table. The wicks crackle gently in the black, speckled wax and transfix my gaze, heralding another rush of memories: candlelight – my favourite voluntary way into the astral world. If I stare at it for too long, I know what will happen. Peter is sitting now and follows my gaze, immediately realising the potential implications.

"Close your eyes," he whispers, but I am already there, my eyes squeezed tightly shut. Goodness knows what Mary and Boo must be thinking, but it is the least of my worries.

"Is the light troubling you?" asks Muriel abruptly.

"Yes, it is," says Peter before I can reply.

"We can do without." Muriel wets her fingers and extinguishes the candle with a gentle hiss.

My eyes flutter open. I make out the concerned faces of Boo and Mary opposite, give a weak smile, and their expressions relax.

"There will be no Ouija board," says Muriel suddenly. "And no table tapping, automatic writing, ectoplasm or dramatic ghostly projections. I will be a conduit for the spirits. They will speak through me. Now, join hands and do not let go. The formation of the circle brings the spirits and keeps them earthbound. Do you understand?"

We whisper our affirmations, and she begins. "Spirits come to me. Join us, speak with us, and bring us news from beyond. Use my body to convey your messages, speak to the living, bridge the gap between life and death."

Muriel speaks confidently, her words loud and robust. She is in command, in firm control of the six people hanging on her every word. While I don't believe in spirits, I can't help but take Muriel seriously. That she might fail is almost inconceivable.

"I am here." A deep manly voice booms from Muriel's mouth. We stare at her, marvelling at the change in timbre.

"Thank you, spirit. Will you speak with us?"

"I will." The hairs on the back of my arms stand to attention.

"Announce yourself," says Muriel.

"I was known on earth as John Dee."

She has lost me. I know enough about history to have heard of the notorious Elizabethan alchemist and astrologer. Why must mediums overreach themselves? Almost any other name might have convinced me, but a famous occultist seems contrived.

"Who are you here for?"

"The other man."

"His name?"

"Peter."

Peter's hand tenses in mine. While I know he will be as cynical as I am, he is nonetheless taken aback by this personal approach.

"What is your message?"

"Don't trust him?"

"Don't trust who?" Peter breaks the silence of the circle and stares at Muriel, who is sitting with her eyes closed.

She speaks in John Dee's voice. "You know who. Trust your instincts, but do not trust him. That is all."

"Do you have another message?" Muriel's voice returns. She has finished with Peter and is moving on.

"I do."

"To whom would you speak?"

"To Madam Yeats."

Carrie gasps audibly.

"What do you wish to tell her?"

"I bear a message from her husband."

The light is faint, but it provides enough illumination to see Carrie's eager face, gazing longingly toward Muriel. A frisson of anger snaps through my body at this woman taking advantage of the recently bereaved.

"He says there is no mystery to his demise. It was entirely natural, and you are not to worry. He is happy in the other world and will watch over you until you are together again."

A tear trickles down Carrie's face and plops onto the table. "I miss you," she whispers, her voice thick with emotion.

"I miss you too. Stay here where you are safe and loved."

It is too much. Carrie breaks the circle, puts her head on her arms and sobs as if her heart would break. Peter scrapes back his chair and strides angrily towards the light. He presses the switch, and the chandelier flickers as the room illuminates.

"Are you alright, dear?" Boo is on one side of Carrie and Gay Curnow on the other.

"I'll fetch a brandy," says Mary, rushing away.

"That's why I didn't want to come," hisses Peter as he watches Carrie's crumpled form.

Muriel raises an eyebrow and shoots a glare Peter's way. She waits for Carrie's sobs to subside, then asks, "Did you feel him? Your husband was in the room."

Carrie raises her head. "I did. Oh yes, I did. He was standing behind me."

Muriel nods. "That's right. Did it help?"

"More than you can ever know. I miss him so much, and it is enough to know that he isn't suffering and loves me. I am so grateful to you."

Muriel gazes triumphantly at Peter. "And that is why I do it," she says.

91

CHAPTER TWELVE

Penhallow House

Monday, October 17, 1932

Penhallow House has lost none of its appeal, and my heart gladdens as we pull into the driveway, and I lay eyes on its charming grounds. Laura is waiting by the door and rushes out to see us, throwing her arms firstly around Mary and then around me as if we were long lost friends. Her awkward kisses landing close to but not touching Boo's cheeks suggest an air of frostiness, but if Boo notices, she doesn't react.

"And this must be Peter," says Laura, offering her hand.

Peter accepts it with a broad smile. "Pleased to meet you," he says, exuding charm.

"Well, come inside then," says Laura as she guides us into her orangery. I recline on a rattan chair in temperatures more often found in Mediterranean countries and immediately remove my cardigan. Laura's butler enters, bearing a large cake stand, returning moments later with pots of coffee and tea.

"Thank you, Jonathan," she says as he leaves the room.

"Such a treasure," she remarks when he is safely out of earshot. "I don't know what I'd do without him."

"I'm sure you'll never need to worry about that," says Mary.

We pass a pleasant half-hour chatting and enjoying an excellent carrot cake, Peter having taken several slices.

Mary tells us about her latest painting trip abroad, and Laura listens, basking in her words.

"I do so love hearing your stories," she says, not in the least envious of Mary's travels.

"The hotel was just like the one we stayed in when we went to Gibraltar," says Mary.

"How lovely."

"And what have you been doing with yourself, other than the obvious?" asks Mary.

"Mostly gardening and a little walking," says Laura.

"And dancing?" Mary's eyes flash mischievously.

Laura blushes, and she looks down at her lap, momentarily lost for words.

"Oh, Laura. Please don't feel embarrassed on my account. It's been nearly two years since Crawford disappeared. You're entitled to be happy."

"I wanted to tell you before you heard it elsewhere. How did you know?" Laura and Mary are speaking as if they were alone.

"Gay Curnow saw you at the tea dance and put two and two together. Now, what is his profession, and when do I get to meet him?"

"He's an accountant," says Laura. "And you'll meet him when I'm more certain about our friendship."

Mary raises an eyebrow.

"Soon, I promise."

The momentary awkward silence is soon broken by Boo Lyons seamlessly changing the subject into her opinion of the latest fashions. It is controversial, and Mary and Laura are soon arguing good-naturedly. I zone out, fashion not being my strong point. Soon, Laura stands and offers a plate of biscuits around the room. My eyes are growing heavy from the excessive heat, and Peter prods me to break my reverie. I snatch a biscuit even though I am full, vainly hoping they might think I was paying attention and not just about to drop off – my ruse fools nobody.

"Shall we go outside?" asks Laura.

"It's rather cold," says Boo, with a mock shiver. "Haven't you just extended your workroom? I would rather see that."

"You must go outside to get there," says Laura.

"Isn't it part of the house?"

"No. I built it against Crawford's old writing room. I couldn't bear to get rid of his things, so I added an extension to the building instead."

"Do you paint too?" I ask.

Laura nods. "A little, but it's only a hobby," she says modestly. "I wouldn't dream of trying to sell them."

"They're good enough," says Mary.

"You're too kind. It's enough to know that I can keep my hand in. Now, do you really want to look?"

"Absolutely," says Boo enthusiastically. "I could do with some ideas for Cormorant House. Gulliver has finally agreed to let us take over the old glasshouse. It will need considerable adaptation to be fit for purpose, and any ideas are welcome."

"Come along then," says Laura. "Connie, Peter – won't you join us?"

"Do you mind if I don't?" Although I am half asleep, my hip is still throbbing, as it sometimes does in cold and damp weather.

"Not at all."

"I'll stay with her," says Peter, reaching for another biscuit.

"I don't know where you put it," I say when the three women have left. You ought to look like Billy Bunter."

"Hollow legs," Peter says with a grin. "Now, tell me why you didn't want to go outside. It's most unlike you."

"My hip honestly hurts," I say.

"And?"

"And I've been in the workshop before. I opened Crawford's

trunk when I was there. It had a false bottom."

"Oh yes, I remember you telling me. Didn't you find a Calcium Aureum robe in there?"

"Yes. And Mary passed me a burned journal for safekeeping."

"The one Laura found?"

"Correct. It was almost spoiled beyond recognition, but the fire had missed a few pages containing symbols. I can't help feeling that Newson was involved with the sect somehow."

"Poor devil," says Peter. "How long do you think they'll be?"

"A while, I should think. It's a five-minute walk to the workroom."

"Then let's have a look around. Otherwise, you'll fall asleep."

I grab my stick and show Peter into the drawing-room, where he admires the paintings. Then we pass through the dining room and slink past the kitchen, where Jonathan is whistling while he works on the other side of the door.

"Look at this, Connie," says Peter as we pass the door to the library. I follow his gaze and see a room filled floor to ceiling with dark mahogany bookshelves and a substantial oak desk in the centre.

"This must be Crawford's study," I say.

Peter is almost speechless, transfixed by rows of leather-bound books on shelves so high that the Newsons installed a sliding ladder to reach them. "I want one," he says, using slow, staccato words.

He walks towards the nearest shelf and strokes the gold leaf-covered spines. "Crawford must have spent a fortune. I wonder if Laura has read them all?"

"She couldn't have," I say. There are thousands of books in the library, more than anyone could get through in several lifetimes unless they did nothing else all day.

"What I wouldn't give for a few months in here," says Peter.

I pluck a book from the shelf. The exquisite binding hides a surprisingly old book written over a century earlier. It is a

95

treatise on moral ideals and not worth further inspection, given that my reading material is mostly fiction – anything else I find indigestible.

Peter moves over to the finest bound books, extracts one, and then his face falls in disgust. "Why they're not real," he says, holding the husk of a book, perfectly bound but with its inners missing. "They're moulds, fakes. How disappointing."

"Not all of them," I say.

"Even so. There are plenty of old books around with which to furnish a library. Crawford Newson is all show." Peter purses his lips, genuinely offended at the deception.

"It would cost a fortune," I say. "Look. I bet these are real." I point towards a row of books, out of kilter with the even rows of similarly bound books on the other shelves.

Peter walks over. "I bet you're right. It's because he penned them." He picks up a book and inspects it. "Ah. Belle of the South Seas. This was Crawford's last book, published posthumously, you know – the one they made into a film."

"I remember," I say. "Though I've yet to see it."

Peter shelves the book and picks up another. He takes it towards the window and perches on the little window seat, turning one page, then another, his forehead furrowed in concentration. I know I have lost him for a moment and content myself trying to identify the false books from the real ones. I am offering internal congratulations on my high success rate when Peter speaks.

"I've seen this style of writing before," he says.

"I should think so. You introduced me to the Cornish trilogy."

"No. This book differs greatly from his usual work. And the subject matter bears no resemblance to any I've read before. You know how Newson writes, very much in the Boy's Own style, all heroic adventuring or irreverent comedy. Well, this couldn't be further from that type of writing. It's a gothic horror, more in the style of Henry James, and could almost be a different author, but now and again, a familiar expression appears, a way with words that make it classic Newson."

"Are you sure?" I ask.

Peter shoots a withering look. "I spend most of my life reading and analysing books, and I'm telling you now that this differs from Newson's usual style, but I've seen something similar recently. Even down to the name of the country house in which he's set the story. Look at this – Doubledown Manor." Peter pushes the book under my nose and jabs his finger into the middle of the page.

"It seems a normal enough name. Not that uncommon."

"It's not just the name – it's the way of writing. I'd swear they were the same. If only I could remember where I'd read it."

"Come on, Peter. We'd better get back to the orangery. Laura will be back soon, and I don't want her to think we've been poking around."

"Blast it." Peter returns the book to the shelf with a scowl. We return down the corridor and are almost back where we started when Peter tugs on my sleeve and hisses triumphantly. "That's it, Connie. I've remembered. I read the story in this month's edition of The London Herald, and if Newson didn't write it, then someone went to great lengths to copy his style."

CHAPTER THIRTEEN

The Four Musketeers

Wednesday, October 19, 1932

We've been in Bosula for several days when Mary brings the post inside and hands me two letters over the breakfast table. The first is from Mrs Ponsonby, who feels the need to tell me that one of the chickens is egg bound. Other riveting news from the Ponsonby pen includes Elys' first attempt at a lemon meringue pie which, unusually for her, ended in failure and reports on Mr Brookbank's latest attack of gout. Mrs Ponsonby must have acquired the latter piece of gossip from Dolly as she seldom visits the hotel for any other reason, appearing to disapprove of it for reasons I can't fathom.

Peter, sitting next to me, scoops the last forkful of scrambled egg, which he quickly dispatches before patting his lips with a napkin. "Who's sent that?" he asks, and I hand the letter over, hoping it will keep him distracted long enough for me to read the second missive without him noticing. I know before I open it that it will be from Sebastian. No one else knows I am here. Sure enough, the long cursive script is as I expected. Sebastian has invited us for dinner at the Lamorna Wink, conveniently close to Cormorant House. Unless he hears otherwise, he will collect us at six o'clock tonight. I lower his letter and chew my lip, wondering whether Mary will mind if we go out without her. But that is the least of my worries. I have barely mentioned Sebastian to Peter except in the context of an investigation, of which Peter strongly disapproves. He hasn't met Sebastian and will not, I am sure, be keen on the idea of dining with not one but two perfect strangers. I must handle this tactfully.

I leave Peter with Mrs Ponsonby's letter and look for Mary, drying dishes in the kitchen with her mother. They are giggling like two schoolgirls in cahoots, and a jealous rage surges through me at their easy relationship. For the umpteenth time, I wish I had known my mother.

"Hello, my dear," says Mrs Newson with all the joy of a life untouched by tragedy, even though this is not the case. "I was just telling Mary that a hedgehog has been using St John's best hat for its business."

"He shouldn't have left it outside," says Mary.

"It could have been someone else. Still, he's not back for a few days yet, and I might try to clean it."

"Otherwise, he'll howl like a banshee," says Mary. "You know how easily offended he gets."

"I'll deal with St John," says Mrs Newson, polishing a glass that she adds to a long row of similar glasses on the windowsill above the sink. "Not much point in putting these away now that Gulliver has opened the box of claret."

"Shall I help?" I ask, not wanting to intrude on Mary's time if I can't be of assistance.

"Absolutely not. You're my guest."

"I don't mind."

"Then pop these on the aga to dry," says Mary, handing me a collection of damp tea towels. I lay them across the warm range, then lean back against it, enjoying the residual heat.

"What are your plans today?" asks Mary.

"That's what I came to speak to you about," I reply. "Well, not so much my plans today, rather this evening."

"Oh, yes?" Mary raises a curious eyebrow.

"I've been invited to dinner," I say.

"Really. By whom?"

"A friend from Newquay. I don't think you know him."

"Try me."

"Sebastian Letwin."

"You're right. I don't."

"Well, anyway. He has invited me to The Lamorna Wink."

"How lovely," says Mrs Newson. "You should go."

Mary shares none of her mother's enthusiasm and chews her lip anxiously. "What does Peter think?"

"I haven't told him yet, but Sebastian knows he's here and has asked him to join us."

"Oh, good. In that case, I agree. Go along and have a lovely time."

"What about you?"

"I've got plenty to do. And Boo is determined to press on with this new garden workshop before Gulliver changes his mind. She wants a hand sketching out her ideas, and I'm more than happy to help."

"Splendid," I say. "I'll tell Peter." And I leave the kitchen feeling excited. Cormorant House represents a freedom so often denied to me by Mrs Ponsonby. I can do anything, go anywhere when released from the confines of Pebble Cottage and Mrs Ponsonby's iron grip. Now just the small matter of Peter to deal with.

As expected, my suggestion does not go well. "What on earth is that man doing here?" asks Peter coldly when I show him the invitation.

"He's visiting a friend in Mousehole."

"Did you know he was going to ask you?"

"He might have mentioned it."

"Then why didn't you tell me?"

I wordlessly shrug and hold my hands wide, motioning to Peter that I knew he would react badly, hence the deception. He scowls but appreciates my point.

"Must we attend?" he asks.

"I would like to."

"And presumably you will go alone, whatever I say?"

"Well, yes. Tony Harding has a car with him, and they're coming to collect me, so why not?"

"Oh, Connie. You are so trusting. You'd go off with two soldiers, one you barely know and the other you've never met. No wonder Mrs Ponsonby keeps you on a tight leash."

My mouth drops open as I stare at Peter, wondering how he has the audacity to talk down to me as if I were a child. "How dare you," I hiss. "What gives you the right to judge me?"

"You're only here because I agreed to come with you," says Peter. "Otherwise, you'd be having this conversation with Vera."

"Don't call her by her first name," I say petulantly. "Peter. I'm a grown woman, and all I want to do is join a friend for a meal. I'm not running off to Gretna Green, and it's not an unreasonable request. Sebastian has asked you to join us, so what exactly is your problem?"

"Fine," says Peter. "Have it your way. I'll cancel my arrangements."

"What arrangements?"

"Never mind." Two spots of red blaze across Peter's cheeks.

"I do mind. What arrangements? Did they include me?"

"It doesn't matter."

"Peter. Tell me."

"Carr is having some problems. We were going to discuss them over a meal at the hotel."

Peter looks at the floor, then the window, then past my ear – anything to avoid my eyes.

"You like him, don't you?"

"We're friends," says Peter. "I don't need to meet him tonight. We've got another week."

"Nonsense," I say. "You go out as planned. Sebastian is coming here, and you can meet him before I go. That should keep everyone happy."

"I really shouldn't," says Peter. "I promised Mrs P." But he is wavering, and one more push from me ought to do it.

"It's bad manners to back out of an engagement," I say. "Think of Carrington."

Peter chews his lip. "If you're sure you don't mind."

"Positive," I say.

#

I am watching from the window when Sebastian arrives in a big blue Triumph with a loud engine which backfires only yards from Cormorant house. The attractive driver stops the car and tips me a regretful salute. I wave back and walk towards the reception hall, arriving moments after Boo, who has already let them in.

"Well, what have we here?" she purrs, looking both interested and aloof at the same time.

"Ah, Connie," says Sebastian as I enter, and Boo's face falls.

"Are they your friends?"

I nod.

"Lucky you," says Boo, disappearing into one of the painting rooms. She closes the door as another opens, revealing Peter, dressed in evening wear.

He starts to speak, then stops, and I realise he doesn't know Sebastian from Tony Harding, neither of whom he has met. I quickly introduce them and am about to tell Sebastian that Peter won't be joining us when Peter unexpectedly takes control of the conversation.

"Good of you to invite me," he says, thrusting his hand towards Sebastian. "I'm delighted to join you for dinner."

I stare at Peter, perplexed, but he ignores me and carries on chatting. Peter seems the soul of cheerfulness, good-natured and gregarious, but I know him better, and his smile does not reach his eyes. Beneath the Bonhomie lurks immense frustration. I am yet to learn whether it's because he feels compelled to babysit me or whether something else has happened. But as Peter will now join us at the Lamorna Wink, there is no reason to hang around at Cormorant House. So, I pointedly collect my coat from the stand, and Sebastian helps me into it, and then we walk to the car.

Sebastian opens the rear door, and I climb inside, stowing my stick beneath my feet. The leather upholstery smells new, making me feel slightly queasy before we even set off. This is not improved by Tony's offer of a cigarette, which we all decline, but he lights one and puffs away regardless. I don't mind the smell of cigarettes, although I have never tried one. But on the rare occasions that I've travelled by car, I always feel nauseous even if I'm not actually sick. I know they say that cigarettes are good for the health, but I wish they would make them a little more tolerable in confined spaces. I wind the window down a fraction, hoping that nobody will notice.

"What have you been up to?" asks Sebastian, turning to face us. "Did you manage a boat trip, Connie? I know you wanted to."

"Not yet," I say. "But we're here for another week. There's plenty of time."

"Me too," says Tony, inhaling a plume of smoke and flicking ash through the window. "Then I'm off on my travels again."

"Sebastian is also going away," I say to Peter. "Back to Gibraltar with his regiment."

"You'll have better weather than this," says Peter. Dusk is rapidly approaching, and a fine drizzle has settled in. Tony flicks a switch, and the windscreen wiper darts across the driver's side. I watch, hypnotised for a few moments, before tearing my eyes away.

"Are we nearly there?" I ask plaintively. The moving wiper has exacerbated my nausea, and I am dangerously close to disgracing myself by being sick.

"That's it over there," says Tony, pointing to a distant light. "Just a couple of minutes."

103

I slide my hand between the narrowly open window and the car roof, feeling the cold air wash over my skin. It is enough to stave off the sickness, and I feel relieved when Tony parks the car under the window of a large stone building.

Tony applies the hand brake while Sebastian darts out and opens the door. He escorts me into the hostelry while Peter and Tony chat behind us. Moments later, we are sitting at a table, clutching our menus. Peter and Sebastian order a glass of scotch while Tony and I settle for wine. We glance at the menu, give the waitress our meal choices, and settle down to talk. Then Tony steeples his hands and leans forwards. "So, I hear you are interested in our late friend Hugh," he says.

"I am," I reply, blushing furiously. The way Tony has approached the subject makes me feel like a nosy intruder, and it's a fair point.

"Why?"

I take a deep breath. "Because I don't like mysteries," I say, eventually.

"And what makes you think you could help resolve this one?"

"She makes some pretty good guesses," says Sebastian.

"So, I hear." Tony lights another cigarette and then rummages in his pockets before withdrawing a blue bound copy of *The Man with Two Left Feet*, which he places on the table. I regard the book with interest. Any novel gets my immediate attention, yet I am perplexed. Although I often want to read at the table, especially in dull company, it's considered bad manners. Surely social conventions haven't changed that much.

Tony breaks my reverie. "I suppose you are wondering why I've brought this," he asks.

I open my mouth to speak, but Peter interrupts. "No doubt you've heard about Connie's reading habit," he says, sporting his first genuine smile of the evening.

Tony laughs. "Do you like PG Wodehouse?" he asks.

"I like all writers," I say. "Though I'm not familiar with this novel."

"That's because it's a collection of short stories," says Tony. "But that's beside the point."

"Then what is the point?" asks Sebastian.

"This belonged to Hugh," says Tony. "And strictly speaking, it still does, or at least to his estate. I borrowed it and missed the opportunity to give it back."

"That's a shame," I say. "But a nice memento for you, at least."

"Quite," says Tony. "And even more so when I reached page 183, *A Sea of Troubles*. Look what I found. Tony flips open the book, which naturally falls open to the page in question because of a photograph marking the end of a chapter. He lifts it from the book and places it on the table, turning it first towards Sebastian, then towards me.

"Well, look at that," says Sebastian, a slow smile spreading across his face. "The four musketeers. Well, I'll be damned."

"It's the same as the one in his dining room," I exclaim. "Only smaller."

"I remember you mentioning it," says Sebastian. "Fancy him keeping two copies."

"Digger Brown took the picture," says Tony. "Do you remember?"

"How could I forget? He photographed us during our last year at RMA Woolwich," says Sebastian, trying to give context to Peter and me. "We were so young, then. And now one of us is dead before the age of thirty. We've had a year to get used to it, but I don't think I will ever resign myself to Hugh's death."

"Nor I," says Tony. "Hugh was the type of chap you'd expect to go on and on. I'm not surprised he married well."

"And the only one of us who has," says Sebastian.

"Oh, I don't know. Drake got quite close to a girl a few years ago. Nothing came of it, though."

"There would have been a wedding by now," says Sebastian.

"I'll ask him about it when I next see him," jokes Tony. "You can come too if they haven't sent you back by then."

"It will have to be soon," says Sebastian. "I've only got a few weeks left in blighty."

"Drake is in Hampshire now. You can go whenever you like."

A delicious smell precedes the arrival of our food, which comes as a relief. Tony and Sebastian have taken a turn down memory lane as if they have forgotten that Peter and I are there. I don't mind, but Peter looks bored, and as he has already sacrificed his plans for the evening, I must jolly things along. We tuck into our food and order another round of drinks.

"This is delicious," says Peter, looking happier by the moment.

Tony pushes the book to the table's edge and cuts into his steak.

"How do you propose conducting this investigation?" he asks.

I swallow a mouthful of fish and contemplate my words. "By examining the facts," I say lamely.

"The police did that," he replies. "To no avail."

"And I'll talk to a few of the people concerned. Sebastian has offered to help."

Sebastian gives an encouraging smile. He must have discussed my interest in the case with Tony Harding, but Tony seems cautious, bordering on hostile, and I wonder if he finds my interference distasteful. I confront the matter head-on.

"Do you mind?" I ask.

"A little," he says, frankly. "Hugh was a dear friend. I would have liked to have seen the cause of his death resolved at the inquest. And however talented you are at assembling facts, or whatever you do, I can't help feeling you are picking private matters apart with no hope of progress. It bothers me."

"I understand," I say.

"I can vouch for Connie," sighs Peter, seemingly frustrated at his need to defend me.

"Look, it doesn't matter," says Tony. "Just because I feel uncomfortable doesn't mean you shouldn't do it. Who am I to sit in judgement, anyway? But you seem like a nice young lady and ought to know what you are dealing with. Hugh was a man of the world."

"Tony." Sebastian shoots a warning glance.

"No, my old friend. Don't keep things from her. Hugh was what he was. There's no point in pretending. It will all come out in the wash."

"What do you mean?" I ask, picking a bone from my fish and placing it on the side of the plate.

"He led a full life. Frances did too."

"I don't know what you mean."

"I thought not. The Chevis' had, how shall I put it? They had what you might call an open marriage."

"You mean?"

"Yes. Hugh and Frances were blissfully happy, but he saw other women, and she saw other men."

"While they were married?" I ask.

Tony nods. "Before and during their marriage."

"And neither minded?"

"No. You must understand that Frances led a very cosmopolitan life. She was an heiress and wanted for nothing. Hugh was a Training Instructor at Aldershot, and as you know, they lived together in Blackdown Camp. But as far as Frances was concerned, Hampshire was in the middle of nowhere. So, she kept her flat in London and her children, by her previous husband, lived there with their nanny. Frances spent the week with Hugh and returned to London at the weekend."

"What a strange life," I say.

Tony puts his cutlery down and steeples his hands. "To you and me, perhaps. But it was perfectly normal to them. Hugh kept up his friendship with..." Tony breaks off and clicks his fingers, struggling to remember.

"Iris Coates," says Sebastian.

"That's the one," says Tony. "A nice girl. Very accommodating. Frances turned a blind eye, and in return, he didn't make a fuss when she found an escort in London."

"When you say escort?"

107

"A long-standing lover," says Tony. "I don't know who it was, and I'm not sure Hugh did either. She was coy about the name, but it didn't matter. Hugh wasn't the jealous type. The arrangement suited them both very well."

"Thank you for telling me," I say. I don't know how it will help, but unexpectedly uncovering a lover would undoubtedly have thrown me off track had I found out mid-investigation.

Peter clears his plate and dabs his mouth with a napkin. "I could eat that again," he says.

"Well, I hope you kept some room. The desserts are magnificent."

Silence falls while the rest of us clear our plates. I am the last to finish, and no sooner does my fork hit my plate than the efficient waitress arrives to clear away our dishes. We order desserts, each making different choices, and wait for them to arrive.

"Do you know anything else that might help?" I ask.

"Not really."

"What about the telegrams?" asks Sebastian. "Don't you have a theory?"

"Quite the opposite," says Tony. "Bloody press – excuse my language."

"What about them?" asks Peter, looking interested. Peter feels protective of the press, given that his cousin is a reporter.

"They blew the telegrams out of all proportion," says Tony. "Now, if you don't already know, Hugh's father received a telegram on the day of Hugh's funeral. They had only just released the news of Hugh's death, yet someone sent it the day before, most likely his murderer. It was a cruel thing to do to a grieving man."

"What did it say?" asks Peter.

"Hooray, hooray, hooray," says Tony. "The envelope contained a Dublin postmark and came from The Hibernian Hotel. It was signed by a J Hartigan."

"And they never found him?"

Tony shakes his head. "Not for want of looking. The police

got to it quickly, interviewing every guest at the hotel, to no avail. A few days later, a second telegram arrived at the offices of The Daily Sketch, asking why they published a photograph of the first telegram. And four days after that, Sir William Chevis received the third and final missive containing a simple message.

It is a mystery they will never solve. Hooray. J Hartigan.

"Hooray," I say. "What a strange thing to say."

"Not really. Sporting types give three cheers all the time. It amounts to the same thing."

"I know," I say. "But it lends an air of joviality to an otherwise serious matter. Do you mind if I write this down?"

"Be my guest," says Tony. He repeats the salient points, and I scribble them on the back of the menu, which I fold and place in my pocket.

"It does, you know," says Peter.

"What does?"

"Trivialise matters. The telegrams seem contrived somehow."

Peter does not elucidate further. He is interrupted by the waitress, who asks if we would like coffee to finish. The three men opt for cognac, but I am glad of the opportunity for something non-alcoholic. I am still tired as I have been for the last few days, and anything more would send me to sleep.

"What now?" asks Sebastian when we have finished our drinks. "Would you like to go to a bar?"

"Do you mind if we don't?" I feel rude for bringing the evening to an early close, but we've been in each other's company for three hours now, and I am ready to go home. Peter looks relieved as I say my piece – he is not much of a bar fly either. Sebastian pays the bill and refuses our attempt to contribute. Then Tony Harding takes my hand and escorts me to the door. I flop onto the back seat of the car, exhausted. Tony pulls away, and before long, the men have fallen into a tedious discussion about the strategic military implications of Iran joining the League of Nations. Peter is interested, but I am not, and I doze against his shoulder.

Time passes, and I wake with a jolt. It seems like hours but can have only been minutes, and they are still droning on about the same boring subject. I sigh and detach myself from Peter, hoping that he didn't hear my groan of boredom. He doesn't even look at me as I pull away, so I reach into my pocket to examine the menu I stashed earlier. My hand disappears through one side and out of the other. I try again, but this time, it melds into the fabric. Then I realise. I have fallen into a waking dream without trying. And it's the first time in ages that I've done it publicly. I gaze around, feeling uncomfortable and embarrassed, but I know from previous experience that they can't see me. Moved to test my theory, I shimmy upwards until I am half in, half out of the car roof, watching my sleeping body still curled against Peter. I close my eyes and will myself back again, but it is not to be. So, I push back through the roof and try once more – still nothing. I can't remember the technique I used previously, that memory joining the dwindling few that remain entirely elusive. I count to one hundred with my eyes tightly shut, and at the end, I open them before plunging my hand through the window to test. It shears through the glass like a knife through butter, and I begin to panic.

We are only a few miles from Cormorant House. What happens if I can't reoccupy my body in time? Will I lie there as if comatose? Will they think I've died? A vivid memory of the barn at Trenhorne Farm flashes through my mind. This happened before while I was trying to help Annie Hearn. And the only way I could return home was to go somewhere dark. Somewhere utterly pitch black. And as I think darkness and imagine inky skies, I am lifted upwards in a sudden swirl of energy as if carried through the eye of a tornado to a place I know well – the astral plane.

I haven't seen it for a while, mainly because I took to keeping my eyes tightly closed while travelling. But watching stars push timorously through the tenebrous firmament brings a host of lost thoughts and abandoned recollections: robes and insignia, Coralie Pennington, and Felix Crossley. Slavering jowls sexually charged rituals and unspeakable evil. And I know without question that I am part of their plans. This newest memory shocks to the core – Coralie, you were my friend, and now your life is bound to his. Why? Does Mrs Ponsonby know? And if so, why are they still friends? They must be. I know because I saw a letter addressed to Coralie propped up on the sideboard only last week. All these thoughts swirl randomly around my head as memories ebb and flow.

A tidal wave of despair descends on me as I slow and hover in the vortex, seemingly tied to the astral plane. I don't know where I'm going or whether there is a final destination. Or will I be stuck here for eternity like Tantalus, reaching for the fruit which always eludes his grasp? Perhaps that is my fate – forever in orbit with no doors in or out. I wait and watch while I linger. Then he comes. He is a shadow in the distance, moving slowly at first, so far away that I can't even be sure he is human. But as he draws near and I see his round face, the bald head, and the glint of metal on the unicursal hexagon he wears around his portly neck, I stiffen. I feel the false sensation of a heartbeat only present in my earthly body, the echo of an intangible surge of adrenalin, and I gasp aloud. That sound, that sudden movement, saves me. He is only yards away when a searing tug at the back of my skull tears me away, hurtling me back to earth, where I wake with a jolt.

Peter sniggers. "Having a nightmare, were we?" he asks. "You all but screamed, Connie."

"Something like that," I mutter, recognising the driveway to Cormorant House. I have returned in the nick of time.

Tony parks, and then Peter offers them a nightcap, as much out of politeness as a desire to prolong the evening. Sebastian declines and then turns to me in concern to ask if I am alright. I thank him for the evening, and we make brief plans to meet again, if not here, then in Porth Tregoryan. They leave, and I am alone with Peter in the hallway.

"What's wrong with you?" he asks.

"Not here," I hiss.

Peter opens the nearest door and glances inside. "It's empty," he says, screwing his nose up at the smell of oil paints that permeate the room. We slip inside, and I take a seat at the paint-spattered table. Peter sits opposite.

"What is it?"

"I wasn't asleep," I say.

"Oh. You mean…?"

"Yes."

"Are you sure? I couldn't tell."

"Absolutely certain. It happened in the car, and I couldn't remember how to get back into my body."

"You just touch it," says Peter.

I look heavenward. Of course. How could I forget such a basic fact?

"What did you do?" he asks.

"I remembered getting stuck before and got past it by concentrating hard in complete darkness. So, I used the same method, and it took me to the black, where I met Crossley."

"Did he see you?"

"I don't know. He came towards me but didn't get close enough for me to tell one way or the other."

"This is serious. I hoped your memory loss would keep you from all this danger."

"It's mostly back. The only things I can't bring to mind are the memories I long to know the most."

"Jim?"

I nod.

"About that," says Peter, but doesn't get to finish. The door opens to reveal Gay Curnow.

"What are you doing here in the dark?" she asks, reaching for the lamp chain.

I blush to my roots. We have ignited a small oil lamp, but it must look odd whispering together under what might be

112

construed as romantic lighting.

"It seemed wasteful to light the mantle," I say.

"A fair point," says Gay. "Do you like it, then?"

She points to a picture of a sandpiper at the end of the table.

"Yes, it's beautiful. Is it one of yours?"

Gay nods. "Wildlife is my thing. I'm exhibiting in London next week."

"Like Mary?"

"In a different gallery in another part of town. But I can't wait to be there. I have friends to catch up with."

Gay reels off a list of people, and I know Crossley will be one of them before she says his name. Peter visibly starts when he hears it, but I sit there resigned to a truth I could see coming. Gay is still talking.

"Yes, Felix wrote last week. He came back to England from Germany – well, he's been here for a good while actually, but this is the first I've heard of it. Felix is a good sort, odd and somewhat spiritual, but fun to be around and an excellent host. I shall look forward to chatting with him before he comes to Cornwall."

CHAPTER FOURTEEN

Something Deadly This Way Comes

Friday, October 21, 1932

We left the following day, driving without a break and arriving back at Pebble Cottage just after lunch. Elys and Mrs Ponsonby were clearing dishes when we came and immediately jumped up, fearing the worst from our sudden arrival. Peter's cover story about our rapid departure due to his concern over my frail physical health did not help their disquiet.

And now, a whole day later, I cannot get any peace from Mrs Ponsonby's anxious ministrations when she looks like she ought to be in bed herself. Elys is no better and brought breakfast to my room, even though I had been up and about for hours, only laying down fully clothed to read a brief chapter from my book. It is all too much.

Peter slunk home at the earliest opportunity, knowing I was cross with him. From the moment he realised that Gay Curnow was friendly with Felix Crossley, my time at Cormorant House was under threat. Peter had practically packed my bag for me before graciously allowing me to tell Mary that I was poorly and must go home. I naturally protested, feeling I was as safe in Bosula as anywhere, but Peter disagreed, threatening to contact Mrs Ponsonby if I didn't cooperate. The only thing worse than breaking my holiday early would be my guardian dragging me away like a spoiled child. And having no other dignified choice, I agreed. But as much as I understand Peter's reasoning, he could have dealt with things better, and I will happily do without his presence for a few days while my anger subsides.

I take a mouthful from the bowl of porridge Elys delivered earlier, but the gloopy mess is tepid and tastes like sludge. Pushing it away, I reach for my book, but my mind isn't on reading. I hear a scrabbling at the door, which opens to reveal Teddy. He bounds onto my bed and greets me with a wet kiss. I missed him a lot while I was away, and he evidently felt the same, having hardly left my side since I returned. If he hadn't needed a comfort break, he wouldn't have left my room at all, and it gladdens my heart to know that something loves me that much. I offer Teddy the porridge, and he takes a mouthful or two before turning away. Even the little cocker spaniel can't muster the enthusiasm to finish it, and I make a mental note to ask Elys not to serve porridge again. I cuddle Teddy for a moment, breathing in his warm furry body, and after a while, I feel a little better. Determined to make something of the day, I delve into my secret stash of things Mrs Ponsonby knows nothing about, bypassing the paper with the Netherwood address on it in favour of the menu with the transcript of the Hooray telegrams and the newspaper clippings and notebook. I settle back on the bed and re-read everything I know about the Poisoned Partridges, familiarising myself with details I had already forgotten. Then I note all the people I would like to speak to when I finally get around to questioning them. Once done, I stow everything in my bedside drawer, ready to resume work later. I glance at the clock, whose hands have finally struggled round to ten-thirty and decide not to waste any more of the day indoors. Grabbing my stick and an extra cardigan, I go downstairs and straight into the path of Mrs Ponsonby.

"Good news," she says as I navigate past her and reach my coat from the stand.

"Oh, yes?"

"We're having a visitor."

"Who?"

"Just a moment." Mrs Ponsonby bends over, wincing in pain as she holds her hand over her side. "Oh, dear."

She barely finishes uttering the words when Elys is by her side and manoeuvring her into the parlour.

"Take her arm," hisses Elys. But the notion of touching Mrs Ponsonby is so strange that it stops me in my tracks, and I pause.

"For crying out loud." Elys barges past me, wrapping her arm around Mrs Ponsonby and lowering her onto the couch.

"Fetch my pills, dear," says Mrs Ponsonby.

"Of course." Elys dashes to the kitchen, shooting me a glare as she leaves. I stand awkwardly by the door, watching Mrs Ponsonby and wondering what I should do. She seems distressed, and I want to help, but it doesn't come naturally.

"Don't worry about me," says Mrs Ponsonby, breaking the unnatural silence. "It will pass."

"What's wrong?" I ask, hoping her illness is not of an embarrassing nature.

"Just a gastric complaint," says Mrs P, before a sharp intake of breath temporarily renders her speechless.

Elys returns with a brown bottle and a packet of pills. She puts them on the side table, takes a jug and pours a glass of water, which she gives to Mrs Ponsonby.

"Hold out your hand," says Elys, popping two pills from the packet that Mrs Ponsonby swallows, gulping water to wash them down. "Do you want the medicine, too?"

Mrs Ponsonby shakes her head.

"I've left the spoon in case it gets any worse. Shall I pop your feet up, and I'll fetch you a blanket?"

"No. Just a magazine."

Elys passes her a copy of Country Life, and she settles down to read it. I linger, waiting for her to tell me about the visitor, but Elys jerks her head in a "leave her alone" kind of way and I remove myself from the room and follow Elys down the corridor to the kitchen.

"What's that all about?" I ask when we are safely out of earshot.

"She's poorly," says Elys.

"Yes, but all that fuss for a bit of gastric flu."

"Is that what she said?"

"Yes. And that it would soon pass."

"Then I'm sure she's right." Elys stares tight-lipped at a mixing bowl covered in a gingham cloth.

"What's in there?" I ask.

"Bread. It's proving." Elys is terse and unfriendly. I can't help wondering if I've done something wrong.

"Oh, look at Teddy," I say, trying to lighten the mood. He is standing on his hind legs on the other side of the table, the tips of two paws and a wet little nose peeping over the edge.

"Down," barks Elys, and Teddy retreats, backing towards me where he settles against my leg.

"He didn't mean any harm."

"You should train him," snaps Elys. "It's unhygienic."

I spin on my heel and stalk from the room, wondering what has got into Elys. She is tetchy, and I don't like it. I reach for my coat where it hung from the newel, and I am about to put it on when Mrs Ponsonby calls me in a weak voice, and I go to her side.

"I didn't tell you who was coming," she says. "You'll be so pleased."

"Is it Peter?" I ask.

"Oh no. This isn't a day visitor. We have a staying guest."

Foreboding clutches at my heart. "Who?"

"Coralie. Coralie Pennington. She's arriving on Sunday. Now, what do you think about that?"

#

What do I think about that? What a ridiculous question. Mrs Ponsonby has taken leave of her senses, allowing that woman in our house with the associations she keeps. I charge towards the cave, walking more quickly than my health allows. Tired and weak, I pull up some fifty yards before the cave and stop to catch my breath. Panting in rapid shallow gulps that make my fingers tingle, I wobble dangerously against the stick, and, for a moment, I think I might pass out. I am on the verge of sitting down when the worst of the panic passes. Just as well, as I don't like my chances of easily getting up from the sand when my legs are too tired to carry me. Resisting the urge to hurry into the cave, I force myself to wait. One hippopotamus, two hippopotamuses. I count a hundred of the weighty mammals before risking a slow amble across the beach. Slowly and steadily, my cave moves into view. I stumble inside and throw myself on the chair, snuggling under a blanket until my heart rate normalises.

It's blowing a storm outside. I hadn't noticed with the shock of hearing Mrs Ponsonby's words. No wonder I struggled against the wind, spending more energy than is usually necessary. It's cold, and the blanket is inadequate. I grab another from the matching chair and stare into the horizon, marshalling my thoughts. Coralie Pennington will be in Porth Tregoryan in less than forty-eight hours. What does Cora want here? Is she coming for me, and how afraid should I be? I know she's involved with Crossley, but she doesn't know that I know. She might be here for nothing more than a visit – a chance to catch up with an old friend. If so, I could simply carry on as before. But I'm not a good actress. Peter says I wear my heart on my sleeve, and he is right. I would never make a poker player. And the thought of pretending everything is fine and dandy when I know Cora indulges in Crossley's horrid rituals is something I could never overlook. Damn Gay Curnow. If only I were safely ensconced at Cormorant House, I could miss Cora altogether had Peter not practically marched me back from Bosula.

I watch the gulls swooping overhead. So many of them, cackling like mischievous children, and I consider my situation. Crossley has reared his very unattractive head three times in close succession. He is a friend of Gay Curnow. I saw him on the astral plane last night, and today I discovered that Cora Pennington is en route to my home. They are too many coincidences for comfort. Crossley is creeping back into my life, and I'd better not be here when his creature, the once lovely Cora, arrives. I'll have to leave. But how?

I can't ask Elys. Apart from the fact that she is behaving strangely, bordering on overtly hostile, Elys has never completely forgiven me for running away to Croydon. I can't ask Peter. We are barely speaking, and he wouldn't let me go. In fact, I wouldn't mind betting that he would rush to tell Mrs Ponsonby, and I don't know whether I can trust her either. Her so-called illness could be a ruse for some nefarious purpose I can't yet fathom. Sebastian is still in Cornwall, and Jory will tell Elys if I ask him for help. There's only one thing for it. I'll have to go alone.

The thought terrifies me, and I shiver beneath the double blanket, wondering how I could possibly cope by myself. Years of Mrs Ponsonby's dominance have made me dependent on others. And my inconsistent physical frailty means I can't be sure of the extent of my abilities. Yet I can't stay here. I'm not safe, and it's not as if there was any doubt about what I saw when I finally remembered the extent of Cora's association with Crossley. The memory is clear and present. Cora dressed in robes, quaffing wine with the fat man, aloof and superior to the other women in the room, staring at Crossley in thrall to his power. No good could come from her presence in my life now, however much I once admired her.

I have only been in the cave for a quarter of an hour, but that is long enough to be sure of the momentous decision I've just made. I will depart Porth Tregoryan tomorrow at the latest and won't come back until the coast is clear. But I must plan carefully, and I will leave a note behind this time. My departure is not a selfish act. I am not flouncing away in a huff like last time. Sadness envelopes me as I think about leaving Pebble Cottage behind. But one thing is sure. I will not leave Teddy, no matter how difficult it makes things. I cannot bear to be completely alone in the world, and if he travels with me, I will have something of Jim for the lonely autumn nights. A tear steals down my face, and I wipe it away, angry at my moment of weakness. I cannot afford to be sentimental while danger draws ever closer. I put my face in my hands and think until my brain hurts. And by the time I lift my head, I have formulated a plan which might just work. Then I take a slow walk back home and write a couple of letters, one for Elys and the other for Peter.

CHAPTER FIFTEEN

On the Run

Saturday, October 22, 1932

It is four o'clock in the afternoon, and I am sprawled across the seat in a train compartment I chose because it was empty. To my disgust, an elderly man opens the door and joins me. Sighing, I arrange myself in a manner more suitable for company, and he regards me with the look of someone wondering if he is sharing a space with a half-wit. Teddy is sitting beside me and generally behaving well. But because he is a spaniel, he cannot sit still for two minutes, and every time he moves, Teddy knocks my stick, which goes flying across the compartment. This has happened three times now, and I ought to lie it down on the floor, but I don't. It might roll under the seat, and the thought makes me feel insecure.

I departed Porth Tregoryan this morning, waiting until Mrs Ponsonby left the cottage, before taking Teddy and a small suitcase and boarding the bus. This time, I didn't sneak away and left letters for Elys and Peter in the hallway. They will know that I've gone and I'm safe, so my departure should not provoke the panic that it did last time. Peter can, if he wishes, take a reasonable guess at my destination. Whether he will try is debatable. The letter I wrote to Peter is more detailed than the one Elys received. I have told him in general conversational tones that Coralie Pennington is coming to stay. Anyone reading the letter would assume I am imparting news, but Peter alone will understand the danger. And if the letter falls into the wrong hands, nobody else will be any the wiser. Because Peter knows I must avoid Coralie at all costs, he will probably leave me well alone and not draw attention to my location. I have told him I will be in touch, and he will hopefully allow me to proceed unhindered.

Teddy yawns, making a faint little whimper as he closes his mouth. An amused smile flickers across my travelling companion's face, and I decide he can't be all bad. People have been kind to me today, making an arduous journey possible. I boarded the bus with difficulty, juggling a suitcase, a stick, and a leashed dog. It was a terrible struggle, and I almost gave up until a young schoolboy rushed toward me and took my case while offering his hand to help me up the stairs. His good manners and kindness almost brought me to tears, and he was equally solicitous at the other end, this time walking Teddy down the stairs while carrying my case. I thanked him and offered him a penny, but he shook his head and strolled away. I took his kindness as a good omen, and so it turned out. My second stroke of fortune was running into another dog owner at the station. A woman of about forty was also travelling to London to spend a few weeks with her sister. She, too, had a travelling companion – a curly-haired golden retriever. Teddy and Sampson rubbed noses, as dogs do, allowing us the opportunity to converse. And after a brief discussion about our travelling plans, it felt natural to sit together. My new friend, Matilda Wright, was a solicitors' typist living and working in Truro but formerly from Fulham. An engaging companion, she was easy to talk to and, most importantly, eager to help. I didn't need to ask for assistance. She noticed my stick and quietly helped without drawing attention to my difficulties or making me feel like a burden. And when we arrived at Paddington Station, she insisted on waiting until I boarded my next train. And here I am now, missing her already but having not spent a moment worrying about how I will cope. My journey has gone swimmingly, and apart from a lurch of panic when we pulled into Paddington and I realised how close I was to Crossley's lair, I could not have wished for an easier time of it. The next bit will, of course, be much more challenging.

Time passes, and the train pulls into its final destination. I stare from the window as the platform draws closer. People are waiting, casting anxious glances toward the train as they hope for a glimpse of their loved ones. Nobody will wait for me, for nobody knows I am coming. I dare not ask if I can visit in case the answer is a resounding "no". I chew my lip in anticipation as the train draws towards the platform. And there I wait for a moment or two until the crowd of passengers begins to disembark.

The man sitting opposite stands and lifts his case from the webbing above. He slides open the compartment door and then turns to face me. "May I help you, young lady?" he asks.

"Yes, please," I say, feeling relieved. I didn't expect him to offer, and I couldn't bring myself to ask for assistance, though I badly needed it. Despite the long hours of sitting, my legs are wobbly, and I'm weak from lack of food. I thought of almost everything except packing some sandwiches or even a bag of fruit. Had Teddy not been with me, I might have been able to purchase something at the station. I wasn't without funds, with a few pounds of my own and having dipped into the housekeeping tin for extra. And as shameful as that sounds, I took the money, intending to repay it, and made sure that nobody else would look guilty. I shoved a note inside promising to pay Mrs Ponsonby back, even if I needed to take a job to do it. But regardless of my solvency, I couldn't purchase food.

Neither of the station cafes allowed dogs, and that was that. So, I am weak and hungry, as Teddy probably is too.

"I'll take your case," says the man. "Can you manage the dog?"

"Yes, thank you." I trail behind him as he steps from the carriage, then he turns and takes my arm, which I've slipped through Teddy's leash.

"Is someone meeting you?" he asks.

I shake my head.

"Then where can I take your bag?"

"To the nearest telephone box," I say.

"Are you sure?"

"Quite sure."

We arrive at a row of payphones, and the man puts my bag down, tips his hat, and then is gone. I stare around the station, feeling lonely. My heart beats as I remove a card from my pocket and place it above the brass bells. I pick up the receiver and then dial the number hoping that somebody is at home to answer my call.

#

"Wimbledon 251. Can I help you?"

I recognise his voice at once. It is familiar and comforting, though whether it will be in a few moments when I tell him what I've done is another matter.

"It's Connie," I say. "How are you?"

"Connie, my dear. You've remembered me. Are you feeling better?"

"Yes," I say. "Much better."

"How is Peter?"

"Fine," I say, mildly irritated that Fox is interested.

"Good, good," he murmurs. There is a slight pause, and then he speaks again.

"And your guardian?"

"Also fine," I say, trying to work up the courage to tell him where I am.

"How about your memory?" Oliver Fox is fishing, and I

wonder why.

"Mostly back," I say.

"I'm pleased to hear it," he replies, but his tone indicates the opposite. "I hope you're not calling from the cottage."

"No, I say. I'm using a public telephone box."

"It's just as well," says Fox. "Can't be too careful, you know. But even so, I don't think it's a good idea for us to be in touch. Didn't young Peter tell you? Crossley is on manoeuvres again."

"Manoeuvres?"

"Yes. It all went quiet while you were poorly, but the manifestations have returned, worse than ever."

"I know, but things have changed."

"It shouldn't make any difference. You must forget all about us, Connie. With luck, you will be safe in Cornwall."

"Well, I'm not."

"Not safe?"

"Not safe and not in Cornwall."

"Where are you?" Oliver Fox snaps the words out with unexpected urgency.

I take a deep breath. "I'm at the railway station."

"Where?"

"Wimbledon."

Fox gasps, and the line goes silent.

"Mr Fox?"

"Yes, I'm still here."

"I'm sorry."

"It's too late for that. Oh, Connie. Worple Road is the last place you should have come to, but I can't leave you at the station. I take it you're alone?"

"Apart from Teddy."

"Who?"

"Jim's dog."

"Of course. Look, I'm coming to get you. Find a seat somewhere as public as possible. I'll be with you in ten minutes."

I replace the receiver, hook my stick over my arm and make

a beeline for a bench a few short yards away. I sit down, placing my case beneath the seat and holding Teddy close to my legs, watching as a train pulls out of the station while I contemplate Fox's words. From the lost memories that have spewed forth over the last few weeks, I know that Worple Road has held some horrors. But before then, it was a haven. And although I know London is unsafe and that getting in touch with Fox is risky, I never expected the level of danger that Fox suggests.

I sit quietly, processing my thoughts, and after a few moments, I notice a dark cloud rolling across the sky, bringing the threat of rain. But instead of a downpour, a wave of foreboding descends, heralding an acute sense of despair, the like of which I have not felt since the early days of Jim's loss. The sky is dark and oppressive, the light wind circling with sinister intent. Teddy whines, a pitiful cry like a wounded bird, and I shiver. Something is wrong – Crossley is close. Dark forces lurk nearby.

I tighten my grip on Teddy's lead, my eyes darting towards the entrance, searching for Fox's familiar face. As the minutes pass, my sense of unease increases, and then a gust of wind whips a spray of fallen leaves across the platform, taking my gaze from left to right. And when they settle, something has changed. Part of the platform moves, rippling slightly in a black and bumpy way. I stare, transfixed. It runs like a tide, pushing forward, and though it outwardly appears like a regular road surface marred by a heat haze, it lacks the usual qualities of tarmacadam. This surface, which should be stationary, is a carpet of movement, comprising not one thing but many. Tiny arachnid bodies surge as one, pushing towards me like a mini tidal wave. They march in an eight-legged battalion, each identical to the other, moving with malicious intent. They mean to harm me, and my heart almost stops from the shock of it. Teddy whimpers and cowers against me as the sea of creatures approaches. My mind splits into a thousand plans of the many ways I could escape this nightmare. I could try to focus long enough for astral travel, but that would mean leaving Teddy, and I won't abandon him. I close my eyes and rest my head on his furry neck. If we go, we go together. But just as the heaving mass comes close enough to touch, a voice bellows from across the station.

"Connie. Don't move."

I look up, still clutching Teddy, to see Fox running across the platform, brandishing a bag he hurls into the writhing mass of creatures. They evaporate as if they had never existed.

A man standing a few yards away looks up. "Bloody lunatic," he says to his young wife. Clearly, they cannot see what Fox and I have suffered.

Fox reaches me. He is panting, and his face is florid. He pulls out a handkerchief and mops his brow. "We must go," he says, grabbing my case. And before I have time to think about it, we reach the safety of his car.

CHAPTER SIXTEEN

Under Attack

"Oh, Connie. What have you done?" Oliver Fox bundles me through the front door and slams it behind him. Then he turns and throws not one but three bolts, two of which are new.

"I'm sorry. I didn't know."

"He should have told you."

"Who?"

"Peter."

"Don't blame Peter. He was very clear about Crossley, and I was happy to heed him. But I didn't know it was so dangerous here, and as I said, things have changed."

"Not in any way that could make Worple Road safer than your home."

"Good evening." The substantial form of Hilda Grady hoves into view, interrupting Fox's excitable tirade. Already of Amazonian proportions, she has gained an inch or two around her girth since we last met.

"Hello," I say cautiously. I have never been sure of Hilda's feelings towards me. One minute she is friendly, and the next, she is staring at me as if I were a problem to be solved.

"Would you like a nice cup of tea?"

"Yes, please," I say, just as Fox replies.

"Not now," he snaps.

Hilda raises a shaggy eyebrow and regards him sternly.

"Alright. Tea then. Come with me, Connie."

I follow Fox into his study and sit at my old desk.

"Where is Bertha?" I ask, surprised that she hasn't come to greet me.

"At her sisters."

"Will I see her?"

"No. She's far away. And if you don't mind, I'd rather not say where she is. I've sent Bertha away. It's too dangerous here."

I look at Fox's drawn and anxious face as guilt floods through me. "I'm sorry," I say.

He sighs, and Teddy whines. "Can I feed him? He hasn't eaten all day."

"Have you?"

I shake my head.

Fox strides to the door, opens it and shouts up the hallway. Moments later, I hear Hilda's gruff voice. "What is it?"

They exchange bellows, the net result of which are instructions for Hilda to cook me some supper and bring food for the dog with our tea.

"Well, then," says Fox, as he retakes his seat. "What has prompted this exodus from Cornwall?"

"Coralie Pennington and Felix Crossley."

"Please explain."

"I found out yesterday that Cora Pennington is coming to stay at Pebble Cottage. She will arrive tomorrow."

"Oh, dear. And you fled because you were worried. So many secrets. What a shame. It was completely unnecessary."

"Unnecessary," I exclaim. "She's knee-deep in it with Crossley."

Fox opens his mouth to reply, but the door opens, and Hilda

bowls in, carrying a large metal tray. She places a dish of meat scraps on the floor, followed by two cups of tea and a large plate of biscuits on the table. "I'll heat up a suet pudding," she says.

Fox nods. "Yes. That will do nicely."

Suet pudding is not my supper of choice and would ordinarily turn my stomach, but I am ravenous and would happily eat the contents of Teddy's bowl, which he is currently wolfing down as if he'd been starving for weeks. I cram a biscuit into my mouth before burning my lips on the hot tea. Macfarlane butter bar biscuits have never tasted so good. I take two more and break them into small pieces, so I don't look quite so greedy."

Oliver Fox reclines in his chair. "Why were you worried about Crossley?" he asks.

"His name came up in conversation while we were at Mary's."

"Really? How unexpected."

"And unwelcome. Crossley is a friend of Gay Curnow's. I don't know her very well, and our paths barely crossed the last time I was in Bosula. But my sixth sense was in overdrive, and I almost expected it. Especially as I'd seen him on the astral plane."

"Are you travelling again, Connie?"

"Yes. One by choice and twice unexpectedly."

"Perhaps that's why Crossley is stronger."

"I don't understand."

"Neither do I. But you have a connection with Crossley, and it is vital that we keep you away from him."

"We?"

"Stella McGregor and the Cult of the Shining Path."

"You've stayed in touch, then?"

"We've been working night and day to find out more about Crossley. He grows bolder with each passing hour. Calicum Aureum attacked the Shining Path headquarters again last week. Fortunately, their psychic defence skills were equal to his attack. But it only takes one or two weaker members to let him into their midst and access their secrets. It simply doesn't bear thinking about."

Fox visibly shudders at the thought. "This friend of Crossley's – how does she know him?" he asks.

"Gay didn't say. But she was on her way to see him in London and intends to invite him back to Cornwall."

"Immediately?"

"I don't know. But Peter insisted we leave, and that was that."

"Does he know you are here?"

I shake my head. "No. We haven't spoken for a few days."

"Then he doesn't know about Cora?"

"Not yet. I've written to him but haven't said where I intended to go."

"Small mercies," mutters Fox. "The fewer people that know, the better. Now, I'll be honest with you – there's little choice left but the truth. No more secrets. My house on Worple Road has been under attack for weeks."

"Why?"

"Because Crossley knows our connection and thinks he can get to you through me."

"Then I've brought terrible danger to your door."

"No more than usual. Crossley's creatures will appear here with or without you. But they mustn't discover you when they arrive."

"They already know. You saw the spiders at the station."

"It's possible," admits Fox. "But it's more likely that they were coming for me. I was heading to the station, and we'd spoken on the telephone. They sensed my arrival, not yours."

"Why do you think that?"

"Did you see anything untoward before you called me?"

"No. Nothing."

"Then we must assume I am correct. Now, Connie. The worst always happens at night. Dusk will soon fall, and it's too late for you to leave. You can stay here tonight and go in the morning. But while you are here, you must obey my instructions. I will remain in the front part of the house, and you can have your old room back, providing you let Hilda watch over you while you sleep. The manifestations will save the worst of it for me, and perhaps you will escape their attention altogether. Whatever happens, you must not leave your room after dark, no matter what you hear. Do you promise?"

"Yes," I whisper, feeling sick with dreadful anticipation. Fox is holding nothing back, and he wears his concerns about the night ahead through his clammy pallor. "How will you manage alone?" I ask.

"I have practised for a long time under Stella's tutelage," says Fox. "My defences are robust. I have only faltered once, and Hilda stopped me."

"Can she see them?" I ask, intrigued.

"It's better if you don't ask."

"You said no more secrets."

Fox raises a weak smile. "Perhaps one or two. Now, it sounds like Hilda is laying the table. Let's fuel up in the dining room. We're in for a rough night."

#

"Try to sleep," says Hilda as I shift awkwardly under the covers while still fully dressed, with a solidly built cocker spaniel wedged behind my knees. Sleep! Chance would be a fine thing. Although I am now replete, the suet pudding was neither light nor fluffy and sits in my stomach like an undigested brick. It is causing night sweats, not helped by being clad in day wear. I am uncomfortable and feel excruciatingly self-conscious about being babysat by someone I neither know well nor understand.

Hilda is pacing the room in anticipation of the night's events, and I realise she knows far more about the old enemy than I do. Hilda must be in Fox's confidence to a large degree. That he trusts her is evident, but whether he should do is far from clear. I'm not sure I do, yet part of me is glad to have her here, knowing that danger may be close by. I raise my head and peer toward the window. The tightly shut curtains block views across the garden. Hilda has set two nightlights on either side of the bed, and the comforting glow provides misguided security. But it is enough to make me feel drowsy, and I feel myself drifting away.

I settle into a dreamless sleep and then wake to the sound of tennis balls against the windowpane. While navigating the path between sleep and wakefulness, I dozily wonder if children are playing outside. I rub my eyes and prop myself onto my elbows before rising to a seated position to find Hilda next to me on the bed. She clutches my arm, hissing, "shhh."

I am properly awake now and watch as she gazes anxiously toward the window – thud, thud, thud. The tennis ball noise is increasing in intensity.

"Shouldn't we see what's happening?" I whisper.

"Certainly not," says Hilda. "Don't move from this bed under any circumstances. They must not see you."

I wait with a fluttering heart until the noise stops and a wary silence settles. The wind whistles, louder and louder, until it changes into a hypnotic hissing sound. And I know beyond doubt that a serpent, hostile and menacing, lurks behind the curtain. I pull the covers over my shaking body, lean down, and reach for my stick. Teddy squirms closer to me, burying his head in my chest. The snake's song is rhythmic and beguiling, and I sway to its ebbs and flows. I am dancing, gently moving – its sweet music calling me home. Snatched memories of slow dancing with Kit Maltravers at the Potts' supper party flash past. I recall the heady smell of his cologne and how secure I felt in his arms. He is back, and we move towards the light, gracefully swirling towards safety. Another man steps in, takes me, and holds me. I look into his eyes. It is Jim. He is home, and I fling my stick away, needing it no more. I am with the man I love, and we are running across the sand, hand in hand, free as gulls in the sky.

And then I fall backwards as a burly arm flings me to the bed. I struggle, desperate to get away, but I cannot move under the sheer bodyweight of my assailant. I twist and turn, arms flailing. A dog growls, and my eyes open to see Teddy, teeth bared and ready to bite as Hilda Grady pins me to the bed.

"Where are you?" she commands.

Kit is gone, Jim has vanished, and I am not on a beach. "At Worple Road," I whisper.

"Good girl." She releases me from her hold and shuffles from the bed. Teddy casts a threatening look her way, then snuggles into me.

"What happened?"

"Was it the snake?"

I recall the hissing sound. "Yes," I say.

"It's one of the worst manifestations. Don't blame yourself."

"Why were you holding me?"

"Because you hurled your stick across the room before trying to get out of bed, presumably to open the window. A good thing your dog stopped you."

"He tried to bite you."

"I know. But at least you couldn't get past him. He kept you safely on the bed. God only knows what would have happened if you'd opened the window."

"Can they get inside?" I ask, remembering the spider manifestation that almost reached me the previous year in Pebble Cottage.

Hilda nods. "It depends. With training, we can shut them out."

Her voice, always on the gruff side, drops a measure, and I stare at her in alarm. Something is wrong, and my heart wells with distrust. I am alone in a room with a woman who has pinned me to the bed and now sounds like a grizzly bear. Teddy cocks an eye and curls his lip.

I panic, gaze around the room, and reach for my stick, which Hilda placed on the end of the bed.

"Leave it alone," she says.

I shift uncomfortably, eyes darting this way and that, searching for an escape route. My heart thuds and I prepare to scream, hoping that Oliver Fox will come to my aid. Hilda notes my fear and extends a meaty hand toward me. I flinch away.

"Please don't," she says, looming ever closer.

I open my mouth, but the scream won't come. And it doesn't need to.

Hilda sighs, accepting defeat and extends her hand again. "Lieutenant Harold Grady, Number one Special Defence Unit, psychic division," she says. "And for all that is holy, stay put, shut up and don't bloody move until dawn."

CHAPTER SEVENTEEN

Deep Undercover

Sunday, October 23, 1932

Sleep somehow took me in the early hours of the morning after a night of horror, of unspeakable manifestations swirling like dervishes behind the curtain. I saw them only once when the windows rattled from the surge of bodies trying to push through the glass. When Hilda, despite herself, felt moved to check the window's construction for fear that the creatures would break through. She only opened the curtains a fraction, but it was enough to see swathes of dense, black ungodly forms wreaking havoc across the garden, squeezing, compressing, forcing themselves into the tiniest space. I cannot adequately describe the terror. I wanted to flee into the astral realm, but Hilda, or should I say Harold, and I had already spoken of this before the worst bombardment. And he warned me of the danger in no uncertain terms. So, I resisted, even when the urge came unbidden, tearing at the base of my skull like a branding iron.

And somehow, despite it all, I enjoyed an hour or two of blissful sleep.

Dawn has now broken, and I am lying under the bed covers watching Hilda doze in a chair. I uncurl my legs, knocking Teddy awake, and he yawns loudly and jumps from the bed. Hilda starts awake at the sound of his claws skittering on wooden floorboards. She rubs her eyes sleepily, realises where she is, and jumps to her feet before cautiously pulling the curtain to one side. The early morning sun drifts into the room. Gone is the hissing, the thumps, and thuds of last night's attack, now replaced by gentle bird song and clinking bottles from a milk float. Hilda visibly relaxes.

"Glad that's over," she says, her voice an octave higher than last night.

"What do I call you?" I ask, coming straight to the point about a matter that bothered me despite all the terror surrounding us.

"Hilda or Mrs Grady," says Harold. "I am deep undercover. I should not have revealed my identity, and I wouldn't have done had you not looked likely to take off."

"I wouldn't have got very far," I say, nodding to my stick.

"You wouldn't need to. These are powerful forces. It was enough to make me lose my concentration, which alone was dangerous. Crossley would have whipped you off to God knows where if you'd taken a step outside last night."

I shudder, knowing that he is right. Last night's danger was real and present – no figment of our imagination.

"I must find Fox," says Hilda abruptly, first striding straight-backed towards the door, then slowing and hunching as she gets into character. I climb out of bed and follow slowly behind.

I have only just left the room when Hilda bellows further down the corridor. "Fetch a jug of water, quickly now."

I return and retrieve the item from my bedside table, then walk to Fox's room as quickly as possible. Hilda is waiting outside the door and snatches the jug from my hand. I follow her inside to see Oliver Fox slumped in a chair by the window, with his head lolling across his shoulder.

"Is he alive?" I ask in a trembling voice.

Hilda nods. "Only just," she says. She raises his head and sits him upright before gently slapping his face. Fox's clammy features are grey, and his eyes remain shut for all her efforts. Hilda takes the jug and sloshes water into his face. The shock of the cold liquid revives him a little, and he opens bleary, unfocused eyes.

"Wake up, man," says Hilda, firmly patting his cheeks.

Fox brushes water from his eyes and shakes his head, trying to dislodge the fuzziness inside. He succeeds.

"Have they gone?" he asks, looking anxiously at Hilda.

"For now."

"The worst yet," says Fox, lifting the jug and drinking the remains of the water straight from it.

"I'm afraid it's time," says Hilda.

"Please, no. I can withstand it a while longer."

"No, you can't. We've gone as far as we can alone. It's back to HQ."

"No. I won't do it. This is my home. I must earn a living."

"And so you shall, when this is over."

"I can't just leave. I work for the civil service."

"Which makes it a darn sight easier for my department to arrange a period of leave. No one needs to know why. And you can write all day long if you like."

"But where will I live?"

"Headquarters, as I said. You've been there. You know they have apartments in the building. There's no choice."

"What about me?" I ask timidly.

Fox and Grady exchange glances.

"No," they say in unison.

"But?"

"No buts. Look – we've had a long night. I don't know about you two, but I'm so hungry I could eat that dog." Hilda Grady points towards Teddy, who cowers into my legs.

"I'll make some breakfast, and we'll talk," says Hilda.

"Freshen up and meet me in the dining room in half an hour."

#

I am the last to arrive and cautiously sidle into the dining room, feeling out of my depth. The table is groaning with bacon, poached eggs, and a large plate of buttered toast. A small bowl on the edge of the table contains a chopped sausage.

"For the dog," says Hilda. "I'm rather fond of him."

"Oh yes. You fed him when Jim was at work, didn't you?"

Hilda scrunches her face. "How did you know that?"

"Never mind," I say, realising that she might know about astral travel but may not be a practitioner, or she would have seen me spying on her last year at Jim's. My heart skips with relief at the recovery of another memory. Surely, I must be close to discovering what happened to my dear friend by now.

"Tuck in," says Hilda, heaving herself into the seat usually occupied by Bertha Callaway. Oliver Fox sits meekly beside her. In a few short hours, there has been a complete role reversal.

We sit in silence for a few moments, devouring the food as if we hadn't eaten for days. Then Hilda swallows a barely disguised belch, quaffs her tea, and pushes her plate away. Fox and I are still eating, but she carries on regardless.

"Now, cards on the table. This is far from an ideal scenario."

Oliver Fox nods vigorously. "Far from it," he echoes.

"But you're here now, you know too much, and we must make the best of it. First things first. Everything you hear in this room is in the strictest confidence. You must not reveal any part of this discussion to anyone outside of The Shining Path."

"I promise," I say. "But how will I know?"

"Know what?"

"Whether the people I meet are members of this organisation."

"You won't. You don't need to. We know who they are, and that is enough."

"Am I coming with you?"

Hilda sighs and shakes her head. "In for a penny..." she mutters. "Alright. Point taken. Things are changeable, and you might meet someone from the Shining Path while we are not around. I'll give you the latest password, but it changes monthly. When this one expires, we'll find a way to let you know the new one."

"What is it then?"

Hilda stands up, opens each door, and the window, peers outside, and returns to her seat.

"Watchers of Avalon," she whispers in a barely audible voice.

"So, I can trust anyone who says that to me?"

"For the next few weeks."

"But what about now?" Oliver Fox leans forwards and steeples his hands.

"We are going to the Shining Path Headquarters in Bayswater," says Grady quietly. "But it's less than a mile from Crossley's current location, so there's no question of taking the young lady."

"Why not, if it's good enough for you?" I ask.

"Because we have both extensively trained in psychic defence, and you have not."

"I know a little."

"But not enough."

"How will it be any safer for you in London?" I say churlishly. If I can't go with them, I don't see why I should make it easy for them to leave without me.

"Because we will have Stella McGregor and the other members of The Shining Path, not to mention a couple of our military chaps. There's safety in numbers."

"Are they also disguised as housekeepers?"

"No," says Hilda. "But then they never learned to cook. I am uniquely qualified in that regard." Hilda pushes her shoulders back with an air of pride. But I have no intention of basking in her glory. I want to go with them to London. I would feel much safer with Stella McGregor.

"Please, can I come?" I ask.

"No," says Oliver Fox firmly.

"But Crossley's coming to Cornwall."

"First, I've heard of it," says Hilda.

"Sorry. I should have mentioned it," says Fox. "That's why Connie's here."

Hilda nods her head. "It complicates matters. I don't suppose you know when he's travelling?"

I shake my head.

"Then neither place is safe. Is there somewhere else you can go?"

I rack my brain, then think back to my original plan of investigating the Chevis poisoning. "Actually, there is. I'd like to go to Deepcut Barracks?"

"Whatever for?"

"Does it matter?"

"Not really. But that's my old stomping ground from my training days. I know a lodging house in Frimley – my old digs, in fact. I'll write you a letter, and they'll give you a warm welcome. Now, excuse my frankness, but have you sufficient funds?"

"I think so," I say.

"Take this." Hilda reaches down her top and removes a small bundle of notes. She peels off two and hands them to me. "That will pay for your accommodation for a week or two. We'll know more by then. Will it do?"

"I glance at Fox, looking for reassurance, and he nods.

"I'll drive you there," he says.

"Are you sure?"

"We can't risk the train. It should be safe?"

Hilda nods. "Hopefully." Her tone is far from convincing.

"Right. I'll do it," I say, heading upstairs to pack.

CHAPTER EIGHTEEN

Tracking the Cook

Monday, October 24, 1932

Oliver Fox was as good as his word and drove me to Frimley yesterday. But there was no mistaking the fear on his face as he careered down the road at breakneck speed, on a circuitous route that meandered every which way, leaving me thoroughly car sick. I wanted to tell him to stop being silly and drive in a straight line. That the people he feared did not take to the roads but were busily cruising the astral plane, a fact he knew full well. But Fox was taking every precaution because he felt thoroughly guilty at leaving me friendless and alone in rural Hampshire.

"Then take me to London," I had said, and he had responded with the anxious gaze of a bloodhound who has lost the scent and must report back to his master.

"I can't," he'd replied.

"You mean you won't."

"It's not wise."

"Then this is the only option, so please don't waste more time going around in circles."

He had slowed the car, and I suspected he would change his mind if I pushed the matter. But I had already resigned myself to the Hampshire visit. And having re-read my notes about the Chevis death, my interest had sharpened. I was ready to pursue the case, letting Fox off the hook by staying silent.

I wasn't prepared to drop Hilda's presence in the household, though. The more I thought about it, the more absurd it seemed. While working in Worple Road, I had observed their relationship, and Fox had undoubtedly treated her like an employee. I had remembered the Callaways discussing Hilda's interview and their initial reservations about employing her. If Fox had known her real background, he must have lied to his wife. So, yesterday I asked him outright as the car journey was too long for him to squirm out of telling me. Fox said he did not know that Hilda Grady was anything other than a housekeeper in the beginning. But since he found out, he had come to rely on her. It had been Hilda's idea to tell Bertha about the manifestations, and she'd encouraged Fox to persuade Bertha to leave home for her safety. While that seemed reasonable, Hilda's random appearance as their housekeeper did not. It was far too much of a coincidence, and I demanded an explanation. Fox had eyed me apologetically and attempted to divert my questions. But I wasn't having it, and he eventually capitulated. It took a while to understand his explanation, not because it was complicated, but because Fox insisted on whispering, even though we were travelling at speed in a car with a noisy engine. I could barely hear myself think, much less concentrate on what he said, and neither Crossley nor his minions would have stood a chance. I eventually heard enough to piece things together.

Oliver Fox had a friend called Anthony Bridgewater with whom he confided about his astral travels. On returning home after our first meeting, he had told his friend about me in the strictest confidence. Bridgewater already enjoyed a close friendship with Stella McGregor, and Fox hadn't realised its extent. By the time he had asked Bridgewater to introduce him to McGregor, she was already familiar with his interest in astral projection and knew of his friendship with me. Stella McGregor was no fool. Crossley considered himself a master of the astral plane, and any skilled traveller would likely come to his notice. The Callaways' need for domestic help gave her a perfect excuse to get someone in the house and observe the situation. And that someone came in the guise of Hilda Grady.

The revelation had left me bursting with questions, but Fox batted them away. "I've said enough," he'd muttered. "And I don't know the half of it."

I had persisted. "But are there others spying on you? Or me too, for that matter?"

"Yes. That's why there is a password."

"And what about Calicum Aureum?"

"I don't know how they identify themselves."

"I didn't mean that. How many members are there? And more to the point, where?"

Oliver Fox had stalled, literally stalled. With increasing discomfort from avoiding the question, he'd removed his foot from the peddle, and the car ground to a halt. This had instilled a fresh fear in him, and he'd darted to the front, winding the starting handle as if his life depended upon it.

I had waited for him to return to his seat and tried again.

"Are they all in London?"

"Probably not," Fox had replied. "But they don't know where you are. They've never known."

"And if they did?"

He snatched a sideways glance. "They would come for you."

The rest of the journey had passed in silence, and Fox had swiftly settled me into the boarding house, then left with a warning.

"I will be in contact with Peter. Someone must know where to find you," he said. And I had felt comforted at the thought and didn't argue.

That was yesterday, and I am now sitting in the lodging house dining room wondering what to do next when Mrs Travers appears. Betty Travers is my host and a jolly good sort to boot. From the moment she clapped her eyes on my stick, she made it her business to keep an eye on me, offering to bring meals to my room if it was easier than coming down. Feeling subdued and nervous, I took supper in my room last night but knew I wouldn't get anywhere by hiding away. I awoke this morning to a dry but chilly day and decided to make the best of it. So, I came downstairs and braved a busy dining room, even joining another young woman at a table instead of sitting alone. But Angela had almost finished and left shortly after introducing herself. I am now sitting alone, feeling more than a little self-conscious, when Betty arrives with a teapot.

"Don't mind the men," she says when she sees me sitting quietly. "They are all officers. I don't take any lower ranks here."

I raise a weak smile, wondering why she feels moved to say such a thing. Privates and lieutenants are all the same to me. I am not a snob. But as I gaze around the room, I realise she is trying to be kind. Now Angela has gone, I am the lone female among many men, unsurprisingly for an establishment that mainly caters for soldiers. She must be trying to reassure me they are safe to be around.

"Thank you," I say, and she smiles.

"Would you like some kippers?"

I shake my head. "Can you rustle up some toast and jam?"

"Is that all?"

"It's more than enough."

"Of course. Cook made some lemon curd. Would you like that?"

"Rather." My mouth waters at the thought. Though an excellent cook, Elys has never mastered the art of preserves, and ours, therefore, comes from the shop. But Isla Tremayne occasionally makes lemon curd, and I must stop myself from taking a spoon to the jar and polishing it off in one fell swoop.

As I stare around the room, trying not to drool, I accidentally catch the eye of a young officer. He lowers his cup and smiles. I glance away, embarrassed, and pretend to examine my nails. I am still looking down when Betty Travers returns with my toast.

"There you go," she says. "And I've put extra curd in the pot. Ellen was down to her last jar, but she'll make some more later, so you've got the lot."

"How kind," I say. "Please thank her for me."

"I will." Betty disappears through a door, and I spread my toast with delicious curd, which envelopes me like a warm hug as I devour it, bringing back happy memories of the Tremaynes and Pebble Cottage. For a moment, I am transported back to more innocent times, when astral travel was a nightly dream and Crossley hadn't reared his ugly head.

"Good day."

My thoughts return to the present as the young officer passes my table and greets me on his way out.

"And to you," I reply, watching as each man leaves the room. Soon I am alone, feeling deserted, but not for long. Betty reappears, brandishing another pot of tea.

"Mind if I join you?" she asks.

"Not at all," I say gladly. I haven't planned my day, and I can do little without help. A better acquaintance with the kindly landlady could yield results.

Betty plants her plump behind upon the wooden seat and tops up my cup before pouring hers. "Was it any good?"

"The lemon curd? Simply delicious," I reply.

"Good. Now, tell me. What's a young lady like you doing in a place like this?"

The question catches me unawares. I can't tell her what I'm doing here, but I must start my investigation, so I settle for a half-truth. "I've come here on behalf of a friend," I say. "He lost a colleague last year and asked me to pay my respects."

"Oh, I see." Betty casts an eye at my walking stick. "A pity he didn't escort you."

"He can't get away," I say. "And I was visiting anyway, so I agreed."

"Well, that's very good of you. It can't be easy."

"You mean my leg? It's true. I can walk short distances, but not terribly far. But I'll manage if there's a good bus service. Do you have one?"

"It depends where you're going."

"Deepcut Barracks," I say.

"Oh?" Betty eyes me curiously.

"Yes, Sebastian's friend lived there. He died under peculiar circumstances."

"Let me guess. He was poisoned."

"That's right."

"With a partridge."

"Yes. I suppose you must know all about it, living so close."

"And what is Sebastian to Lieutenant Chevis?"

"One of his best friends. They went through training together."

"They didn't bury Hugh Chevis here," says Betty.

"It doesn't matter. I'm not here to visit his grave. It's more about following in his footsteps, seeking out his bungalow, that sort of thing. It will comfort Sebastian to know how he lived. They hadn't seen each other for a few years, with Hugh being at Deepcut and Sebastian abroad in Gibraltar.

"Right." Betty smiles, and I can see that she has bought into my story. "Well, you should visit my kitchen in that case."

I eye her quizzically, and she laughs.

"I share something in common with Lieutenant Chevis," she says. "Her name is Ellen Yeomans. His former cook is now mine."

#

Betty's words ring in my head as I brush my teeth in the first-floor bathroom, which I share with four other guests. Fortunately, they are all out, and I am alone with no need to lock the door. I pace around the creaky wooden floor as I brush and think, marvelling at the incredible piece of luck that has brought me within a few yards of the Chevis cook. I wanted to go to her straight away, but Betty Travers does not run a profitable hostelry without good reason. A canny employer, she will not allow me to distract her cook while she is preparing the evening meal. But Betty said that Ellen would take a break at lunchtime after making the sandwiches, and I can visit her then.

I occupy myself in the meantime by going for a short stroll around the town, where I find a row of stalls selling sweetmeats. I pay half a penny for a toffee apple and eat it on a bench by the green, then return to re-read my notes once more. But the toffee has unpleasantly coated my teeth, and I cannot scrub hard enough to remove it. I squeeze another blob on my toothbrush and start the process again, finally satisfied with my oral hygiene. I return my wash bag to my bedroom and while away half an hour, watching the world go by from my upstairs window, which overlooks the town.

The clock chimes midday, and I grab my stick and traverse the shallow stairs. I am lucky to find easy access within this ancient building. Often stairs in older properties are too steep for me, with the bannisters usually inadequate. But not here, and I navigate the stairwell with ease and head for the dining room. The tables are unset, except for the smallest below the window containing cutlery for one, and I take a seat there and wait. I am still waiting ten minutes later, wondering whether they have forgotten my request for a light lunch, when a stout woman wearing an apron approaches me. She is carrying a tray.

"Are you Miss Maxwell?" she asks.

"Yes. Please call me Connie."

"I've made lunch for you. Tuna sandwiches and soup unless you'd rather have salt beef?"

"No. Tuna will do very well."

"Right you are. I'll give you twenty minutes to eat, and then I'll return with a pot of tea. Mrs Travers says you want to ask me some questions."

"I do. And thank you. That will be marvellous."

I wait until Mrs Yeomans is on the other side of the door

before opening the sandwich and checking the contents. It is a bad habit and not very ladylike, but I prefer to know exactly what I am eating, especially when it comes to fish. Three years spent trying to avoid Elys' Stargazy pie has put me on high alert for all things piscine. I open the sandwich to reveal slices of tomato, which I peel away before examining a layer of tuna sitting atop heavily buttered soft white bread. It all looks edible, and, satisfied with my examination, I take a large bite. The sandwich looks better than it tastes, so I dip it in the vegetable soup, immediately improving the flavour. Fifteen minutes later, all evidence of lunch is safely inside me, and I wait impatiently for Mrs Yeomans to return.

Her timekeeping is excellent, and she arrives exactly when promised, bearing tea and biscuits. She sets it to one side while clearing my plates and swaps them onto the tray.

"They'll be alright there for a few minutes," she says. "Do you mind if I sit down?"

"Of course not," I say. "It's very good of you to indulge me."

"I understand your young man wants some information about his friend."

I blush beetroot red. "He's not my young man," I say.

"But he's a friend of Lieutenant Chevis?"

"Yes. A very good one. Sebastian is one of the four young men in the photograph on Lieutenant Chevis' sideboard." I make the statement aware that she might ask me how I know. But I feel the need to establish Sebastian's credentials and deem it worth the risk.

"Well, well. The master mentioned a young man called Sebastian once or twice. And another with a name like a duck. They trained together; I believe."

"That's right. You must be thinking of Drake Mallard. And the other is called Tony. What did Lieutenant Chevis tell you?"

"Good Lord. He didn't talk to me. I'm only the cook – but he chatted about it to Nicholas, his batman. Inferior in rank, of course, but another soldier and all boys together when it came to reminiscing."

"Oh, so he was informal with the other ranks?"

"Not at all," says Ellen. "But he had a knack of chatting without losing his authority if you know what I mean."

"Yes, I do," I say, thinking of Kit Maltravers and his ability to move seamlessly between being a knowledgeable family doctor and a charming yet unobtainable friend.

"Well, what can I tell you?" asks Ellen.

"I'm not sure what Sebastian would ask if he were here," I say, setting myself up for a detailed interview. "So, perhaps I can just ask you questions as if I knew nothing about it, with the understanding that you won't answer if you feel uncomfortable."

"Alright."

"Do you mind if I take notes?"

Ellen sits back in her chair and eyes me suspiciously. "You're not a reporter, are you?"

"Absolutely not," I say firmly.

"Are you sure?"

I cast a steady look towards my stick, turning my leg around far enough to show an eyeful of my built-up shoe.

"Oh, my dear," she says. "Were you always like this, or did you have an accident?"

I am taken aback for a moment, but I find her candour refreshing. Most people skirt around the issue of my damaged leg, leaving both parties uncomfortable.

"I don't actually know," I say, parrying her frankness with an honest one of my own. "I can't remember much of my earlier years, and I have no mother to ask."

Her face softens. "Then I'm sorry I mentioned it," she says. "Of course, you are not a reporter. I'll help in any way I can. I wouldn't have said anything, but loyalty is important to me. And I don't want to let Mrs Chevis down by speaking out of turn."

"Do you still see her?"

"I've only recently left her employment. She asked me to continue working for her when she moved back to London, but I didn't like it there. I'm a country girl at heart. I heard Mrs

150

Travers was looking for a cook, wrote to her and here we are now."

"Good for you," I say. "I can't imagine living in a city. Were you with the Chevis household for long?"

"Hardly any time, really," says Ellen. "You must think I'm flighty, going straight from Mrs Chevis to Mrs Travers, but I led a stable life until then. I was landlady of The Fox Inn, Farnborough, for nigh on twenty years and ran it alone for a long time after my dear Albert passed away. I kept going until my boys grew up and left home, then took up the cook's position with Lieutenant Chevis in the hope of an easier life. Well, the last thing I expected was to become embroiled in a murder."

"I suppose you couldn't see it coming?"

"No. There were no clues at all. They seemed a happy couple, and I never heard a cross word between them. Not one."

"Did you like your employers?"

"I can't say I thought much about it. I spent little time with Lieutenant Chevis, and Mrs Chevis left the household management almost entirely to me. She spent long periods in London during the week. I think she found Hampshire rather too quiet."

"Did you decide to serve the partridges, or was it her idea?"

"I really can't remember," Ellen says abruptly, and I realise she is still sensitive about the matter. Having read the newspaper clippings, I know they questioned her extensively about the provenance of the meat, and I will need to tread carefully to avoid antagonising her.

"Perhaps you decided between you," I say diplomatically.

"Possibly. Sometimes she wrote out the weekly menu, and sometimes I did. But it often changed, especially if the butcher had something special on display."

"But someone would have ordered the partridges?"

"Yes. It was Mrs Chevis. She telephoned Colebrook's and placed the order."

"And the poulterer would have handled them."

151

"The poulterer trussed them and gave them to William Noyes, his driver. Noyes brought them straight to me, and I put them in the meat safe."

"In the kitchen?"

"No. Outside."

"Front or back?"

"At the front."

"Oh. So, anyone could have looked inside."

"In theory, yes. But in practice, I'm not so sure. They would need to have walked up the front path in full view."

"Only if someone was passing. Was the bungalow overlooked?"

"Not particularly," says Ellen. "There were other properties nearby, but they weren't built on top of each other, you know."

"Of course not," I reply. "And as the cook, I presume you collected the meat from the safe when it was ready to prepare?"

Ellen nods. "I did."

"Did you clean the birds?"

Ellen thinks for a moment. "No, they came oven-ready."

"And looked normal?"

"Completely normal. This is rather a lot of detail for your friend to consider?"

"I don't know what he needs," I say, doing my best to look diligent.

"I understand," she says, but with a newfound wariness. I will need to change tack.

"Do you mind telling me what happened after you served the birds?"

"Well, the partridges were back within a few moments of going out. Mr Boulger, the batman, came sailing in, dumped them on the table and told me to put them straight into the fire. 'The fowl is foul,' he had said, and not in a jokey way, but with a lofty air that I didn't appreciate. I'd worked hard on that meal, and I thought he was having me on at first. But he was adamant. The master had said I was to burn the partridges in case one of the dogs got them."

"Why should they?"

"I don't know. Common sense, I suppose. And quite right, as it happened. That poor spaniel."

I stare at Ellen, wondering if she is referring to Teddy, who I have left asleep upstairs. "What spaniel?" I ask.

"Why, the Evereds' little dog. It died from strychnine poisoning the same day as Lieutenant Chevis."

"But how did that happen if you burned the partridges? And who are the Evereds?"

"They were the next-door neighbours, and nobody ever got to the bottom of the dog's death, but the vet was certain it ingested strychnine."

"Well," I say, genuinely puzzled at this turn of events. "Did you wash the birds?"

"Funny you should ask that, as the police did too. And it's fair to say that the Evereds' dog would drink water from the drain. But the birds came fully prepared, as I said. There was no need to wash them, and I didn't. I simply laid them in a tin with some dripping and cooked them on the gas stove for forty-five minutes. Apart from basting them every now and again, I barely touched them."

"And nobody else could have?"

"I never left the kitchen."

"At all?"

"Not for a single minute. From the moment I took the birds from the safe, they were in my eyesight at all times."

"So, the poison must have been in the partridges before you cooked them?"

"Yes, except..." Mrs Yeomans' words trail away, and she stares unseeingly towards the door.

"Except what?"

"Well, I tasted the gravy like any good cook. And there was nothing untoward. It was perfectly pleasant if I say so myself."

"Were you ill?"

"No. Not in the slightest. The poison must have been right inside that one bird until Mrs Chevis carved it open."

"Yes. I wondered if it might have been in the dripping, but obviously not."

"If that were true, we'd have lost the entire household. The dripping was from the Sunday roast – a nice joint of lamb. And we'd been using it all week. I'm partial to dripping on toast, and Mr Boulger even more so. We'd have been the first to go."

"Can I ask one more question about the meat safe?"

"Go ahead?"

"Tell me what it looked like and how they packaged the partridges."

"Well, the safe itself is like a large box attached to the north wall with a door that swings open. I put the birds outside on a plate with a mesh over to keep off the flies."

"So, the meat was visible with the door open?"

"Yes. But as I say, nothing could have got to it, for all the attempts by the local cats."

I think of Mr Moggins and smile. He would have broken into the meat safe at the drop of a hat if he were in the vicinity.

"It's not a laughing matter. I take food hygiene very seriously," says Ellen.

"Of course, you do. I was thinking of my cat."

"Have you anything else to ask me? Time is pressing."

"Yes," I say, screwing up my courage for the big question by throwing in an uncomfortable starter.

Ellen cocks her head and waits.

"Who do you think did it?"

A long, deep sigh follows while Ellen considers my question. She opens her mouth, guppy-like, as she searches for the right words. "I just don't know," she says. "I mean, only three of us had access to the meat safe that day, me and Mr and Mrs Chevis."

"And the driver," I add.

"Yes, but why would he have done it?"

"Why would you? It didn't stop them asking, did it?"

"No, but they soon cleared me for that reason. I could have lost my job when Lieutenant Chevis died. Fortunately, Mrs

Chevis kept me on, but my prospects were poor for a while."

"Were you fond of Mrs Chevis?"

"I didn't know her long enough to care for her one way or another."

"Then may I ask an indelicate question?"

"You may?"

"Sebastian seemed to think that his friend enjoyed something of an open marriage."

Ellen's mouth clamps firmly shut, and her neck speckles red. She stands up suddenly, scraping the chair back with unnecessary force. "I know nothing about that," she mutters, grabbing the tray. "Now, I must press on before I upset Mrs Travers. Nice to have met you."

Ellen stalks off into the kitchen, leaving me staring at her broad behind. I mishandled the question and embarrassed her. She is well and truly off-side.

CHAPTER NINETEEN

Drake Mallard

I finish scribbling notes from my earlier conversation with Ellen. Before that, I started from scratch, handwriting everything I had learned so far about the Chevis case and putting it into date order in a brand-new notebook I had popped out to purchase from the next-door stationer. I completed my task, thoroughly pleased with myself for not only producing an accurate timeline but for managing alone in a new town. I regret all those years of thinking that I couldn't cope when I can. If I'm sensible and stick to short trips, I can manage as well as the next person. Frimley feels as safe as Porth Tregoryan, and thoughts of Felix Crossley and his dark forces couldn't be further from my mind. I dress for supper and go downstairs with a full heart and an empty stomach.

My newfound happiness evaporates at the sight of the dining room. I should have left for dinner sooner, but I wanted to finish my task. All tables are now occupied, with barely any spaces remaining. Angela sees me and shrugs sympathetically. She is sitting with Major Cameron, a gruff old gentleman long retired from the Indian army, and there are no spaces left on their table. My panicky eyes dart around the room. If I want to eat, I must join a table, and they are all occupied by army officers. I am still standing like a rabbit in headlights when the young officer who smiled at me during breakfast jumps up and approaches.

"Would you care to join me?" he asks.

I smile with nervous relief. "I would, thank you."

The officer has excellent manners and pulls the chair out before offering to take my stick. I decline, preferring to keep it close by, and he resumes his seat opposite me.

"Would you like some water?" the officer asks, and I accept, but his companion has barely raised a smile, making me feel unwelcome. I study the short menu and try to exude a confidence I don't possess.

Betty Travers approaches with a paper and pen. Though she owns the establishment, she is very involved with all aspects of the service, including waiting tables, even though another young girl is also taking orders in the dining room.

"What can I get you?" she asks.

"I'll have the lamb cutlets, please."

"Will you want a dessert?"

I turn over the menu and remind myself of the offerings. "Semolina pudding, please."

"Your fruit cobblers will be along in a minute," she says to the men. The less friendly of the two dabs his moustache with a napkin and drops it on his empty plate.

"No need. I've changed my mind," he says abruptly. "I'll be off, old man," he continues. "Enjoy your evening," then he winks and leaves.

I blush to the roots of my hair, and Betty shakes her head, raising her eyes heavenwards.

"Don't mind Bluey," says the young officer. "He's always that way."

"Bluey," I repeat. "What a peculiar name."

"It's short for Blumenthal. We all get nicknames."

"Do you have one?"

"Of course. Mine is Drake."

I almost drop my water glass before snorting with amazement. "Surely not Drake Mallard?"

"How do you know?"

"Sebastian told me."

"Well, I never. Why was the old boy discussing yours truly?"

"He wasn't. Tony was."

"Tony Harding?"

"Yes. I recently dined with them."

"I have no words. You have left me well and truly speechless."

"They said you were billeted at Deepcut. I should have thought to look you up."

"I'm only here on secondment from Woolwich, hence why I live in digs. But any friend of Sebastian's is a friend of mine. How is he? Still hobbling around on that stick."

Drake's hand flies to his mouth as the words leave his lips. "Oh, I say. I'm awfully sorry. I wasn't thinking."

"Don't worry. I'm not offended."

"I know, but it's a bit much. I should have thought before I spoke."

I cast my mind back to the Potts' supper party and Edgar Sutton's description of me as a poor little cripple. His words were offensive, but these are not, and I try to relieve his concerns once again.

"Please forget it. I'm not upset. On the contrary. I'm happy to meet you."

Drake smiles and offers his hand. "Let's begin again," he says, taking my hand and brushing his lips against it.

"Charmed, I'm sure," I say, not knowing the correct etiquette for a hand kiss.

Betty arrives with my cutlets and Drake's cobbler. She places them down and then returns with a custard pot and a jug of gravy.

We eat while chatting easily about his friendship with Sebastian and Tony, and I avoid discussing Lieutenant Chevis, knowing that the subject will inevitably arise. And just as I'm digging into my second cutlet, it does.

"Of course, there were once four of us," he says sadly.

"I heard. I'm very sorry."

"Do you know how Hugh died?"

I nod. "A truly terrible way to go. His poor wife."

Drake shakes his head. "Yes. She's gone back to London. Met another chap already, by all accounts." He shakes his head bitterly.

I don't know what to say, so I continue eating.

"A chap she met on the boat to India..." he continues before his voice trails away. I can see the pain written across his face and quietly empathise, visions of Jim flickering through my head. I couldn't give myself to another man so soon, and I still can't remember the exact nature of our relationship. It must be equally hard to watch a friend's widow move on quickly.

"I'm sorry," I repeat. "I suppose she wants to forget all about it. How dreadful that somebody poisoned your friend, and they never caught the killer."

"Clever blighter," mutters Drake. "And the more time passes, the less likely they will catch him."

In a few short moments, Drake Mallard has gone from a charming, cheerful man to one who seems broken with grief. I feel responsible in a way that I shouldn't and badly want to help.

"I have some experience in solving crime," I say.

"You?" Drake's eyes widen in ill-concealed surprise.

"Yes. It must seem odd for a woman with my limitations," I say. "But I have had success in this field." I am grossly overstating my position, having believed Annie Hearn was innocent and not remembering the outcome of the Croydon poisonings. But Drake Mallard seems weighed down with grief, and I feel moved to cheer him up.

"How?"

"It's difficult to explain," I say. "But that's why I'm here. I will do my utmost to bring the killer to justice."

Drake finishes the last of his cobbler and places his spoon in the bowl. "Can I help?" he asks.

"Of course."

"What can I do?"

"I've spoken to the Chevis cook already," I say. "She works here."

"I know."

"And I'd like to see the bungalow and speak to the neighbours if they are still there."

"I can take you." Drake volunteers enthusiastically. "And perhaps we can go for a drive afterwards. I'd do it tonight, but I've got an appointment to keep. Will tomorrow do?"

"That will be perfect."

Drake checks his watch. "Dash it. I've spent too long in your charming company. We'll catch up at breakfast tomorrow and take it from there. Please excuse me."

"Of course."

Drake nods and strides across the room. He is rangy and athletic, and if Jim's disappearance had not consumed me with grief, I might be interested in an altogether different way. But things are as they are, and I am glad of the acquaintanceship, brief as it is. I am no longer alone and can rely on Sebastian's friend for help should the need arise.

I finish my cutlets, push my plate into the centre of the table, and then wait for the pudding to arrive. But when it does, Ellen Yeomans carries it, and Betty is elsewhere.

"Thank you," I say as she places it in front of me. I expect her to grunt and turn on her heels, but she doesn't.

"I've thought of something else," she says. "Well, rather someone else. I ought to tell you about him, though it's all hearsay. I've only met him once or twice."

"Who is it?" I ask.

"Not here," says Ellen. "I'll finish in an hour. Come to the kitchen, and we'll talk there."

#

It's pointless going upstairs again just to come back down, so I take a short walk outside and settle in one of the two small armchairs in the foyer. Someone has left a book on the side table, so I occupy myself by reading a few chapters until enough time has passed that I can justifiably interrupt Ellen. I make my way to the kitchen, push the door open, and peer inside. Ellen Yeomans is sitting at the kitchen table nursing a cup of tea. Her eyes droop, and she is about to fall asleep.

I tap my stick on the floor and cough. Ellen's eyes widen, and she holds her hand to her heart.

"My goodness. You surprised me," she says, heaving herself from the chair. "Sit down, and I'll pour you a cup of tea."

She places an unsavoury brown brew in front of me, and I know before I taste it that the tea will be tepid, having stewed for some time. But if I'm to curry Ellen's favour, I must be polite, so I sip the tea even though it is as disgusting as I feared.

"What did you want to tell me?" I ask.

"Nothing," she says crisply. "I'd rather forget the whole sorry affair, but I can hardly discuss it without mentioning Major Jackson."

"I know that name," I say.

"Yes. Your friend probably knows him. Major Jackson was Mrs Chevis' first husband."

"That's it. I've seen the name in the papers."

"What have you read?"

"Only that they considered him a suspect, but he had an alibi."

Ellen nods. "That is correct. His alibi was unimpeachable."

"Then why would my friend need to know about him?"

Ellen Yeomans pulls a handkerchief from her sleeve, dabs her nose, and folds it into a square. Then she places it in her apron pocket and stares at her hands. I wait patiently, hoping she will soon break her silence and eventually, she does.

"I wasn't completely honest with you earlier," she says. "Loyalty to my employer, whether past or present, is in my nature. I was reluctant to give an opinion, and when you mentioned their personal lives, well, it quite threw me. But I've been married, and I'd like to think that I'm a woman of the world. I don't know why your friend is so interested in the smaller details of their lives, but I assume it's because of the injustice. The murderer is still at large."

"Exactly that," I say enthusiastically.

"I thought long and hard while I was making the dinner and concluded that I should be frank in what I know. But I warn you, some of this information is second-hand."

"It doesn't matter. Anything is helpful."

"Right. Well, you remember me speaking about Nicholas Boulger, the batman?"

"Yes, I do."

"On the night of the murder, Nicholas and I cleared up when the lieutenant and Mrs Chevis left for the hospital. And afterwards, we sat down and talked over a cup of tea. Well, that's not quite true, and I promised I'd be honest, so I will. We helped ourselves to a brandy each. We were tired out and still in shock from the night's events. Well, tongues loosen after a drop of alcohol, and it's fair to say that we discussed our employers more openly than normal. By then, we were certain that Lieutenant Chevis had been poisoned, and I asked Nicholas who might have done it. Trev Jackson, he said."

"But the major's alibi was unshakeable."

"Yes. But we didn't know that then. Anyway, I had only met Major Jackson a few times. He was Mrs Chevis' first husband, and she shared children with him. They lived in London with the nurse but occasionally visited the bungalow, and Major Jackson sometimes collected them. I remember opening the door to him."

"What is he like?"

"Very polite," says Ellen. "And perfectly charming with the children. He treated Lieutenant and Mrs Chevis respectfully. I couldn't help but like him. But he looked rather silly, dressed in plus fours. I think they look ridiculous on a man."

"He enjoyed golf then?"

"Oh, all sports. He was very fond of cars and horses, of course. He rode to hounds – still does, I shouldn't wonder. But then he is a veterinarian."

"Oh really. Then he must have had access to drugs?"

"Well, that's what Nicholas said. And that's what started us talking."

"Well, if Major Jackson was her first husband, and he's still alive, there must have been a divorce. Was it acrimonious?"

"So Nicholas said," Ellen replies, leaning forward conspiratorially. "He knew a chap who worked with Major Jackson and said that the major contested the divorce. And that when they didn't swiftly resolve it, it came to the notice of the newspapers."

"So, he didn't want to lose his wife?"

"No. But she was in love with Lieutenant Chevis and wouldn't take no for an answer. Now, Mrs Jackson, as she was then, was an heiress and had plenty of money. So, to a certain extent, she could do as she pleased. According to Nicholas, she had Major Jackson followed by a private detective who found him staying with a certain Miss Bradley at a Brighton Hotel. And Miss Bradley wasn't the only woman in his life. They named three others in the divorce proceedings."

"So, he was as disloyal as she was?"

"It looks that way, doesn't it? But Nicholas said that it was all for show."

"I don't understand."

"Major Jackson fought against the divorce for a long time, but Mrs Jackson was determined. And she had protected her money from him and could afford to fight until she got her way. Nicholas says that the major realised he couldn't win and allowed the story of his unfaithfulness to run uncontested."

"Why would he do that?"

"So, he didn't run out of money. And also, because, like many of us, he didn't want to air his dirty laundry. He was the type of man who preferred the stiff upper lip approach. My

Arthur would have liked him."

"But why are you telling me this if his alibi was unbreakable?"

Ellen ignores the question. She gulps the rest of the now cold tea and pours herself another. I put my hand over the top of my cup to signal my lack of interest in a refill.

"According to Nicholas, Major Jackson always spoke well of Mrs Chevis," Ellen continues. "And she of him until the lieutenant's death. But after the poisoning, she disparaged his character, even calling him a scoundrel."

"Why would she do that?" I ask.

"Why indeed?" Ellen raises an eyebrow, and the penny drops.

"Oh, my goodness. Surely you don't think…?"

"I don't think anything," says Ellen abruptly. "But what conclusions you may come to having heard this is a matter for you."

"I think I understand," I say slowly, processing her words in my head. Then I remember something Tony said.

"In the spirit of frankness, may I ask you something I touched on earlier?"

"About the open marriage? I can't comment on it because I saw nothing of that nature. Mrs Chevis was always loving towards the lieutenant."

"Somebody told me she had a lover in London."

"I wouldn't know. You'd have to ask Ivy Thorne."

"Who's she?"

"The nursemaid. She still works for Mrs Chevis at her flat in Knightsbridge."

"Can I have the address?"

"Basil Mansions. But I can't guarantee she'll speak to you. She's very fond of Mrs Chevis. Unusually so."

"Thank you. That's helpful."

Ellen looks up abruptly and gazes straight into my eyes. "Nicholas said that he heard she was seeing the chauffeur," she blurts out as if quickly speaking negated the remark. "But she

couldn't have been. At least not our chauffeur. He was too old."
I open my mouth to speak, but Ellen has clearly had enough. "I must press on," she says. "You know as much as I do now."
I take my cue and leave, eager to see Teddy, who has spent the evening alone in the bedroom, dutifully waiting for my return. I open the door, and he rushes to me, and I return his loyalty with a couple of dog biscuits. Then I take a seat at the dressing table and add Ellen's tale to my notes. Once finished, I lie quietly on the bed, rehearsing the conversation in my mind. Ellen, still loyal to the end, was reluctant to say too much about her employers. I had seen them myself while in astral form, bearing witness to events at the bungalow and seeing nothing to suggest the husband and wife were not deeply in love. Even if Tony Harding was correct, any adultery was by agreement, so why had Ellen taken such pains to discuss the major who couldn't possibly have committed the crime? It could only be to give me an insight into Frances Chevis.
"What did I learn?" I ask aloud, and Teddy responds by nuzzling my hand.
"She's single-minded," I say, and Teddy wisely stares as if listening to my whirring brain. "Yes. She is self-centred, capable, and rich enough to afford anything she wants or needs." Teddy jumps from the bed, and I resume an internal dialogue. Frances Chevis may or may not have been having an affair. But without stating it, Ellen has implied that the grieving widow was capable of murdering her husband. But given their open relationship, what possible motive could she have? I am still mulling it over long after I undress and get into bed.

CHAPTER TWENTY

Unwelcome News

Tuesday, October 25, 1932

I decide to risk taking Teddy to the dining room for breakfast. I had thought he was content to be left unattended in my bedroom, but on waking this morning, I noticed marks on the door, which turn out to be deep scratches on closer inspection. Teddy has been pawing at the paintwork, causing significant damage. I wake, dress, and ponder the situation. He has exposed the woodwork, and I don't want to receive a repair bill when I leave. Having painted nothing in my life, I don't know where to start, but I have a bottle of talcum powder with me, and I wonder if that will do. I liberally coat my hands and rub it into the door. The result is far from perfect, but it's disguised the worst of the damage. Pausing only to wipe the floor with a damp cloth, I leash Teddy and go downstairs, hoping no one will see me take him in.

I'm earlier than usual today, and only two other people are in the dining room, neither of whom I know. They both see Teddy but don't raise an eyebrow, and I slink to the end of the room and park my little dog in a corner where he sits quietly chewing a dog biscuit. I should get away with it if he doesn't bark.

I order my breakfast and wait patiently for Drake Mallard to arrive. He eventually bowls in after I have finished my cereal and while I am nibbling my second piece of toast, then apologises profusely for his tardiness.

"I met a pal last night," he says. "Six rounds of cards later, I almost lost my shirt and drank far too much. Jolly nearly slept in this morning," he continues. "Thank goodness I set a second alarm."

"Make sure you eat a good breakfast," I tell him.

He grins. "What, to soak up the alcohol?"

"To feel right," I say. "Are you well enough to drive?"

"I'd better be," he says. "I must meet with the commanding officer after our little jaunt."

"Don't waste time on me if you're busy," I say, noting a frisson of concern in his voice.

"Nonsense. I said I'd take you, and I will. It's not very far, and it won't take long. We'll have plenty of time for that drive I promised."

"Oh, good," I say. "I discovered some interesting facts about your friend last night, and I must tell you all about it."

"Capital," says Drake. "I will look forward to it. Ah, here comes Mrs Travers with my breakfast."

"But you haven't ordered it."

"No need. I always have the same thing. You can't beat starting the day with a couple of fried eggs on toast."

He digs in, and I watch while sipping the last of my tea. Teddy, patiently hiding in the corner, sidles over to Drake and rubs his head against his leg.

"Is he yours?" asks Drake in surprise.

"In a manner of speaking," I say. "That won't be a problem, will it? I know some people object to dogs in cars."

"Not me," says Drake. "Not that I'm a dog person myself.

My father has an allergy," he continues.

"Oh, dear. Not you, though?"

"I have several allergies – hard work, corked wine and pilchards. I can't stand the bloody things."

I laugh. "That's exactly how I feel about them." I am about to launch into a monologue about Elys and her obsession for Stargazy pie when Teddy suddenly bolts from the table, dragging his lead behind. I grab my stick and jump up about to follow him when he stops and stands, tail wagging for all it's worth at the foot of a man who has just entered the room. A man I've known for years. What on earth is Peter doing here?

#

I stare agape as Peter spies me and marches over.

"Ah, Connie. We must talk," he says.

"Why are you here?" I am rooted to the spot, torn between anger and embarrassment.

"Is everything alright?" asks Drake.

"Sorry to intrude," says Peter. "But I must speak with Connie."

"Not now. We are about to go for a drive."

"Not wise," says Peter abruptly. "Just give me five minutes of your time."

"Must I really?"

"I wouldn't be here otherwise. Do excuse me, Mr - er, whatever your name is."

"It's Drake Mallard," I hiss. "Sebastian's friend."

"Good Lord. Pleased to meet you. I'm Peter Tremayne." Peter offers his hand, and Drake takes it uncertainly.

I sigh and reach for Teddy's lead, still trailing on the floor. The young waitress stares disapprovingly across the room as I crouch and pick it up. I stand and brush my dress down. "Will you wait for me?" I ask, looking pleadingly towards Drake, hoping Peter's terse approach hasn't put him off our drive.

Drake glances at his watch. "Yes, but don't forget my appointment with the CO."

"This way," says Peter, and I trail in his wake as he strides across the room. He turns back, remembers my limp, and slows down. "Sorry, Connie," he says. "Time is pressing."

"Too right it is," I say, a little more loudly than necessary. "You've made me look every kind of fool. Now, what is it?"

Peter shakes his head. "Can we go to your room?"

"I suppose so."

I stomp upstairs with as much drama as I can muster, unlock my room and gesture for Peter to sit on the chair by the dresser. Teddy bounds onto his lap and tries to sit down, but he is too big and pushes against Peter, who nearly loses his balance on the chair. "Down, boy," he says and tickles Teddy's ears to reassure him he isn't cross. But I have no time for Peter's ministrations to my hound.

"What was that all about? Drake must think I'm stupid."

"I don't see why," says Peter.

"Because he's taking me for a drive, and suddenly you appear out of the blue."

"Which was self-evident," says Peter mildly. "And as you didn't know, he can't possibly hold you responsible, ergo no stupidity on your part."

"Even so," I huff, still angry at the interruption to my morning.

"Don't you want to know why I'm here?"

"Not particularly."

"Fine. Enough now, Connie. This is serious."

I examine his face, so familiar to me, yet grey and etched with more frown lines than I remember. And my fractious mood vanishes. Peter wouldn't hare down here without good reason, and I should know better than to greet him with peevish ill-will. "I'm sorry," I say.

"Don't be. Just listen."

I take a seat on the bed and wait.

"Felix Crossley is in Cornwall," says Peter. "He has been for a day or two."

"We knew that would happen. It's hardly a surprise."

"No. But it means that you can't return to Cornwall while he's here."

"I wasn't going to."

"You know that, but how would I? You bolted without discussion."

"I sent you a letter."

"Well, it was better than nothing, but only just."

"I suppose Fox told you where I was? He said he would."

"Naturally," says Peter. "He wired me straight away."

"Then why did you rush down?"

"Mary's keeping an eye on things in Bosula. She's seen Crossley and even spent a few hours with him. I've taken her into my confidence. No choice, really. But it puts her in a tricky position. Crossley doesn't know about your connection to Bosula, and you've only been a few times, so he shouldn't work it out. He knows you by sight and even by reputation in terms of astral travel. But I doubt he knows your name. If he did, he'd have tracked you down long ago."

"What's that got to do with your sudden appearance?" The words sound ruder and more ungrateful than I intended, but my need for information leaves my thoughts unfiltered.

"Crossley is taking a week's break on his way back to London."

"Where?"

"She doesn't know. Mary is trying to find out, but she can't ask questions, as you will appreciate."

"Well, there's no point in worrying until we find out."

Peter cocks his head. "Really, Connie. You should know better. Mary has no training in the art of information gathering. Crossley may choose to keep his movements to himself. But Hampshire is between London and Cornwall. How close do you think he would need to be before he sensed your presence?"

I think about the many times our paths have crossed. "It could happen anywhere," I mutter, unwilling to acknowledge Peter's concerns.

"It's not worth the risk."

"Then what do I do? I can hardly return to Cornwall."

"Definitely not," says Peter. "It must be somewhere else."

"I don't know anywhere else. I'd be better off going to London."

Peter's eyes narrow while he thinks. "That's not such a bad idea," he says.

"Isn't it? Won't Crossley's acolytes be all over the capital?"

"They are not as powerful as he is, and London is the last place they would look."

"I'll do it."

"That's a quick decision. Is there some ulterior motive of which I am not aware?"

"Only that I would like to call in on Ivy Thorne."

"Who is she?"

"A nursemaid in the employ of Frances Chevis."

"I see no reason why not," says Peter. "And I would also like to pay a visit."

"Where to?"

"The London Herald office."

"Oh. Are you checking up on that writer?"

Peter nods. "I'd like to talk to him and find out why he's copying Crawford Newson's style. Perhaps it's for professional reasons, but it would be good to know either way. But for the difference in his author's name, I can't tell his work from Newson's.

"We must tell Drake. He was about to take me to the old Chevis bungalow."

"Why?"

"So, I could get a feel for how close it was to the neighbours and an exact location for the meat safe."

"We'll drive past if you like."

"I do, but I must make my excuses to Drake."

"I'll come with you."

We return downstairs and back to the dining room, where Drake Mallard is still sitting and staring moodily into a cooling cup of tea. He sees me and jumps up from his seat.

"Ready to go?" he asks affably.

"I'm sorry. I can't. An emergency at home," I explain. "I must return to Porth Tregoryan."

"That's a pity." Drake looks genuinely upset.

"Perhaps we'll bump into each other again," I say, fighting down a surge of guilt for taking up the time he could have spent getting ready for his meeting.

"I hope so," says Drake. He presses my hand and then gives Peter's a vigorous shake. "Goodbye for now," and then he is gone.

"Best go pack," says Peter, and he takes Teddy for a walk while I do just that.

CHAPTER TWENTY-ONE

Basil Mansions

It is not until we are on the outskirts of London that Peter comes clean with me about what he did on his dog walk. They didn't go for a long stroll around the green, as Peter implied. Instead, he crammed Teddy into a public phone box and telephoned Oliver Fox at home, who was unamused to receive his call.

"I didn't know what else to do," Peter had said, discussing Fox's reminder about allowable modes of communication. But when Peter explained his concerns and our intended trip to London, Fox had relaxed, listened, and finally agreed that it was the best course of action. He also insisted that Peter and I familiarise ourselves with the Shining Path premises in Bayswater and how to reach them should the need arise.

"I don't see why we need to worry if Crossley's in Cornwall," I say.

"You can't be too sure," Peter replies with an air of superiority.

We discuss where to stay and settle on a respectable

boarding house in Somerstown. It is too far to walk to Bayswater, at least for me, but we have the car and travel shouldn't be a problem until Peter mentions refuelling.

"Is it expensive?" I ask and then remember Hilda Grady's accommodation allowance, which I'd initially handed to Betty Travers. When I sought her out earlier and explained my sudden need to leave, she had refunded me the balance, which was now in my purse. "I have funds," I say brightly.

"You mustn't worry about money," says Peter. "I've just been paid."

"Shouldn't you be at work?"

"My grandmother is poorly," says Peter grimly.

"Running out of excuses?"

"Yes. And this is beyond the pale. Both my grandmothers died years ago, but I didn't know what else to say on the spur of the moment."

"It's good of you to bother. I know it's a risk."

Peter squeezes my hand, glad of the appreciation which I should have given sooner. We trundle into London, driving past great and glorious buildings. I stare transfixed as Peter provides a running commentary. I have never been to London, and it is vast and considerably more handsome than I could have ever imagined, but Peter is an old hand. When his father was alive, he frequently went to the capital in the course of his work, often taking Peter and Isla with him. Though it's been many years, Peter's memory is excellent, and he tells me the stories his father told him while I listen, enraptured. And before long, Peter parks in front of our intended lodgings, a place he has used before, and we approach the reception desk and ask for rooms. It is quiet in the capital in the autumn months, and rooms are plentiful and cheaper than we anticipated. We take our room keys and unpack, then meet in the communal lounge room, which is basic but perfectly adequate.

"Where shall we go first?" asks Peter.

"To see Ivy Thorne?"

"Where?"

"Basil Mansions, Knightsbridge."

"That's the other side of Hyde Park from the Shining Path HQ," says Peter. "Should fit in nicely."

"Must we go?"

"I promised we'd drive past. That's all. Don't you want to go inside?"

"Not without Fox," I say. "After what I saw at Worple Road the other day, I want to forget all about that part of my life."

"Was it awful?" asks Peter.

"Terrifying," I reply.

"Oliver Fox doesn't think I'll ever see the manifestations," says Peter.

"Most people don't unless they travel the astral plane."

"I wonder why?"

"I don't know, Peter. Once, when I was working for Fox, I read a paper on the theory of psychological suggestion. I'm undoubtedly vulnerable to that, and Crossley is a master of persuasion, but there's more to it. Those things are real. They leave traces behind."

My lip involuntarily curls in disgust as I remember the slime from the spider beast that forced itself into my bedroom last year. While travelling in the safety of daylight, I can hardly believe it happened, but the memories return with fearful clarity at night.

"Can we stop talking about it?" I attempt to change the subject. But Peter persists.

"We'll go to Queensborough Terrace first," he says. "Get it over with, and then you can interview your lady. Will she see you?"

"I don't know," I admit. "And I must be careful. Ivy won't speak in front of her mistress, which could be tricky. It may take several visits."

"We should be here for a few days," says Peter cautiously. "I'll telephone Mary in a moment. Let her know where we are. Then she can get hold of me if the situation changes."

"Good old Mary," I say, wishing I was with her. Then I

remember where Crossley has gone and shake the thought away.

Peter's stomach growls, and I realise he hasn't eaten. While I was busily devouring cereal, Peter was driving, and he must be starving. We call into a coffee house close to where he parked the car. Peter buys a steak and kidney pie while I have a scone, and we eat it in the car. When he has finished, Peter pulls away.

We make our way across town and onto Queensborough Terrace. It is a pleasant road full of handsome townhouses, and I feel confident about its normality. Peter locates number three, a similar property to its neighbours, which couldn't look less ordinary if it tried. Then we pull away again, paying attention to the route as we drive alongside Hyde Park before arriving at Basil Road. Peter stops the car in front of an impossibly attractive building, oozing wealth, and privilege.

"I can't possibly go in there," I say.

"Nonsense," says Peter. "You're well clothed, and nobody would know."

"I rather think you are missing the point. There's a doorman. He'd want to announce me, and I've no reason to be here."

Peter sighs. "Then what are you going to do?"

"Wait," I say. And we do.

#

After twenty minutes, Peter is getting decidedly tetchy. He checks his wristwatch every few minutes and emits a series of painfully deep sighs. The conversation has ground to a halt, and I am running out of ways to start it again. Just as I am about to rethink my strategy and consider finding a way to access Basil Mansions, a stout woman appears dressed in a smart coat holding hands with a pair of young children. I grab the newspaper clipping of Frances Chevis leaving the inquest and compare it with the person before me. The slender figure of Frances bears no resemblance to the woman I'm looking at, but another individual photographed standing to the left is a close match.

"I wouldn't mind betting that's Ivy Thorne," I say excitedly.

176

"Great. Now, what are you going to do?"

"I don't know. See if she'll speak to me, I suppose."

"What about me?"

"Stay here for now. I'll signal if I need you."

"Are you sure?"

"Perfectly."

I grab my stick and make my way toward the figure, who is now hurrying down the road. I will never catch her limping along at a snail's pace and decide to wave to Peter for help. But just as I am about to raise my hand, I see a woman dressed in a grey uniform rushing towards them from the other direction. "Where have you been?" asks the woman, whom I hope is Ivy Thorne.

"Sorry. I was delayed,"

"Better late than never. Now, children. Off you go, and mind you, behave." She hands them over to the uniformed woman who escorts them along the road, then spins on her heel straight towards me.

I am flustered for a moment and don't know what to do, but as she approaches, I step into her path. "Excuse me. Are you Ms Ivy Thorne?"

The woman looks me up and down. "Yes. What of it?"

"May I speak to you?"

"About what?"

"Lieutenant Chevis?"

"Go away," she says sternly.

"I beg your pardon."

"I'm sick to death of your lot, hanging around the place and upsetting people."

"I'm not a reporter."

"Oh. Then what are you?"

"A friend of Sebastian Letwin."

Ivy's face softens. "I know him. He was a friend of the master's."

"That's right. And he's still very upset. He was out of the country when Lieutenant Chevis died and knew very little about it."

"There isn't much to tell. The whole thing is a mystery."

"So, I hear. And that's the problem. Sebastian badly wants to know more about it."

"Then why isn't he with you?"

"He's hurt his leg and is recovering at Bodmin before returning to his battalion in Gibraltar. I'm here in his place."

Ivy looks me up and down, and her eyes settle on my stick. I know what she is thinking, although she is too polite to say it.

"What do you want from me?"

"To talk. It will only take a few minutes."

She moves off again towards Basil Mansions, and I position myself to her left and try to keep up.

She is silent for a moment until we reach the entrance before stopping outside the wrought-iron fence.

"You can't come in," she says.

"Then talk to me here."

"Certainly not. It's common."

"There's a little coffee shop further down the road."

"I don't want a coffee."

"Then come and sit in the car for a moment. Please. It's important."

"Where is this car?"

"Over there." I point to Peter, who has parked only a few yards away.

He must look agreeable as Ivy nods her head. "Very well," she says. I'll give you ten minutes of my time."

We reach the car, and Peter jumps out and holds the door open. Ivy sits in the back, and I join her.

"Shall I wait outside?" he asks.

"Not on my account," says Ivy. "Now, what do you want?"

There is no point in fluffing things up. Ivy Thorne is direct and to the point. I must be the same, even at the risk of upsetting her.

"Sebastian would like to know how his friend came to die."

"He ingested poison," says Ivy. "But you know that. Are you

asking who did it?"

I nod.

"I don't know."

"But if you had to speculate?"

"Fortunately, I don't. But I'll give you the benefit of my opinion. I think someone contaminated the birds before they ever arrived at the bungalow. Lieutenant Chevis died accidentally."

"Oh. You're the first person to say that."

"Who else have you spoken to?"

"Ellen Yeomans, the cook."

Ivy Thorne snorts. "You're not likely to get an objective opinion from one of the suspects, are you? Who did she blame?"

"Nobody. She was very careful not to."

Ivy waits and scrutinises my face. I feel uncomfortable and move my gaze away. The woman with whom I am sharing a car is highly intelligent and frighteningly perceptive. She is waiting for me to continue, and I do.

"But she implied that Mrs Chevis might have other interests."

"I see. And you want me to tattle about my employer's private affairs?"

I swallow. "Yes."

"And how would this benefit your friend?"

"He only wants to know the facts. And not by reading a gratuitous account of it in the press. Sebastian has heard that the Chevis marriage was unusual and wants to know the truth."

Ivy rests her hand on the door handle, and for a moment, I think she intends to leave. But instead, she turns to face me. "It's true. Their marriage was unconventional. They both saw other people and allowed each other total freedom. For that reason, you can safely assume that Mrs Chevis is innocent. She had nothing to gain from her husband's death. Do you understand?"

I nod. "Yes. Frances Chevis was wealthy in her own right and allowed to do as she pleased."

179

"Quite. So, Mrs Yeomans should keep her silly opinions to herself."

"I suppose so. Do you know the name of Mrs Chevis' gentleman friend? Only, Mrs Yeomans thought it was the chauffeur."

"It was not the chauffeur," says Ivy disapprovingly. However, I wouldn't be surprised if the suggestion of it was a joke on her gentleman friend's part to conceal his identity. Although Lieutenant Chevis knew of his existence, he didn't know his name."

"Why?" I ask.

"I don't know. Part of the game, I suppose."

"Game?"

"Their way of living. But it doesn't matter. Neither of them minded."

"Did you meet her lover?"

Ivy shudders. "Gentleman friend," she reiterates. "And no, I didn't."

"He never came to the apartment?"

"Of course not. The children live here."

"And you don't know his name?"

"No, I don't. And it suits me that way. The upper class has different standards than the rest of us. Why do you feel the need to know? I suppose you are hoping I will say he was called Hartigan?"

I smile. Ivy Thorne evidently has a sense of humour.

"I'm sure the police would have tracked him down by now if he bore the same name as the sender of the Hooray telegrams."

"I'm not sure they know very much about him at all. And a good thing too. They would jump to conclusions about her behaviour."

"It sounds like you didn't approve?"

"It's none of my business what Mrs Chevis does. And she didn't keep me in the dark. My employer confided certain general matters, and I was happy to lend an ear when she wanted to talk. But this did not include intimate details of her personal life or the names of her escorts. And if I knew more, I wouldn't tell you. Loyalty matters. Nothing I have said today is harmful to Mrs Chevis. Quite the contrary. Now, ten minutes are up. I've said enough. I wish you a good day."

And with that, she opens the door and strides briskly towards Basil Mansions.

I relocate to the passenger seat and glance at Peter, who has sat quietly throughout the conversation.

"What do you make of that?" I ask.

"Plenty of food for thought," he says. "We should talk about this later. And while we're about it, I'd like to look at those telegrams. Do you have copies?"

"Copies of one and notes of another."

"That will do," says Peter. "Now. Let's pop along to the London Herald offices and see if we can track down that writer."

CHAPTER TWENTY-TWO

Living in Fear

Our visit to the London Herald offices was successful, producing an immediate result that took only moments to achieve. Peter had passed a clipping to the girl on reception, who took one look at it before proclaiming it to be the work of Norman Leslie of Clerkenwell. She happily gave his address without asking Peter why he wanted it, and we drove straight there, hoping to see him. But that was where our good luck ended. We had expected a house, but Norman Leslie lived in a lower ground-floor flat in a bleakly depressing building in a less than salubrious area. Peter had insisted that I stay in the car while he tried the doorbell. But after several minutes of knocking and ringing, nobody answered. Peter had then tried to peer through a small window at the rear, but something blocked the view from the other side.

"I'm sure there's someone in there," he had said. "But he won't answer."

"We'll have to leave it then," I had replied. "What a pity."

"Isn't it? Damn. I would love to have met him."

I had mulled this over for the rest of the afternoon. It is now early evening, and I have found a solution. Whether Peter will go along with it is another matter.

"How much do you want to track down Norman Leslie?" I ask.

"A great deal – I was curious before, but now we can't get hold of him, I'm even more interested. I was keen on Crawford Newson's books before you met his sister, and now I'm intrigued to find another writer so similar in style. But it is not to be. The flat is like a fortress. Norman Leslie must be a recluse."

"You don't think it's worth visiting again?"

Peter shakes his head. "A waste of time, I would say. The fellow was in there. I could hear him. He didn't want to answer the door."

"Did he see us?"

"I doubt it. He's just generally unfriendly."

"There is a way," I say.

"What?"

I hesitate, and Peter reads my mind.

"Absolutely not."

"You'd be here watching me."

"I said no. It isn't safe."

"But Crossley's in Cornwall."

"How does that make any difference? You could come across him on the astral plane. He hones into you like a hawk in pursuit of a dove."

"But you'd be here watching me. You can bring me back as you did before."

"No."

"I'll do it with or without you."

"Don't start that again, Connie. It isn't worth it."

"I think it is."

Peter pushes away his coffee cup. It is half full, but he seems to have lost all appetite for it. "Oh, Connie. Here we go again."

"I'll go straight there, and it will work because I know where I'm going, and I should be able to get there quickly. You'll need to say the address out loud."

"I don't believe this," mutters Peter.

"Come on then. Let's get it done."

"Absolutely not. Oliver Fox would have a fit if he knew. We'll have a civilised dinner and talk some more."

#

Two hours later, stuffed to the gills with lemon chicken and roast potatoes, I sit on my bed while Peter paces nervously around the room. Teddy follows behind him with the concerned look of a hound who knows something is amiss.

"I'm still unhappy about this," says Peter, a picture of abject misery.

"Don't worry. I will be careful."

"Aren't you frightened?"

"A little," I say. But I don't mention that I am also strangely excited at the prospect of another controlled dream walk. Peter doesn't understand what it's like to be restricted by bodily frailty. He can run for the bus, cycle to work and skate on an ice rink if he chooses, but I cannot. Yet, I am footloose and fancy-free in the astral realm. I can do anything, be anyone, and for all the risks, it is liberating.

"Sit down, Peter," I say.

"Must I?"

"If I'm to concentrate."

"Perhaps it won't work," says Peter, hopefully.

"Come on. Say your piece."

Peter chants the Clerkenwell address while I stare at the candle we'd lit moments earlier. I watch the flickering flame, wishing I felt sleepier. But as I relax into the pillow, propped up to give the perfect view of the flame, I feel myself slipping into a place where Peter's mantra drifts further and further into the background. And suddenly, it takes me. I fall backwards through the bed, the floor, and the hotel, descending on my back before gravity slowly flips me the right way. I keep my eyes tightly shut, not even risking a peep, feeling an inherent safety in my ignorance. And within moments, I come to a gentle halt and find myself standing on what would be *terra firma* if I had solid legs. Once I stop moving, I open my eyes and inspect my surroundings.

I have executed the perfect plan, and I can't help grinning at the sight of the building we'd parked outside earlier today. I am precisely where I hoped to be. It is early evening and dusky but not dark enough to find strange creatures lurking in unlit corners. I feel safe. Crossley is far away, and I cannot feel his presence anywhere. I move towards the door that Peter couldn't access earlier, marvelling at the swift smoothness of my progress. I am a different person on the astral plane, strong and independent, with a regular walking gait. Determinedly, I power through the front door.

I am in a small, poorly lit hallway. The front door has a window which ought to provide light, but there isn't any because someone has placed a wooden panel over the glass. Three hefty bolts seal the door tightly shut, and the middle bolt has the added security of a padlock. Norman Leslie lives in fear. He is hiding from something or someone. I glide into the tiny kitchen, but it is empty. Lamb chop bones rest upon a plate on the draining board with the dregs of a claret bottle nearby. My eyes drift to a box of wine on the kitchen floor, which is also full of claret. The flat is rudimentary, but the kitchen contents indicate that the owner of this property has means. He is not as poor as the location and shabby property exterior suggest. I leave the kitchen and head towards the sound of a radio playing classical music in the background. As I pass through the door, I almost walk into the recumbent form of Norman Leslie, who is lying asleep on the sofa with a newspaper clutched to his chest. The living room occupies the corner of the property with windows on both sides. Norman Leslie has shut the curtains save for one, which provides a tiny chink of light. I approach it and try to peer outside, but metal bars obscure my view.

For a moment, I wonder if this man is a prisoner, but the chunky chain of keys lying on a low table in the centre of the room suggests otherwise. I leave the window and walk towards the sofa, standing above the sleeping man for a good view of his face. He looks familiar and is heart-stoppingly similar to Mary's photographs of her dead brother. This man is a relative, a doppelgänger, or Crawford himself. But why would a man of his means and renown hide in a low neighbourhood like this? And why all the bolts? And then I realise. If I am in the presence of the missing Crawford Newson, he likely faked his death. And given that he lives his life in fear, he must be running away from someone or something. A vision of purple robes in the false bottom of a trunk flashes through my head. Robes with the Calicem Aureum symbol embroidered on the reverse. Is Crawford Newson hiding from Crossley too?

The sleeping man emits a deep sigh and rubs the side of his nose with his finger. He lies there in a dreamlike state, eyes fluttering as he negotiates the stages of sleep. He is peaceful now, but evidence of his fear lies across the flat. And with sudden clarity and a stab of guilt, I realise I am the last person in the world who should stand before him. I, who Crossley has chased through the astral plane, could lead him to this man who has locked himself away from the world. I close my eyes and bow my head into my hands, searching for an inner darkness not quite present in the room. It works. I hurtle backwards and sneak a peek to ensure I am on the astral plane. Stars glint through inky blackness, and I sigh with relief, waiting for a swift return to my body. But something is disturbing the uniformity of the stars. They tremble and quiver, flickering in and out of sight as if obscured by something. And then I realise. There are many somethings – eight-legged bodies skittering towards me in a hairy mass of evil. As my pulse quickens and fear courses through my veins, I feel my beating heart. I must be within touching distance of my body, or I wouldn't feel the tangible effects of my terror. Trembling, I wait and hope my parts merge before the creatures reach me. I stop still, clutching my arms around my body in a natural attempt to protect myself, for I have nothing else to use. They surge closer and closer, and I recoil, but I will disappoint them this time, for I wake with a terrified gasp to see Peter sitting casually in the seat, looking for all the world as if he is about to drop off.

"Did you see anything?" I bark, clutching my heart, which beats fit to burst.

"What?" asks Peter, bleary-eyed.

"They found me."

"Oh, God – Crossley?"

"No. His creatures. Couldn't you tell?"

"No. You looked perfectly calm. And only a few seconds have passed since you fell asleep."

"Really? Time is peculiar. It doesn't match the length of my experience."

"We already know that. Are you alright?"

"I am now. But I was frightened, and I must not do it again, Peter. Crawford Newson and Norman Leslie are the same."

"I knew it," he says triumphantly. "Nobody can imitate Newson's unique writing style that well. How do you know it was Crawford?"

"I've seen photographs and a painting," I say, remembering Mary's tribute to her brother, painted after his death. Except that he hadn't died at all and had bunkered down in London the whole time. "I can't work out why he's in the capital if he's hiding from Crossley."

"Why would he be avoiding Crossley?"

I remind Peter of the robes I had found the previous year.

"I see. If Crawford Newson was involved with Calicem Aureum, he must know Crossley. No doubt about it."

"But why come to London?" I repeat.

"Because he didn't know Crossley was here."

"Oh. Good point. Crossley was living in Berlin when Crawford disappeared."

"Quite."

"Then what is he hiding from?"

"Can he dream walk?"

"I don't know. Perhaps?"

"I'd say so if he's a member of the organisation. Even if he only practices it at the most basic level."

"Then Crawford erected the bolts and bars to keep out Crossley's creatures."

"Exactly."

"Which means they know he's there."

"Not necessarily. Crawford might have secured his flat with bars in anticipation of an attack."

"Yes, of course. Crawford knew the danger before he left Cornwall. But Peter. I ran into the manifestations again on the astral plane. I might have given Crawford's hiding place away."

"Did you see them while you were at his property?"

"No. I felt perfectly safe there."

"Then the creatures sensed your presence while travelling," says Peter. "As we feared they might. You really shouldn't have risked it, Connie. Thank goodness you got away."

"I won't do it again," I say. "Peter. I'm going to splash my face in the bathroom. I suddenly feel quite overcome."

"Shall I help you down the corridor?"

"No. I'll manage. Wait for me here and keep an eye on Teddy."

I leave the room and hobble towards the bathroom, my legs unusually stiff. Perhaps the shock of my near miss or the knowledge that I have been foolhardy makes them slower, but I have learned a valuable lesson. No matter what the reason, I won't risk myself again. I complete my ablutions and return to the bedroom to find Peter with his nose to the window.

"What are you doing?"

"I heard a noise, and I'm surprised Teddy's whines didn't reach you down the corridor."

"Where is this noise?"

"Outside, obviously." Peter is curt, almost rude, and I huff before stomping toward him.

"I can't hear anything. What kind of sound?" I ask.

"A tapping on the glass."

I am about to look myself when a worm of dread slithers down my spine.

"Close the curtains," I say.

"There's nothing there."

"Close the curtains, Peter. Now."

But it is too late. The dripping mandible of an outsized spider hawks drool across the window before it hangs there, supported by a thick coil of fibre, its front legs jammed against the window. Teddy raises his head and howls.

"Oh, my God. Can you see it?"

"See what?" Blissful ignorance bathes Peter's face.

"That thing."

I point to the window and the gruesome sight before me, but Peter stares blankly.

"Well, can you hear it, then?"

Yes. I told you. Something is tapping against the window, but I've checked, and there's nothing there.

"There bloody well is," I say, using a profanity I last heard when Jory hit his nail with a hammer.

Peter is shocked into action. "Look. I'll show you." His hands are on the window catch, and I cannot reach him in time to stop him from opening it. My body reacts before my brain engages, and I hurl my stick at Peter to stop him. It smashes against the window end first, creating a small but perfectly round hole.

"What on earth?" asks Peter, and then he turns to face me, his features ashen. "What the hell is that?"

The giant spider has taken full advantage of the chink in the window and thrust a hairy leg through it. And somehow, the scales have fallen from Peter's eyes, and he can see what I can see.

"Oh no. This can't be happening." Peter's face turns green, and he looks as if he will vomit. I pull him away from the window. "We must stay in the centre of the room," I command.

"We can't," says Peter. "We must go at once. Look." He

points to a jagged crack caused by the creature plugging a small hole with a large leg.

"Let's go to your room." I grab my stick and Teddy's leash, and we rush down the corridor to Peter's bedroom on the right. No sooner have we shut the door than we hear a rapping at the window, like bullets ricocheting from a gun.

"Is it here?" he asks.

"Don't look. Just stay on the bed."

"I must check. I think I left the window open."

I stare in horror. "It's October. Why?"

CHAPTER TWENTY-THREE

Shining Path HQ

"Oddly enough, I wasn't thinking about the weather," snaps Peter.

"Even so," I remonstrate, but I am stopped in my tracks by a big bulge in the curtains. I stare aghast, my heart in my mouth as the fabric ripples over a large, spherical body.

"Leave now," says Peter, reversing backwards towards the door. I am standing behind him, and, step by step, I mirror his movements, Teddy staying close to my ankles. But we are not quick enough. The curtains fly open just as I place my hand on the doorknob and a large shape launches itself towards us.

"Get out," screams Peter as the spider lands, nose to jaw, sloshing him with gloopy saliva. I take one look and edge backwards and into the corridor. Peter's momentary paralysis ends, and he leaps back, slamming the wooden door into the creature's face with a sickening crunch.

"That should buy us some time," he says. "Now run."

I shoot him a glare before hobbling down the corridor as fast as possible, but my speed is woefully inadequate for our current peril.

"Can't you go any faster?"

"No," I snarl. "Peter, get to the car. Take Teddy and go while you can."

"I'm not leaving you."

"You must. Or we'll both be trussed up in a web somewhere on the astral plane."

"I said I'm not leaving you."

I stop and gulp air. The corridor seems endless, and any exertion makes me feel faint.

"Keep going, Connie. Oh God, it's trying to break out."

Peter is listening to the thumping from his bedroom door that I have been trying to ignore. Large, heavy thuds pepper smaller, more delicate versions.

"There's more than one," I say.

"Keep going." Peter pushes me from behind, but it doesn't help my speed.

"I'll carry you."

"No, Peter. Save yourself."

We hear one almighty clunk, and then the door smashes open, splintering wood along the corridor. A giant spider, followed by a sea of smaller ones, spills from the room before swarming towards us.

"Run, Peter."

"No."

"Run, and I'll meet you there. I'll use astral travel."

Peter turns towards me one last time before taking Teddy's leash and hurtling towards the stairs, dragging the reluctant hound behind him. The spiders are almost upon me when I spy a door, wrench it open and all but fall inside in my haste to escape them. I spin around and examine my surroundings. The suffocating space is a tiny broom closet with no window and a high handle on the door. I wedge my stick between the handle and the floor and throw myself on the tiles in a foetal position.

Ignoring the thumps, the thuds and hisses of disappointed hunters temporarily missing their prey, I close my eyes and am about to enter the astral plane when I realise the flaw in my plan. If I leave my body and let it fall victim to Crossley's creatures, I might as well not have bothered escaping. I must preserve all my parts, ethereal or otherwise, so I get to my feet and search the closet, finding a large metal bin storing tools. Using all my strength, I heave it towards the door and settle behind, wondering if it will protect me from the creatures hurling themselves at the thin piece of wood that stands between us. But the heavy metal bin offers unexpected protection, and they cannot get through.

Ten minutes pass, and then twenty. The noise tails off, and the sense of danger lifts. The creatures have gone, but I don't dare open the door. Then, to my surprise, I hear someone calling my name. It is Peter. He has returned.

"I'm in here," I say.

"Then come out. You're safe," he replies.

"Not until she's paid for the damage," a gruff voice loudly complains.

I try to haul the metal bin away from the door, but it was easier pushing than pulling, and I am nearly exhausted by the time I have created enough space to push past. I take my stick and open the door with trembling hands.

"Thank goodness," says Peter, wrapping his arms around me.

"Who's going to pay for this?" whines a short, dark-haired man, pointing to the door of Peter's room.

"I will," snaps Peter. "Now kindly fetch a glass of water."

"I don't want any," I say.

"Fetch it," Peter commands. The man tuts loudly and walks away.

"The water was just a ruse," says Peter. "Now, we must get away from here."

"You came back for me."

"Of course, I did. I would never have left you. I went to the basement and found a flashlight, then persuaded that odious little toad of a manager to join me, hoping for safety in numbers."

"He wouldn't have seen them."

"We don't know how it works. No manifestation should cause this level of physical damage, yet it has. And this is the first time I've seen one myself. Perhaps they are getting stronger. Anyway, you had vanished by the time we returned, and so had the creatures."

"I locked myself in a cupboard to prepare for astral travel, and then I realised I couldn't risk my body."

"The same thought occurred to me," says Peter. "Not that I would have abandoned you."

"Have we got time to pack?"

"Five minutes only," says Peter. "It's getting darker. There's no time to lose."

#

We leave through the back entrance and throw our bags into the car, having left enough money on Peter's dresser to pay for the room. Then Peter reverses from the car park and drives like a bat out of hell towards Queensborough Terrace. We make it through Clerkenwell, but the skies suddenly darken as we round towards Hyde Park. I peer from the window towards the milky moon, barely visible in the mid-evening sky, and see a dark cloud swarming over it, thousands of wings beating in our direction. Teddy watches my gaze, whimpers, and hides his head in my lap.

"Faster," I say.

"What can you see?"

"I don't know. But it's heading our way."

Peter pumps the pedals and urges the car forwards, swearing under his breath. "I can't go any faster," he says.

I glance outside again, holding my hand over my racing heart. I am sick with fear, and Peter's erratic driving isn't helping. Since my last look, the swarm has grown exponentially, obscuring parts of the sky in a winged eclipse. It moves closer at impossible speeds until I realise it is not a swarm of birds.

"Oh, God. They're bats," I say.

"And sensing us by radar, no doubt. Great. Hold on to your hat."

Peter rams his foot on the floor, and the car lurches down the road, engine squealing. Passers-by leap from the road and cower into the side of the pavement, so brutal is the sound of the speeding car.

"You'll kill someone," I yell, but Peter is past caring. He squints into the distance, his face rictus with concentration and continues the journey at reckless speed. The bats are almost upon us. We hear the high-pitched squeaks inside the car as they slice into our auditory nerves, leaving our heads ringing. Peter winces at the sound, then swerves and hits a tyre on the corner of the road. The car lurches to one side, but Peter steadies the wheel and drives on. The bats surround us, carpeting the roof and windows like a furry cape. One by one, they flop onto the windscreen, obscuring his view. Peter activates the wiper and flips them from the glass.

"Nearly there," he says.

"Is there anything I can do?"

"No. Just keep the windows up." But even as he speaks, the bats start pounding against the rear windscreen. The canvas roof is already bowing under their weight, and it is only a matter of time before they get inside. I take my stick and prod the top, dislodging some, but soon realise that I am in danger of puncturing the rooftop, and I stop. Peter takes the next corner on two wheels, and a slew of bats tumble from the car as we arrive. He slams the handbrake on, and we sit outside number three, covered by a cloud of hissing squeaking creatures, wondering what to do next.

A light appears on the first floor, followed by another, then another. Then suddenly, the bats shriek as if on fire, falling from the car and writhing momentarily on the ground. One by one, they recover and fly away, a gigantic unravelling blanket of evil. I look at Peter. "What happened?" I ask.

The door opens, and a tall, middle-aged woman strides toward us.

"Inside, now," she says. "Chop, chop. No time to lose."

I grab my stick, and Peter takes our bags as we make our way to the handsome five-storey townhouse. The woman slams open the door and pushes us inside, then closes it behind her, throwing one bolt then another, before pulling down a shutter with pentagonal inscriptions. She mutters a few words beneath her breath and then faces us.

"Stella McGregor," she says. "You must be Constance, and I don't know who the hell you are, young man, but come inside, and we'll sort it out."

We obediently follow as she climbs the stairs and ushers us through a door on the first floor.

"Sit," she says, directing us to a cream leather settee. "Let's talk. I hope you don't mind if my concentration is not entirely with you, but I'm on watch duty tonight."

She nods towards a wrought iron surrounded balcony on which a powerful telescope stands. "I saw you coming," she says.

"Oh. I see. How do you know who I am?"

"Oliver Fox warned me."

"Of course. Is he here?"

"No, damn the man. He ought to be. I don't know what he is trying to prove waiting it out in Wimbledon. It's only a matter of time. Probably the influence of that gung-ho fool Harold."

"Hilda," I whisper to Peter.

"I know," he hisses.

"Are we safe here?"

"You're not safe anywhere," says Stella, frankly.

"Why?"

"We don't know. Crossley has a thing about you. No idea why. There's bound to be a reason, but we're currently in the dark. Glad you're here, though. We'll arrange a debriefing session as soon as possible. Of course, you can't stay long though the dog is welcome. I like dogs, and mine are boarding in the country."

"Oh. But surely, I'm safer here than anywhere?"

"Only while Crossley is on his travels. We've staved off his creatures so far, but it's a close-run thing. We need more people and must start bringing them in. But that's an internal matter and not for you to worry about. Now, how do you know Crossley?"

"I don't. I met him on the astral plane, and he seemed to recognise me."

"Interesting. I hear you've been unwell?"

"Yes."

"How enlightening. Details, please."

I sigh. I am hungry, tired and have just escaped from giant spiders and a swarm of marauding bats. The last thing I need is the mental stress of trying to recall an illness, the primary feature of which was acute memory loss.

Stella answers as if she has read my mind. "Oh, leave it until tomorrow, then. Right. First things first, I'll find rooms for you somewhere. You can unpack, and if you look hard, you'll find something edible in the kitchen. If you want something hot, you must cook it yourself. It's all hands to the deck here. Eat, then sleep, and report back here at eight o'clock tomorrow. Just you, Constance. Your friend, Johnny spare, can do as he pleases."

"Peter. Peter Tremayne," I say sniffily. "And I'd prefer it if you call me Connie."

"Whatever. Peter Tremayne. Go to the library and read or something. Stay inside. Connie, we will give you urgent psychic defence training tomorrow morning."

"Can't Peter have it too?"

"Has he been on the astral plane?"

"No, but he can see the creatures."

"Really?" Stella McGregor raises her eyebrows and regards Peter with interest. "That's new," she continues. "A pity we haven't got time to study you. But no, a complete waste of time to teach psychic defence to a novice. Right. Eight o'clock sharp." And with that, Stella McGregor waves her hand and dismisses us.

CHAPTER TWENTY-FOUR

Psychic Defence

Wednesday, October 26, 1932

I report for psychic defence training at eight o'clock the following day with an empty stomach, having managed only a few hours' sleep. I leave Peter in a rudimentary kitchen, trying to make French toast from stale bread and doubtful looking eggs, which I didn't stay around to see opened. Teddy fared better, having received the contents of a sack of dog biscuits that Peter found under the sink. Teddy is with Peter now, and I feel bereft without him. But I don't know what psychic defence training entails, and it seems I must face it alone. I take a deep breath as I push the balcony room handle, open the door, and enter.

Stella McGregor looks at her watch. "Bang on time," she says. "This one can follow instructions."

"Good." The tall, angular man standing nearby eyes me with supercilious approval. "Have you any previous experience?" he asks, fixing me with a beady stare.

"In astral travel, but not psychic defence," says Stella. "She'll need the full course."

"In a day?" His eyebrows dart upwards as he sucks in his breath.

"I am here," I say, feeling a surge of annoyance. This is worse than being patronised by Mrs Ponsonby.

"She's got a point," says Stella. "Right, gather round."

The four other occupants of the room cluster near Stella as the man touches my arm and points towards a day bed like the one in Fox's study.

"Lie down."

"Now?"

"Of course, now."

"In front of everyone?"

"Just do it. There's very little time."

Tears fill my eyes. I try to blink them away, but a solitary drop trickles down my cheek.

"Marjorie, dear. Do your thing," says Stella with a sympathetic glance.

The youngest woman in the room, who must still be in her thirties, approaches me, kneels, and takes my hand. "Don't mind them," she whispers. "We must act quickly, and neither Stella nor Roderick appreciate the finer points of patience and good manners."

"Stay focused," hisses Stella.

"Try to do what they ask you," says Marjorie. "Do it quickly and do it well. There will be time to talk afterwards, and I promise I will answer any questions you may have."

I smile, grateful for her kind words, then lay back on the chaise longue.

"Roderick will help you into the astral realm," says Stella. "Listen to him, and it shouldn't take long."

"It will be quicker with a candle," I say. "But where am I going?"

"Here," says Stella. "Don't roam. At least not until we've

200

joined you."

"I thought you were going to teach me?" I say.

"She asks too many questions," hisses Roderick.

Stella ignores him. "We will – on the other side. Marjorie. Light a candle now."

Seconds later, I am staring at the flickering flame, but I can't concentrate because of a question that is burning in my mind.

"One moment," I say.

"Yes?"

"How will you get to the astral plane if I'm using the couch?"

"We're past the point of needing it," says Stella. "And one day, you will be too. We can access the astral plane at will. Now, enough questions. Please begin."

I resume my concentration on the candle and quickly feel a surge of electricity running through my body. A few minutes, and it's done. I sit up and swing my legs over the side of the daybed, moving them backwards and forwards while watching them meld into the fabric. The action brings a satisfying sense of purpose. The five members of the Shining Path pop into astral form beside me until we are all there, nebulous ethereal bodies standing over or near to their fleshy counterparts.

"Well done," says Stella unexpectedly, and I can't help but smile at the hard-won praise. "Now, approach the balcony, but don't enter it. Tell me what you see."

"A cat," I say, eyeing a ginger moggy perched on the edge of a flowerpot and licking a paw.

"No, you don't," says Roderick.

"I beg to differ."

He raises himself to his full height and eyes me with disdain. "Don't question my judgement, young lady."

"But it is a cat."

"Strictly speaking," says Stella. "But it is also one of Crossley's creatures. Easier to deal with in daylight than the eight-legged variety you saw yesterday."

"You mean it's dangerous?"

"It won't bite your throat out, if that's what you mean," says Marjorie, hovering behind me. "They're spies, really. And quite strong in a group."

"And very difficult to ignore if you touch them," says Stella.

"How do I know it's not a normal cat?"

"That's the problem. You don't. But this cat has been on our balcony for the best part of a month. It's always here and never seems to eat or sleep."

"Can't you shoo it away?"

"You try," says Roderick.

I sigh. "I'm sorry if that was another silly question, but I don't know what I'm doing."

"He means it," says Stella. "Go outside and touch the cat. And when you do, roll the shutters down in your head. Big iron shutters, heavy and preferably in threes. And if you really want to be sure, then fix them with chains."

"I've done this before," I say.

"Really?" Stella cocks her head.

"Yes. Oliver Fox taught me. I've used the technique a few times."

"Not as useless as we feared," whispers Stella to Roderick.

"Charming," I mutter.

"We meant Fox," says Roderick curtly. "Go on then."

"Right." I take a step towards the glass, then through it and approach the cat sitting a bare few yards away. It eyes me disinterestedly.

I wave my hands towards it. The cat sees me but does not flinch and sets its mouth in a challenging grin.

"Go away," I say, gesturing dramatically. Nothing.

I rush forward. "Go. Just go."

Still, it sits there before resuming its cleaning regime as if I didn't exist. I lunge towards the cat and push it in the belly, but my hand goes straight through it. And as my ethereal body meets fur, a black tendril zips from the cat and snakes into my thoughts, flickering like a forked tongue and infiltrating the deepest recesses of my mind. I react at once and slam the metal door hard. The ends of the tendrils break and snicker away into nothingness. The cat yowls and arches its back, fur sticking out like an orange porcupine. Down comes another door, then another, and I wrap it up with a giant chain, fresh from the forge and molten hot. The cat jumps several paces backwards, stares balefully for one last time, and then stalks away. I return through the window and re-join the cult of The Shining Path.

"Good work," says Marjorie, shaking my hand. Her touch is light, like fairy kisses or the faintest zephyr.

"Well. I wasn't expecting that," says Stella McGregor. "And as for the molten metal, nice touch. I must remember that."

"She did well," concedes Roderick.

I glance around the room. The two other unnamed cult members, both male, wear encouraging smiles.

"Next test?" asks Stella. Roderick nods.

"Follow me." Stella walks through the wall and into the hallway before passing through the front door. "Stay close," she warns as I hover beside her. She waits until all five cult members are outside the property and then steps into the road. "Shouldn't take long," she says, nodding to Roderick.

And it doesn't. I hear the bats before I see them rising high on the horizon. Stella exchanges nervous glances with Roderick. "Too many," she says.

"I don't know."

"Far too many. We shouldn't risk it."

"You managed yesterday, alone."

"From inside the house."

"Backs to the wall. If it's too much, we'll retreat inside. Young lady, stay by the door and don't move. Stella and I will be on either side of you. If it's too much and you can't shut them out, fall back through the door. The pentagon will protect you. Do you understand?"

"Loud and clear," I say, with more bluster than I really feel. I am close enough to my body to feel my heart pumping and the clammy prickle of perspiration a few yards away. I watch as the bats bear down on us with a feeling of déjà vu. They surge forward and are upon us in moments. And as the beat of their wings swipes wind into our faces, their high-pitched squeaks lower our resistance as they attack our minds. This time, it is like a tidal wave – an oily black slick of despair, of soul-sucking hopelessness. And as the tide recedes, it steals our secrets, our will to live, our joy. But something deep within me activates, a primaeval, genetic, profound certainty that it doesn't need to be this way. I can stop it; I have stopped it before. Generations before me imprinted their knowledge in my blood, and I know what to do. Once again, the walls come down and this time extend all the way around, boxing in the evil slick and drowning it in a vat of milk and honey. Black turns to white, sour to sugary sweet, songbirds land, bees buzz. The sun comes out. And with a whine of disappointment, the bats fly off, hanging low in the sky as if sapped of energy. I open my eyes to find five people staring at me as if I had forgotten to dress.

"Rarely am I lost for words," says Stella. "But I wonder whether you shouldn't be training us."

\#

"I didn't know I had it in me," I say. "Not like that. I wish I'd realised I could protect myself when the bats descended yesterday."

"Step inside before they return. Come on," says Stella, and we follow her into the front room.

"To your bodies."

I approach mine, touch it, and the two parts meld as if they'd never been apart. Then I take my stick, walk towards the settee, and settle into the comfortable fabric, feeling exhausted.

Stella turns to Roderick, standing quietly nearby. He is gazing into the distance, deep in thought. "Well?" she asks.

"Strength in numbers," he mutters.

"Yes. Of course. We need her here."

"Oh, no, you don't."

My heart sinks into the depths of my stomach. That voice, all too familiar, means we have failed. Marjorie steps aside, opening my view to the doorway. Coralie Pennington is leaning casually against the side in a flared purple trouser-suit. I flinch as if burned, my breath coming in shallow pants. "You've tricked me," I spit at Stella McGregor.

"Tricked you? Don't be ridiculous. What do you mean?"

"She's Crossley's creature," I say, wielding my stick in front of me for all the good it could do.

"Oh, Connie." Coralie moves towards me, arms outstretched and eyes burning with compassion.

"Stay away, or I swear to God I will put this damn stick through your head."

Stella nods towards the blond-haired man near Marjorie, and he gently places his hand on my stick and pulls it away.

"How could you?" I hiss towards Stella, Coralie, and everyone in the room. Then, in desperation, I scream at the top of my lungs. "Peter, help."

"Stop it," commands Stella, stepping towards me. "Too much attention. The last thing we need is a visit from the police."

"Then let me go now. Let me walk out the door with Peter and Teddy, or I will shriek the place down."

"It's not what you think," says Coralie, approaching me again.

"Peter, Peter, help."

I hear a frantic scratching on the woodwork, barking, then whining before the door flies open and Peter appears.

"Look," I say, pointing towards Coralie. "She's here. Get me away."

I struggle to my feet and attempt to walk towards Peter. But before I take a second step, he smiles at Coralie. "I'll take care of this," he says.

I slump down on the couch, mouth agape, almost winded at the disloyalty of my closest, dearest friend. "You too?" I cry and put my head in my hands, tears streaming down my face. Teddy bounds towards me, trying to lick my cheeks, his hot breath panting against my skin. At least I still have one friend, albeit of the canine variety.

"Look up," says Peter, but I ignore him and keep my eyes tightly shut, blocking out the harsh reality of my world. A world in which everything I thought I knew has been turned on its head. I have no friends, cannot trust anyone, and don't know why I am here. A vision of Elys and Mrs Ponsonby pops into my head, and I feel a pang of regret at my lack of appreciation. I wish I were back in Pebble Cottage with Mrs Ponsonby suffocating me with her excessive ministrations. I long to be there, even if it means partaking of Elys' Stargazy pies.

"Connie dear, do as he says." I smell Coralie's perfume wafting towards me. She is close, perhaps crouching to my front. But I still refuse to engage. She sighs. "Very well. Don't look. But you can't avoid listening."

I could, but it would mean removing my hands from my face and putting them over my ears, which would appear childish and remove the safety of not being able to see my enemies.

"Can you leave us?" asks Coralie.

"I'm staying," says Stella.

"Me too." Peter's voice wobbles with emotion.

"The rest of you may leave," says Stella. "But stay close."

The door squeaks open, and several pairs of footsteps proceed towards the hall. I stay hunched over my lap, waiting for the worst, whatever that may be.

"I assume you know of my association with Felix Crossley," says Coralie. My heart lurches at the sound of her voice saying his name. Bile rises in my stomach as another tear slides down my face. I ball my hands into fists over my eyes so they cannot see them shake.

"I was there undercover," says Coralie. "On behalf of the Shining Path."

I shake my head. She would say that, and she won't fool me again. Her ex-husband even turned up at the hotel. Perhaps he's in on it too?

"It's true," says Stella. "Coralie Pennington is a brave woman you'd do well to emulate. She risked everything to infiltrate

Calicum Aureum and nearly lost her life in the process. Thanks to her, we know Crossley is on his way to Cornwall."

I raise my head, conscious of, but not caring about, my tear-stained cheeks. "Not true," I say. "Gay Curnock told us, didn't she, Peter, if that's even your name."

Peter sighs. "Don't be silly." He crouches beside me and takes my hand. "Yes, Gay Curnow said he was coming, but Coralie saw him leave and warned the others."

"How could you know this and not tell me?"

"I found out precisely half an hour ago," Peter says, checking his watch. "When I bumped into Coralie in the kitchen and had a similar reaction to you."

"Is this true?" I stare at Stella McGregor like a spaniel whose mistress has just kicked her, but with nobody else to turn to.

"Yes, it's true."

"But how do you know you can trust her?"

"Because Coralie Pennington joined the Shining Path during its inception in 1920, and we have known each other since school."

I stare at Coralie with a fresh pair of eyes. "Why didn't you tell me?"

"Come here," she says, staring at me as a mother would at an errant child. I rise and walk towards her. She tips my chin, smiles, and envelopes me in a bear hug. "You silly girl. As if I could ever harm you. I would give my life first."

And I sob unashamedly, this time with happy tears, as she cradles me, patting my shoulder and crooning soothing words. When I have finished, and my shoulders have stopped shaking, she guides me to the settee and settles beside me.

"I want to tell her everything," she says, lips pursed in challenge to Stella McGregor.

"Not everything."

"Enough to understand."

"Very well. No names, no pack drill."

Coralie sighs. "None of this would have happened without all the secrecy."

"The secrets are not yours to relate."

"What are you talking about?" I am so relieved to be back among friends that I am losing track of the conversation.

"I'll tell you more another time," says Coralie defiantly. "But all you need to know for now is that I was spying on Crossley from within. I was not the only double agent, and thank God Crossley was halfway across the country before one of his acolytes cornered me with irrefutable evidence of my double life. So, I got out, just in time."

Stella strides over and lifts Coralie's hair, revealing a broad welt across the back of her neck. "An inch either way, and it would have been over," she mutters.

"It's just a scratch," says Coralie irritably.

"Regardless. You must take care now that Crossley has his sights set on you. Still, you'll be safe here, and you saw how well the girl handled things."

"She can't stay," says Coralie.

"She must. Don't be ridiculous."

"He's on his way back."

"How do you know?"

Coralie sighs. "I returned earlier this morning."

"Bloody hell. Tell me you didn't."

"To his flat, not their premises."

"I can't believe he didn't find you."

"I didn't use the astral plane. I took the more traditional method – in person, by taxi."

"How did you get in?"

"I stole his keys a few weeks ago and cut a second copy."

"Good thinking. But barely less dangerous than travelling out of your body."

"No one was home. I know their movements well. Crossley's acolytes spend their days at HQ and nights at the flat. As long as I didn't arrive too early while they were sleeping off the excesses of the night's depravities, I knew I'd be safe."

"But what did you hope to gain?"

"Detailed knowledge of his movements. He intended to

spend a few weeks in Cornwall before a slow trip back to visit old haunts. But I knew that he'd react when they told him about me. I thought he would return, but not this quickly."

"How did you know if the flat was empty?" Stella narrows her eyes, scrutinising Coralie like a sergeant major searching for dust on a uniform.

"Crossley sent a telegram to mistress number three, currently in favour for the first time in a while. He cycles through them, you know. But that's another story. Anyway, Crossley wrote of his plans to take the 9.30 from Plymouth and is undoubtedly closing in on London as we speak."

"Then you're right. Connie can't stay, and neither can you."

"Quite."

"Astral travel is out of the question. You must go quickly and far. Any ideas?"

Coralie sighs and purses her mouth in thought.

"I know a place," I say.

"Where?" Stella shoots a concerned glance as if she can't trust me to think for myself.

"I'd rather not say if you don't mind. The fewer people who know, the better."

"Not Cornwall," says Stella.

"Obviously."

"Or anywhere south or west of London."

"I'm not stupid."

"Will anyone guess?"

"I doubt it. But what do I know? I'll tell Coralie when we're on the road, and if she disagrees, she can choose somewhere else."

"I'll send someone for my car," says Coralie.

"No need. I parked mine outside." Peter, quietly sitting while stroking Teddy's ears, speaks commandingly.

"Good. I don't feel much like driving. But we must go at once."

"Keep in touch," says Stella. "And I'm sure it goes without saying that neither of you must set foot on the astral plane."

"Naturally."

"Well, good luck." Stella nods at Coralie and awkwardly shakes my hand.

"Thank you. Come now." And just like that, I am following Coralie with the same confidence as when we first met.

CHAPTER TWENTY-FIVE

Netherwood Bound

Thursday, October 27, 1932

We pull up at the end of the long driveway I last saw during my astral travels the previous year.

"Well, well," says Coralie. "Good thinking, Connie. But how did you know?"

I contemplate telling her about the deeds I had found in Mrs Ponsonby's secret closet but resist the urge and shrug my shoulders.

"Wait here," says Coralie, slamming the car door shut and heading towards the front door. She pushes it but meets resistance, then takes an elegantly heeled foot and slams it into the bottom of the door. The wood splinters, and the lock pops free. Coralie extends her arm, palm up, gesturing for us to remain where we are. After a few moments, she reappears.

"Should be safe," she says. "But cold and uncomfortable, and I wouldn't look too hard if you don't like spiders. Did I see a couple of picnic blankets in the boot?"

"Yes. And a waterproof cape."

"Good. We'll need something to keep us warm. Peter, bring in the bags, then pop off and find some food, there's a dear. Connie, take Teddy inside."

I grab my stick and move my stiff limbs, flexing my feet to lessen the effects of the journey. Cora and I trail inside while Peter disappears up the drive. We walk through a heavily dust-coated hallway, and Cora, leading the way, turns left towards the drawing-room.

"Don't go in there," I say, remembering the deep hole in the floor that seemed to go on past the foundations.

"Gosh, I'd forgotten. How do you know about that?"

"I've been here before and saw the remains of the attic room, too. It belonged to the Order of the Crescent Moon."

"Shouldn't be possible. You were only a child."

I stop walking and stand stock still. "What do you mean?"

Coralie turns towards me with her eyes fixed on my face. "I've said too much. When were you here?"

"Last year. By astral travel."

"I should have guessed. I'm surprised you suggested it as a safe place after seeing traces of the old enemy."

"I knew it was empty and that no one has been inside for decades."

"Come on then. Let's find somewhere to make a fire."

"We need to talk."

"First things first, Connie. It's been a long day."

#

Having checked the structural integrity of the stairs and disregarded our concerns, Coralie instructs Teddy and me to carefully relocate upstairs while she searches the basement for anything that might make our stay more comfortable. I unleash Teddy, and he adopts a shadow-like presence close to my side while I creep up the rickety staircase hoping that Coralie's assertion that they are safer than they look is correct. I peer into the bedrooms, finally settling on what must have once been a guest bedroom as the least worst option. Opening the one remaining curtain, I survey the room. An old four-poster bed still lies intact, its canopy long gone but hopefully capable of supporting the weight of an adult female and her dog. I test my theory by sitting on the moth-eaten, yellowing mattress and whistle through my fingers. Teddy bounds onto the bed, and I lie backwards, staring at the ceiling rose while he squirms under my arm. I must have been more tired than I realised, as a panting sound suddenly wakes me when Coralie dumps a pail filled with wood onto the bare floorboards.

"Look what I found," she says, holding a box of Bryant & May safety matches. "And that's all that remains of an old packing crate." She nods towards the pail with an expression of satisfaction.

"Your poor heels," I murmur, pointing to deep scratches running up her stilettos.

"Good point," she says before taking one shoe and then the other and snapping the heels off, which she hurls in the fireplace.

"You've chosen well," she continues. "It's not the Ritz, but we should be comfortable enough when Peter returns. Do you know how to set a fire?"

I shake my head ruefully. "Sorry."

"No matter. Have a look for some more blankets."

I head straight towards the main bedroom, remembering the wardrobe from my last visit and the collection of Freemasonry regalia inside. Perhaps I will find a coat or cloak that might protect us from the worst of the cold? The door still hangs from the frame, exactly as I remembered it, but when I reach for the Masonic apron, it crumbles at my touch. I persist and stick my head into the musty void, and my efforts are rewarded when my hand alights on a fox fur coat. I slip it on and lift the collar, marvelling at the warmth. It's a perfect fit, and I keep it on while completing my search of the room. Little remains of the wardrobe contents, save for a pair of ladies' walking shoes which I rescue, hoping they might fit Coralie. I am about to return to the guest room when a deep-seated instinct propels me right, and I find myself outside the nursery door.

I open it to see the familiar wallpaper and dusky pink curtains still hanging by a thread and make my way towards the dust-coated photograph I couldn't quite see during last year's astral travel expedition. Picking it up, I wipe years of dust from the glass with the hem of my dress to see, once again, a family of three, husband, wife and six-month-old child, a girl judging by the clothing. I run my finger along the smooth glass, noting the dog collar around the handsome man's neck and the haunted eyes of the wife beside him. Yet the picture is joyful – a happy family group enveloped in love. I draw the curtains, look from the window across the bramble strewn lawn towards a stone balustrade, and compare it with the photograph in my hand. It's there in the background, faded but discernible. This little family stood there all those years ago, exactly where I'm looking now. Yet they are gone, their house a crumbling mausoleum, their possessions little more than dust. Who are they? Where did they go? And why did they leave this beautiful old house to deteriorate from lack of care? I think about the attic room altar and the symbol belonging to The Order of the Crescent Moon, and nothing feels right. The vicar and his family seem so ordinary that I can't believe he lived a life of subterfuge. The thought of him entangled with the mysterious organisation that ultimately became Calicum Aureum seems ridiculous. His simple life and the secret attic room are too incongruous to be related. There must be more to it. I refuse to believe he is evil.

"Connie." Peter's voice snaps me from my reverie. I thrust the photograph into the pocket of the fur coat I am still wearing and graze my hands on a piece of cold metal.

"I say, Connie. Where are you?"

"Here," I yell, making my way towards Peter, with an anxious Teddy at my side, unwilling to let me out of his sight.

"Bloody hell, damn double damn." Peter lets loose an uncharacteristic stream of invectives, and I emerge on the landing to see him clutching a brown paper bag, his face grim and ashen.

"What happened?"

"The banister I was just holding is lying in the hallway, and I'm jolly lucky not to be with it. This place is a death trap."

"What's wrong?" Coralie's voice bellows down the landing.

"We really shouldn't be up here."

We wait while Coralie stomps towards us, her walking gait awkward from wearing broken shoes. She peers over the galleried landing and into the hallway. "Worse than I thought," she says.

"It's a death trap," Peter repeats. "Seriously. I'm not doing this again."

"Then we'll be very uncomfortable," says Coralie. "There's a hole the size of the garden where the drawing-room used to be, and the rest of the house is stone floors and spiders."

"Apart from the study," I say.

"Study?"

"Next to the drawing-room."

"Is it safe?"

"Yes. And the second set of steps rising to the attic room is still intact."

"I don't think we'll be going up there," says Coralie firmly. "But you're right. I underestimated the damage to the main stairs. Peter, Connie, set up camp in the study, and I'll start bringing our stuff downstairs."

"I'll wait here," says Peter. "You can pass it to me. I'm not leaving you to go it alone."

I take Teddy to the study, marvelling at Peter's assertiveness under pressure. For a quiet librarian, he is slowly coming into his own. And now that I have navigated the heartbreak of disloyalty only to find I was wrong and my enemies are really my friends, my confidence has grown too. Coralie has let slip a childhood connection to Netherwood. And as soon as we've eaten, I mean to have it out with her and make her tell me. But as so often happens, my plans go awry.

#

After a hair-raising descent downstairs with firewood and blankets, Coralie finds a sweeping brush and sets us to work on the study. An hour later, blankets, coats, and an old floor mat from the basement cover the once dusty floor. We cluster around the fireplace, devouring the food Peter purchased from a nearby shop in Westgate Street as if we hadn't eaten for days. I am still wearing the fox fur coat, but the fire is roaring nicely, and I may need to remove it soon.

"Feeling better?" asks Coralie.

"I wasn't feeling unwell," I say.

"I mean, not as upset as you were."

"Not now that I know the truth about your part in this, but the one thing I don't understand is how you can be in two places at once."

"I'm sorry?"

"You were supposed to be visiting Mrs Ponsonby. That's why I panicked and left."

"Oh, I see. Yes, I was, but it didn't happen. Not with all the shenanigans at Calicum Aureum. I couldn't leave, so I sent a telegram to Vera. She replied rather curtly. I must have disappointed her."

"I'm not surprised. She hasn't been well and would have enjoyed a visitor."

"I know." Coralie turns her head and blinks a few times. Her eyes are red when she speaks again.

"Why don't you tell me what you've been doing on your travels? You could have knocked me down with a feather when I heard you were in London."

"It's a long story," says Peter. "You tell it, Connie."

"Well," I say. "It all happened when I met a soldier."

I regale Coralie with the facts surrounding the poisoned partridge case, but Peter clicks his fingers when I mention the telegrams. "Ah, yes," he says. "You promised you'd show them

216

to me."

I reach for my handbag and extract my notebook together with the telegram clippings and handwritten copies.

"Have you got a pen?"

I hand him a pencil, which is the best I can do, and then stare at him, waiting for a response.

"Carry on," he says dismissively, so I continue my story from my time in Croydon to my meeting with Ellen Yeomans, Peter's arrival, and our subsequent escapades around London.

"It sounds thrilling," says Coralie. "Just like old times."

"What do you mean?"

Coralie sighs. "So many secrets. I know Vera would disapprove, but things have changed, and I'm sure you won't tell her."

"Of course not."

"We were private detectives once."

"No." I stare at Coralie with my mouth hanging open. I can easily imagine her as an investigator, but I must assume she refers to Mrs Ponsonby when she says' we'. Stout, solid, mother hen Vera P looks more like a retired headmistress than a private eye.

"Oh yes. Talk about a stratospheric rise. We started our careers in the typing pool of the London County Council. But Isobel often involved herself in less than straightforward matters, and if things became complicated, she invariably sent us to sort them out."

"Isobel?"

"Isobel Smith."

"That name sounds familiar."

"It should. She's… never mind."

"I say. This is jolly interesting," says Peter.

"What is?" I snap, angry that he's just interrupted Coralie as she was about to reveal something noteworthy.

"This telegram."

"What about it?"

"The name. J Hartigan. It feels like it should be an anagram."

"The best minds of the police force and national media have worked on this for months," I say sharply. "The best they can come up with is Raj Hating, and it doesn't help, does it?"

"Then they need to think laterally."

"If you say so. Coralie – what were you telling me about Isobel Smith?"

"Only that she started us off in a sleuthing direction, and when we left her employ, Vera and I set up on our own. Ponsonby and Cream, professional lady's detective agency," she says, her eyes drifting far away to the past.

A thousand questions churn through my mind, but her revelation has literally struck me dumb. I watch her incredulously while trying to form the words to encourage her to divulge more. "But how has it come to this?" I mutter.

Coralie's reverie breaks. "To what?" she asks.

"To you being married and Mrs Ponsonby caring for me."

"My dear Connie. You were our last case."

Her words leave me reeling. "Tell me. I must know everything."

"I can't. Or rather, I will, but not now. I must speak to Vera first. I've already said too much, but I am not a fan of secrecy, and I have never been. Two of us bear the responsibility, and I will not let Vera down, in this respect, at least. Ask as much as you like, Connie, but I won't say any more about that aspect of your life until Vera agrees."

"But you implied a connection to Netherwood."

"I did, and there is one. I'll say more in the fullness of time."

I grind my teeth in frustration – so close to the truth but thwarted again. I try asking more in various ways, but Cora is unwavering in her refusal to answer. The fire is blazing now, and Teddy stretches out contentedly in front of the grate. The weight of the fox fur coat is too much now that the room is warmer, and I heave myself to my feet and remove it, folding it over the arm of the chair. Peter and Cora look up as we hear a tinkling noise on the floor and a metal object rolls towards the bookcase. Peter stands up and retrieves it.

"Is it yours?" he asks, thrusting a bracelet towards me.

"No," I say. "But it's rather familiar. I've seen something very like it."

"Let me look." Coralie all but snatches it away and holds it close to the candle we are burning as dusk draws close.

"I've got it," shouts Peter.

"Filthy thing," says Coralie.

"I'm sure I've seen a similar bracelet," I muse, ignoring the pair of them.

"Connie. It is an anagram."

I turn away from Peter and watch as Coralie surreptitiously slips the bracelet into her coat pocket. She thinks I haven't seen her, but I remember why the silver object is so familiar just as she turns to face me. I rummage in my handbag, remembering the promise I made to Dolly about the bracelet I had found in the cave. My hands close over it as Peter jumps up and thrusts a piece of paper under my nose."

"Connie. Are you paying attention? I've figured it out. Look." He points to a row of capital letters. J HARTIGAN DUBLIN.

"Why have you written it like that?"

"Because the sender posted it from the Hibernian Hotel in Dublin. The letters rearrange to the words, Jubilant Harding."

"So what?"

"Jubilant meaning happy and Harding being…"

"Oh no. You can't be serious."

"Yes. Who do we know called Harding?"

"Sebastian's friend, Tony."

"Also, a close friend of Hugh Chevis."

"I don't believe it."

"Well, you should. I tried it a different way, writing J HARTIGAN as JAY HARTIGAN. Guess what that returns?"

Goosebumps prickle my skin as I watch Peter's earnest face. "I don't know," I say, fearing the worst.

"It reads TRY AGAIN A J H."

And he doesn't need to explain, for I already remember

Tony's full name. Anthony John Harding. "I must contact Sebastian," I say, and Peter nods grimly.

CHAPTER TWENTY-SIX

Alerting Sebastian

Friday, October 28, 1932

I barely slept a wink last night and rose at dawn feeling miserable. I had too much on my mind for restful sleep, but as my eyes grew heavy in the early hours of the morning, I felt the familiar tingling of bodily separation and immediately plunged my hand into a jug of water to shock myself into instant wakefulness. It did the trick, but far too well. Even a gentle doze became impossible, and instead, I replayed all the clues about my former life that Coralie had started but did not finish.

Peter snores gently in the corner of the room, and I try not to wake him as I ruffle Teddy's fur and encourage him towards the door. I open it gently, retrieve the fox fur coat, and cast my eye over Coralie's watch as we pass by. It is a little after six o'clock. I open the rear door with the clunky iron key still standing sentry in the lock despite the long years. It opens with a groan and a squeak and would undoubtedly benefit from a good slug of oil, but it is still functional, unlike the rest of the house. Teddy trots off to one of the few flatter areas and relieves himself while I consider the prospect of locating the exact place where someone took the family photograph. But a few steps in, I realise the brambles are too high to go further without risking damage. Instead, I sit on a low wall and watch Jim's little spaniel as he snuffles through the grounds, excitedly nosing at all the fresh smells. Teddy's wanderings take him towards the side of the house, and I spy a little door in the red brick walls. Grabbing my stick, I negotiate the uneven paving across the rear of the house and make my way towards it, hoping I can get inside. The door is unlocked and creaks ajar, filling my nostrils with stale, mildewed air. I shake my head, take a deep breath, and fling it open to its fullest extent.

Stepping forward, I find myself in a storage room. Decaying goloshes line the floor while moth-eaten waterproofs hang like bats from strategically placed nails. A lopsided shelf holds a cricket bat, a hockey stick and an old cardboard box containing metal hoops. An old perambulator is rusting at the back of the room. I peer inside, but thick webs block my view. Pulling the coat over my hand, I clear the worst of it away and a spider darts across my arm, but it doesn't bother me. I am disappointed to find the pram empty. Not so much as a solitary blanket remains. It is just a carcase – a glimpse of what might have been. I don't know what I expected to find. A child's plaything, perhaps? Or an item of clothing. Something to understand more about the family who once lived here, who I feel attached to through the photograph.

Teddy has returned and is snuffling in the corner by the side of an old wooden box. He whimpers excitedly, scrabbling at the ground. I heave it away from the wall, jumping back in shock as a mouse streaks towards the door. Teddy follows, yapping loudly, and I still my racing heart. When I have recovered, I open the lid of the box and feel a surge of joy at the sight of piles of books. They are not works of fiction. These books are spiritual, some concerned with religion and others with ethics. One is a journal, and I open it with a beating heart, hoping for pages of diary entries, but am disappointed to find it almost empty. Almost, but not entirely. Someone has written a name on the inside flyleaf. Michael Farrow. I wonder who he is. The vicar, perhaps? I clutch the blank journal to my chest, feeling a strong connection to the name, and decide to keep it. Squatting by the side of the box, I am searching through the remaining books when I hear a voice in the distance. I leave my post and hasten to the back door, where Coralie is muttering to herself.

"There you are," she says. "Don't go wandering off alone, Connie. We're not home and dry yet."

"I know," I say. "I had to fight like a tiger not to end up on the astral plane last night."

"Gosh. I didn't think of that. It could have been disastrous."

"Well, it wasn't, but I can't always stop it."

"I hope I haven't misjudged the situation."

"What do you mean?"

"We'd have been better off staying with Stella if Crossley wasn't halfway back to London. And better off in Cornwall without the risk of running into him. Our stay here will be brief. We'll leave tomorrow if I get the right answer from HQ."

"How? There's no telephone, and I doubt the postman delivers."

"I'll send a telegram and collect the reply later today."

"Oh, good. I was wondering how to contact Sebastian. I'll do the same."

"Is that wise?"

"Yes. He's in terrible danger. His best friend is a killer. I must tell him."

"But is he?"

"You heard Peter. Or perhaps you didn't. Perhaps you were too busy hiding that bracelet."

Coralie has the good grace to blush. "Oh. About that. Look, you'd better come inside, and we'll talk."

I whistle for Teddy, and he runs towards me, then straight

through the open door and into the house.

I follow behind, and we return to the study, where I spend the next few moments picking decade's worth of dust and debris from the bottom of my skirt.

"Well?" I say, fixing Coralie with a glare.

"Breakfast first," she says.

"There isn't any."

"Yes, there is." Peter stirs and reaches beneath a blanket. "There are a couple of bread rolls and some cheese in there. I'll go out again later."

"No need," says Coralie. "We've telegrams to send. Then we'll be off again on our travels."

"Where?" asks Peter. "I need to get home if I still want my job at the library."

"We'll leave once Stella confirms that Crossley's back in London," says Coralie.

"But what about me?" I ask uncertainly. Going home is appealing, but it's probably not the safest option.

Coralie and Peter exchange glances. "Bosula is out of the question," says Peter. "And Croydon too, for that matter."

"Then it must be Pebble Cottage. At least you'll be with Vera. If only she weren't so ill."

"What's wrong with her?" I ask.

"She'll tell you herself," says Coralie.

"I doubt it. Mrs Ponsonby goes to great lengths to keep anything meaningful from me."

"Only because she cares."

I snort. "She's controlling," I say.

"She's also very ill, but nobody will protect you the way Vera will. Home it is," says Coralie.

"Not yet," I say.

Cora looks at her wristwatch. "The post office will open soon."

"Not for at least another hour. Show me the bracelet."

"Coralie sighs and retrieves it from her pocket. I search for my bag, rummage in the bottom, and pull out its twin, holding it against the one in Cora's hand so she can see the two together.

"Where did you find that?" she snaps.

"In my cave. Look. They're identical."

"I know. In your cave, you say? In Porth Tregoryan?"

"Yes."

Coralie wanders towards the window and stares outside.

"What does it mean?" I ask.

"It means you shouldn't go home," she says.

"For goodness' sake," Peter exclaims irritably. "Why ever not? It's only a bracelet."

"Look at the inscription." Coralie thrusts the bracelet towards him.

"It's only a pattern. Lots of bracelets look like that."

"On the inside."

Peter turns it towards the light. "Oh," he says.

"Quite. A unicursal hexagon. One of Crossley's people owns this little beauty."

"But it's been in the cave for ages. I found it last year."

"Then they must know where you are. But they can't. Unless…"

"Unless what?"

"Unless it's a coincidence."

"That sounds unlikely," says Peter.

"Not really. The problems between Stella McGregor and Felix Crossley have been rumbling away for years." Coralie is fiddling with her beaded necklace and looking thoroughly disgruntled.

"Tell me about it," I say. "Please."

"I don't know what Calicum Aureum does with its operatives," says Coralie. "But we've had Shining Path members in position since the great schism – sleeper agents lying dormant until required. We knew Crossley was up to no good. The stronger he got, the more precautions we took. Crossley wants power and domination. He is an evil man driven by the worst excesses of human behaviour. We have played a very long game, but Crossley may have had the foresight to do similar."

"By placing one of his people in Porth Tregoryan? Why would he? It's the back of beyond. I could understand it if it was a city."

Cora doesn't speak. Her eyes dart across the room as she considers my words. "A double agent," she says.

"Sorry?"

"We don't use real names outside of headquarters," says Coralie. "We have a register of code names and locations, committing real names to memory. Nobody knows of our affiliation to The Shining Path. Not even our nearest and dearest. My former husband, bless his cold little heart of stone, knew nothing of my connection to Stella and her organisation. He still doesn't, and he's a politician with friends in high places. But just suppose someone has listed the location of our operatives. Then it makes sense to send a Calicum Aureum member to root them out and discover their true identity."

"But if that's the case, they don't know who they're looking for."

"Quite. So, it should be safe for you to return."

"And I suppose your operative must be Mrs Ponsonby?"

Coralie nods. "She's one of them and sacrificed everything to take care of you."

"Why? Why am I so important?"

"Another time. Now, I mean it. Don't ask again. I'm going to send that telegram."

"And I'm coming with you, though what I'll tell Sebastian, I don't know."

"Be careful. Sebastian might still be with Harding," says Peter.

"I'm not risking that," I say. "I'll address the telegram to Bodmin barracks. It's the only safe thing to do."

CHAPTER TWENTY-SEVEN

Going Back to my Roots

Monday, October 31, 1932

I am back home in Porth Tregoryan, having arrived in the early hours of Sunday morning. Peter drove through the night; Coralie having ascertained that Crossley was back in London with no imminent plans to move. Prevaricating throughout Friday and Saturday, she finally decided that me being under the watchful eye of Mrs Ponsonby was the best protection we could hope for. Ordinarily, I would have railed against this. I have always considered Vera Ponsonby an interfering, domineering barrier to my chances of enjoying life. But I have missed Pebble Cottage and its occupants more than I expected, and surprisingly that includes Mrs P.

I have barely seen her since waking up this morning. When I passed the parlour, the door was firmly closed, and Coralie and Mrs Ponsonby talked in hushed tones. Sorely tempted to slip into a purposeful dream walk, I refrained, knowing I must not do it without The Shining Path's protection. Safety in numbers is the order of the day.

"What's got your goat?" asks Elys as I stare at the door waiting for one of the women to emerge. I know they are discussing me, and Mrs Ponsonby, who has only suspected my astral travel abilities up to now, can be in no doubt of the extent of them. I stare at Elys irritably. I am desperately trying to listen from my seat at the dining table, but I can only hear the odd word when their voices rise. But there is no chance at all if Elys is going to chat. She does not take the hint.

"I said, what's bothering you?" she asks. "I thought you'd have lots to tell me, and you've barely said a word."

"It's complicated," I reply.

"Oh. Too tricky for a country bumpkin like me to understand," she huffs.

"That's not what I meant."

"Just don't give Mrs Ponsonby any bother."

"I wasn't going to. Why?"

"She's ill, as you well know."

"So, everyone keeps telling me. But what is wrong with her?"

"I expect she'll tell you when she's ready," says Elys.

"Doubtful. But never mind." I drop the subject and try to eavesdrop again.

"Your doctor friend went to Scotland," says Elys.

I sigh. "Kit Maltravers?"

"Of course. Who else?"

I shrug my shoulders. "On holiday?"

"No. He's there for the next six months. His uncle is poorly and needs someone to run his surgery. No locum, you see. Anyway, Kit has gone."

"What about us?" I ask.

"Dr Arnold will cover while Kit is away. He's a pleasant man."

But not as easy on the eye, I think, though I don't say it. I wouldn't want Elys to know how much I admire Dr Kit.

227

"I'm sure his uncle will be grateful," I say instead.

Elys stops dusting and leans forward with her elbows on the table. "That's as maybe, but someone's not very happy about it."

"Who?" I ask half-heartedly. I'm not in the mood for gossip.

"Charlotte Napier, that's who," says Elys triumphantly.

"Really." My head whips around, and I temporarily forget all about the pow wow next door. "Do tell," I say, eager for more.

"She kicked up a right stink," says Elys. "Proper teasy, according to Clara Bow."

"Clara, who?"

"One of the maids up at Briarwood."

"Her parents' house."

"Quite."

"You have spies everywhere," I say, and Elys grins.

"They were dining with Colonel and Mrs Napier when Kit got the news about his uncle. He summoned a manservant to send a telegram telling the old man not to worry and that he would see him right. Well, Charlotte kicked up a terrible fuss, stormed upstairs and locked herself in the old nursery. Kit left the house alone. She saw him off at the station a few days later, but I hear it was a frosty affair. No kiss, no good wishes, just stony silence. And your friend, slippery Edgar, is coming to see her this weekend."

I shudder. "Doubtless, he'll be sticking the knife in," I say, "loathsome creature. Poor Kit. And he's only trying to help someone out, after all."

"Everyone says she is showing her true colours," Elys continues.

I can't resist a smirk. Charlotte Napier's behaviour has been perfect and ladylike almost the whole time I have known her. But I have never forgiven her for calling me a poor little cripple, and her friends were so unpleasant that Mrs Ponsonby felt moved to defend me. Charlotte may look and sound like an angel, but she is far from it. That others have seen the mask slipping is very satisfying.

I am about to ask Elys for details when the parlour door

opens, and Mrs Ponsonby appears.

"Connie, please come in," she says, and I follow behind with a sense of impending doom.

#

"Sit down," says Mrs Ponsonby, gesturing to the settee. I duly oblige and sit quietly, watching the two women perched like bookends on the armchairs and feeling as if I am about to be interviewed.

"So, I've wasted all these years trying to ignore your potential for astral travel," says Mrs Ponsonby. "Why didn't you tell me?"

"Why didn't you?" I retort.

"Touché." She smiles before her face drops as she clutches her stomach.

"Take this," says Coralie Pennington, passing her a brown envelope. Mrs Ponsonby pops a pill and continues.

"Though there was always a strong chance you might have an inherent ability to dream walk, we didn't know whether you would or not. If we said anything, you might have tried and succeeded. So, we decided to stay silent and keep the subject at arm's length."

"Is that why you don't like newspapers?"

"Partly," says Mrs Ponsonby. "Newspapers publish far too much nonsense, and on a quiet news day, they delve into matters they don't understand. Gutter press, most of them – I've seen all sorts of nonsense about spirits and mediums, so yes. I kept you away from anything that might lead you in that direction. But I don't like newspapers anyway, and I've better things to do than wade through columns of bad news."

"But anyone could have mentioned it."

"Did they, though?"

"Not until I met Oliver Fox."

Mrs Ponsonby squints at Coralie and raises an eyebrow.

"You know the one. You searched for Connie at his house in Croydon."

"Is that...?"

"Yes. He's not a Shining Path member, but that may change. Don't worry. You weren't to know."

Mrs Ponsonby scowls, and I feel an inner gloat. She's very fond of keeping secrets but not so happy when I hide things from her.

"Be that as it may," she continues. "People tend not to talk of such matters, and we kept it secret for most of your life."

"Bully for you," I say. "It's bad enough being lame, but to grow up as a freak, an oddity, knowing that other people don't run across cliff tops in the middle of the night – you might have spared me the worry."

Mrs Ponsonby leans forward and puts her hand on my knee. "I'm sorry. I have made many mistakes with you, my dear. But I only did what I thought was best."

I place my hand over hers, a warm benevolence displacing my surge of ire. "I know. I'm sorry too. But now we're here, won't you tell me more?"

Mrs Ponsonby nods. "I'll tell you a little more, but we are awaiting instructions from on high."

"The Shining Path?"

"Higher than that."

"The British Army – psychic division?"

"I won't ask how you know of its existence, but you appear very well informed." Mrs Ponsonby turns to Cora and opens her mouth.

"No, I didn't, before you ask," Cora says huffily.

"She didn't," I confirm. "And I can't reveal my sources."

"It doesn't matter." Mrs Ponsonby's eyes are flecked with red as if she is suffering from lack of sleep. As if on cue, she yawns. "Excuse me," she says. "Now, Connie. I promised you an explanation, but you must accept the limitations of what I can tell you. We'll get the serious stuff out of the way, and then you can accompany me to Newquay. I must collect a prescription, and I would appreciate your company."

I almost laugh at the absurdity of a shopping expedition hot on the heels of hearing the answers I have pined for most of my life. But I nod my head in acceptance of her terms.

"You came from Netherfield," she says. And I am not surprised. Not one bit. I reach into my handbag where I stowed the photograph that I took from the outhouse.

"Is this my family?"

I pass a picture of the vicar and his wife, and Mrs Ponsonby takes it.

"Perhaps, I never met them," she says.

"Surely you know their names?"

"No. I don't. You were four years old when you came to us after several attempted abductions."

"Of me?"

"Yes. It was only a matter of time until they succeeded. Your parents handed you over in desperation, fearful of losing you forever."

"Why would anyone want to take me away from my parents?"

"I can't answer that."

"Can't or won't."

Mrs Ponsonby's mouth sets in a thin line.

"I see. And you brought me to Cornwall."

"We didn't know what to do with you at first. We considered putting you up for adoption, but your parents wouldn't hear of it. We almost took you to Switzerland, but then Robert Pennington proposed to Coralie, changing everything. I didn't want to continue running our agency alone, and we'd had you with us for several weeks by then. We grew fond of you, Connie. And when Cora decided to marry, I contacted your parents and suggested that I take you on myself. They agreed on the condition that I change your name and that we keep it secret. They broke all contact to keep you safe, and Coralie and I were not permitted to see each other publicly again. We had worked as a pair and would be less easy to identify apart. Stella McGregor was instrumental in liaising between your parents and us."

"But why? What had she got to do with it?"

"Connie, dear. We thought you might have natural talents in astral travel because your mother belonged to The Order of The Crescent Moon."

"Oh no, so did Crossley. Please tell me she isn't like him?"

"She is not. Don't forget that The Order of The Crescent Moon was the predecessor to both Calicum Aureum and The Cult of the Shining Path. They separated in the 1920's schism. Those of Crossley's persuasion followed him. The others, like Stella McGregor, went in the other direction."

"Which way did my mother go?"

"She didn't."

Cora walks toward me and takes my hand while Mrs Ponsonby leans forward. "I'm sorry to tell you that your mother died about a year after you came to live with us."

"How?" I can feel my lip wobbling as I force the word out.

"In an explosion at Netherwood. Your father packed up and left immediately, never to return."

Tears prick my eyes, and I bite my lip, trying to stem the flow.

"There, there," says Coralie.

"Did my father ever try to find me?"

Mrs Ponsonby shakes her head. "Not because he didn't love you, but because he did. He couldn't risk them finding you."

"Them who?"

"Not now, Connie."

And I accept her reluctance to continue. Vera Ponsonby has revealed vast swathes of my life that I thought I might never know. And I am extremely grateful. She could have left me with strangers, but instead, she took me in and sacrificed the best years of her life to keep me safe.

"Is that why you called yourself Mrs Ponsonby?" I ask.

She nods. "I was going to masquerade as your mother," she says. "But somehow, it seemed disrespectful to her memory. By the time I had decided against it, I'd already introduced myself as newly widowed Mrs Ponsonby for a bit of respectability."

"I am grateful, truly grateful," I say. And I mean it. Mrs

Ponsonby has kept her secret well, and I no longer resent her overbearing attitude, recognising it as her attempt to keep me safe. But now I have a secret of my own. Mrs Ponsonby doesn't know my father's name. But I took the blank journal with the name inscribed on the flyleaf, which could belong to him. At least it's something to go on. I know my mother is dead, and I will grieve quietly in my own time. But Mrs Ponsonby didn't say anything about the death of my father. Could he still be alive?

CHAPTER TWENTY-EIGHT

Collapse

Mrs Ponsonby and I pass the journey to Newquay in mutually agreeable silence. I am still reeling from the earlier revelations, my mind processing each new fact and fitting it into the patchwork of my earlier life. As Mrs Ponsonby's idiosyncrasies begin to make sense, I find myself flushing with horror at my previous ingratitude toward her. Part of me wants to throw my arms around her and endlessly apologise. But the stiff formality of our relationship up to now stops me in my tracks. She would be as embarrassed as I would, and I must find another way to express my appreciation.

I can't help staring at her as she gazes unseeingly out of the window. I don't need her to confirm that her mind is elsewhere, probably computing how much danger we are in, which makes this trip to Newquay all the more surprising. I am still watching when she suddenly turns her head and catches me in a full stare. I blush and look at my lap, not knowing what to say. But she speaks first.

"Connie, dear. I hope our earlier conversation hasn't left you too shocked."

"No. I'm relieved if anything. I just wish I'd known sooner."

"But you understand why we couldn't tell you?"

"Yes, I do."

"And I know you have more questions, but now is not the time."

"Of course," I say, wondering why she has brought the subject up during a public bus ride if I cannot mention it.

"Good girl."

The bus pulls in within sight of the chemist, and I dismount first before helping Mrs Ponsonby down the stairs. The small act of reaching for her hand and guiding her safely to the pavement is a turning point in our relationship. Up to now, she has looked after me, even when I didn't need it. But today, for the first time, she's deferred and allowed me to assist her. I feel good about it, more able to deal with my limitations, yet uneasily wondering why she feels weak enough to allow it. Or perhaps it is ultimately a show of strength, a willingness to give me my independence.

We amble towards the chemist, and I am grateful that she keeps to my pace instead of charging off in front, which has often been her way. And when we arrive, she walks to the counter and asks me to choose a few pairs of new stockings. The chemist takes his time attending to her prescription, and Mrs Ponsonby looks an unhealthy shade of grey by the time she meets me at the front cash desk.

"Are you alright?" I ask.

"Fine, dear." She reaches for the stockings and thrusts them towards the teller.

"That's all," she says curtly before handing over a few coins.

"I think we'd better stop for a cup of tea," says Mrs Ponsonby as we exit the building.

"Not for me, thank you," I say, thinking of the drinks that Elys made for us moments before we left.

"We should, Connie. I'll treat you to a cream cake."

I am about to tell her that I'm not hungry when she winces and a cry of pain slips from her lips.

"Are you well, Mrs Ponsonby?"

"I'll be fine," she mutters. "I just need to sit down."

"Take my arm," I say, and she reaches toward me, then collapses to the floor at my feet.

"Mrs Ponsonby. Oh, no. What's wrong?"

I drop to my knees, my stick rolling towards the road, but I don't care. Mrs Ponsonby is lying at my feet, her face ashen and her breathing shallow. Fear clutches my heart.

A man clears his throat beside me. "Can I help?" he asks.

I try to speak, but the words won't come. Instead, I gulp and swallow back tears.

"Shall I fetch a doctor?"

I nod my head and reach for Mrs Ponsonby's hand, clutching it to my heart as I try to remember some basic first aid. Then, I hear a familiar voice, and to my utter relief, Isla Tremayne puts her hand on my shoulder.

"Goodness me," she says. "Out of the way, dear."

She kneels beside me and gently slaps Mrs Ponsonby's face. "Vera, wake up," she says, brusquely. Mrs Ponsonby doesn't move.

Isla snaps open her handbag, reaches inside, then removes the stopper from a bottle of smelling salts and places it under Mrs Ponsonby's nose. It works. Mrs Ponsonby coughs and opens her eyes.

"Where am I?" she asks weakly.

"Don't move, dear," says Isla. "You've had a nasty turn. Stay still, and we'll get you sorted in no time." Isla turns to face the growing crowd of people clustering around Mrs Ponsonby. "Now, does anyone have a motor vehicle nearby?"

"I do," says the man who offered me help.

"Where?"

"Over there." He points to a shiny black car parked only feet away. "That will do very nicely," she says.

"Shouldn't we call an ambulance?" asks a young woman,

neatly dressed in the local tea room's grey uniform.

"No," says Mrs Ponsonby loudly. "I don't want a doctor."

"Don't worry," says Isla. "You can come with me. You and you," she continues, pointing to two young men. "Help me get her up." They duly oblige, and Mrs Ponsonby cooperates with them to the best of her ability.

"Where to?" asks the middle-aged man.

"Compass House," says Isla. "I'll direct you. Connie, sit in the back with Vera. Keep her upright."

I squeeze into the car and gently put my arm around Mrs Ponsonby's shoulders, feeling both protective and intrusive at the same time. But she doesn't seem to mind and smiles at me through half-glazed eyes.

The short drive to Compass House takes less than five minutes, and between us, we get Mrs Ponsonby through the door and onto the day bed in the drawing-room.

"Are you sure you don't want a doctor," asks Isla once the car owner has gone.

"No. Please can you fetch me a glass of water? I've just picked up my prescription, and I'll feel much better once I've taken it."

"Connie, come with me," says Isla as she leaves the room.

I follow her towards the kitchen, and she stops as soon as she is safely out of earshot.

"How has she been?" Isla asks.

"Not very well," I say. "I've noticed her wince in pain once or twice, but she doesn't talk about it."

"Do you know what's wrong?" she asks.

"No. Do you?"

Isla doesn't respond. She fills a glass from the kitchen sink. "Connie, at the risk of offending you, can you make yourself scarce for a moment or two?"

"I suppose so," I say uncertainly. "Do you want me to leave the house?"

"Of course not. Go and sit in the orangery, or better still, look through the bookshelf in the pigsty my son calls his bedroom.

"I will," I say, relieved. I would far rather spend time poking through Peter's magnificent book collection than sitting stiffly in their formal garden room.

Isla retreats to the drawing-room while I climb the stairs and locate Peter's room. Of course, he is not there, and I lose no time in ferreting through his books. I select a dog-eared copy of The Great Gatsby, which I have read before and turn to a few chapters before the end, hoping that I will finish before Mrs Tremayne calls me downstairs. I shuffle onto Peter's bed and recline against his pillows. But as I rest my stick against his bedside table, it slips and knocks a half-empty glass of water which slops down the sides. I quickly strip a pillowcase and wipe away the mess, opening the drawer of his bedside table to check that water hasn't seeped inside. The sight that meets my eyes stops me in my tracks and sets my heart racing. Nestled into the top of Peter's drawer is an envelope addressed to me in a familiar hand. My heart lurches as it triggers a memory, and I recognise the handwriting as Jim's. I snatch the envelope and eagerly read a letter from Jim and an enclosed note from his mother. And I am back, back in Seaford, watching Jim walk towards Grace Duff's house. Memories trip left and right, children, a broken gutter, a vision of Crossley. I am almost there, reaching out for that last little piece of information that will tell me what happened to Jim when the door flies open, and Peter rushes in.

"Oh, God. You've found it," he says.

CHAPTER TWENTY-NINE

Convincing Sebastian

Wednesday, November 2, 1932

I will never speak to Peter again. Not if hell freezes over. He says he only took the letter because he hoped I'd forget how to dream walk and wouldn't find my way back onto the astral plane. He did it to protect me, he insists, yet in doing so, he robbed me of the opportunity to find Jim. And arriving in his bedroom with terrible timing, which couldn't have been worse if he tried, he also distracted me from the memory I was on the verge of reclaiming. The critical moments that might have led me to remember what happened to Jim after leaving the Duff house in Seaford slipped through my fingers. If I felt charitable, I might understand that Peter couldn't appreciate the importance of Jim's letters naming the humble seaside town to which Grace Duff relocated in an attempt to escape her past. But now I know that Jim was there, I finally have a starting point in searching for him. I haven't told the police yet. I want to give them a complete story and must patiently wait for that last memory to return. This will also give me time to think about what to tell them. They won't believe anything I say if I start regaling them with talk of astral travel. Not unless one of them is a member of The Shining Path. I make a mental note to ask Coralie if they have any police operatives. And I will also confide in her about Jim as soon as we get an opportunity to talk. This is not currently an option. Mrs Ponsonby has been in bed since she arrived back at Pebble Cottage, while Coralie has split her time between nursing Mrs P and several trips to Newquay, which, based on a few words overheard outside the bedroom door, involves public telephone boxes. Something is afoot.

I am mulling over what it might be when a shadow looms against the parlour window, and I see a tall, handsome soldier outside. It's Sebastian, and I rush to the door before Elys gets there first and haul him into the parlour, taking full advantage of Mrs Ponsonby's bed rest.

"Did you get my telegram?" I ask eagerly.

"Yes, I did," he says curtly, taking a seat on the couch.

"Well?"

"I'm not impressed. I nearly didn't bother with you, Connie. It's a low trick to play on a chap."

"What?" I am baffled by his attitude. I was expecting some level of gratitude, not a dour expression of pique.

"You should know better than to play with my feelings. Hugh was a good man and a close friend."

"Which is why you need to know the truth."

"What truth?"

"I told you in the telegram."

"It tells me nothing except that you don't know what you're talking about, and you have some sick desire to hurt me."

He unfurls the crumpled piece of paper containing my message. I snatch it up and re-read it. "Tony Harding killed your friend. You are in danger. Avoid him at all costs."

"Oh, I see. I haven't expressed myself very well."

"You haven't explained yourself at all."

"Give me a chance, Sebastian. It's important."

Sebastian looks at his wristwatch. "You have ten minutes to convince me, and then I'm leaving."

"That should be enough. Please wait here for a moment."

I hobble upstairs as quickly as I can, having left my stick lying on the parlour floor. I remove my notebook from its hiding place and return downstairs.

"Two minutes and counting," says Sebastian bristling with hostility.

I ignore it and retrieve Peter's anagram workings with trembling hands.

"Look," I say. Sebastian examines the papers, checks, and double-checks the letters, and then leans back with a sigh. "If, for one moment, I believed this contrived attempt to make the facts fit your theory, I would need an answer to two questions. Why would Tony kill his best friend, and why, having done so, would he risk a capital sentence by purposely leaving a clue?"

"I can't answer the second question," I say, honestly. "But the first is easy. I visited Ivy Thorne at Basil Mansions."

"I'm surprised she spoke with you," says Sebastian. "She's quite the tartar."

"Well, she did. And what she said was enlightening. Forgive my bluntness, but Tony spoke pretty frankly about certain aspects of Hugh's life, and with hindsight, he was probably baiting us."

Sebastian scowls. "Stop editorialising. Just get to the facts."

I ignore the burn of anger, clench my fists, and try again. "Ivy said that Frances Chevis was seeing a gentleman friend in London."

"Yes, we know. Nothing new here," says Sebastian irritably.

"And Ivy is adamant that he wasn't a chauffeur."

"Good. We can safely rule out at least one per cent of the population, then."

"But she says that whereas Frances knew the name of Hugh's lady friend, she kept her escort's name secret."

"So?"

"So, why would she do that?"

Sebastian narrows his eyes as he considers the question. He is silent for a moment. "I don't know," he says. "Perhaps she was embarrassed."

"Why would she be?"

"She might if he was an employee."

"I don't think so. Their relationship was very open. She'd already conducted affairs with working men."

"Point taken. So, what's your theory?"

"That the reason for keeping it secret from her husband is that he wouldn't condone it."

"But he always turned a blind eye."

"How would he feel if she was seeing you?"

"I beg your pardon. Exactly what are you implying?"

"Nothing. Please just think about it and answer the question honestly."

"Hugh wouldn't like it. Affairs were one thing, but he expected loyalty from his friends. Oh, I see what you're driving at."

"Exactly. Don't you think it's a possibility? It's the only reason for secrecy in an open marriage."

"So, you think that Frances was having an affair with Tony?"

"Yes. Where was he last year?"

"In England," says Sebastian. "But I still can't believe it. Do you remember that meal we had together? Tony told us all about their marital arrangements. Why would he bother if he was her lover?"

"To throw us off the scent," I say.

"And he helped enormously with the telegram," Sebastian continues.

For a moment, he has me, but I think of an explanation which I announce with a click of my fingers. "Whoever wrote that telegram was clearly showing off," I say. "They desired recognition and were announcing their cleverness to the world."

"Or their stupidity," says Sebastian.

"Does Tony show off?"

"He's competitive," Sebastian admits. "And a touch arrogant. But really, you have no proof."

"I know. But I had to tell you. You might be in danger."

"What are you going to do with this information? Will you leave it with me?"

"No. I should tell the police."

"They won't believe you."

"Probably not. And I know my theory is flimsy, at best. I may be able to prove it under the right circumstances. But for reasons I can't reveal, now is not the time."

Sebastian shakes his head, and I fear I am down to my last chance. There's nothing more I can say without discussing my dream walking abilities or why I can't currently use them. But Sebastian unexpectedly offers an olive branch. "Look. I can hardly believe this of Tony. We've been so close, and he's never shown the slightest interest in Frances Chevis outside of our friendship with Hugh. But you're right about the affair. Hugh wouldn't have minded anyone else – he didn't have a jealous bone in his body. But we were like brothers – the four musketeers. And yes, he would have felt differently if her lover was one of us. Give me time to ask Drake's advice, and then I'll speak to Tony."

"You can't tell Tony. Who knows what he might do?"

"I must give him a chance to explain himself," says Sebastian. "It's the least I can do. And when I have, I'll come and see you. If Tony can't convince me of his innocence and you still want to tell the police, I'll support you."

"I don't know. Telling him is risky."

"Those are my conditions," says Sebastian, and with that, he turns on his heels and leaves.

CHAPTER THIRTY

A Surprise Visitor

Thursday, November 3, 1932

I potter around the kitchen with Teddy whining at my heels. For once, I am alone, which would ordinarily fill me with joy, but my head is still spinning, and I cannot settle. Coralie has taken Mrs Ponsonby to visit Mr and Mrs Potts, hoping it will cheer her up. She left her bed and dressed in a neat two-piece suit with a modest slash of lipstick which made me think her health must be improving. But Mrs Ponsonby is nothing if not stoic, and I noticed her wince in pain when she thought no one was looking. She is putting a brave face on it, whatever 'it' may be.

I contemplate poking around her room while she is out. It's probably locked as usual, but I can't bring myself to check when she is so obviously ailing. I know there are more secrets to discover – she told me that herself. But now that she has opened up to me, I can't bring myself to cheat. And I owe her my loyalty as she gave me hers. But the mature nobility of my

244

decision is no distraction from my restless state of mind. A maelstrom of suppositions whispers in the quiet corners of my subconscious, leading me down endless rabbit holes. Is my father alive or dead? Should I try to find him? And what does Crossley want with me?

I make a cup of tea and cradle it in my hands as I sit at the table, trying to think things through. If only Mrs Angwin hadn't selfishly tripped over the garden step, Elys would be here for a distracting chat. Goodness knows what Coralie and Mrs Ponsonby would say if they realised I was still alone, but they'd only just left when Jory pulled up in his cart to give me the news. Fortunately, her mother isn't too badly injured, and Elys will be back within the hour, well before they return from the Potts' - a good thing as I wouldn't want her getting into trouble. Besides, what possible harm can I come to in my own cottage in broad daylight?

I stir the tea distractedly as if the act of twirling a teaspoon for no apparent reason might magically provide me with answers. But Teddy objects to my inactivity and starts pawing at my leg. I consider letting him out into our little walled garden, but I begin to feel claustrophobic and decide that a walk in the fresh sea air will do us both the power of good.

I shrug into my warmest coat and take Teddy's leash for effect. He doesn't need it as he did in Croydon, where the roads were busier, but I like to have it with me just in case. I unlock the door and make my way slowly towards the beach. Teddy runs off with a joyful bark as soon as he sets his paws on the sand. But I don't worry as he will find me as soon as he has finished sniffing. He won't have any difficulty catching up with me. Nor, for that matter, would an over-encumbered snail. Fleetness of foot will never be mine outside of astral travel. A shiver runs through me at the notion of dream walking, spiky fears of danger competing with joyful memories of running, arms outstretched along the cliff tops. How can something so pleasurable be so dangerous? I am deep in thought about esoteric matters when I hear the crunch of pebbles behind me. I ignore it at first, assuming it comes from a late-season tourist, but suddenly a hand grips my shoulder. I spin around in fear to see the handsome features of Drake Mallard. He is smiling at me, his eyes twinkling with mischief.

"I thought it was you," he says.

"Well, hello. What are you doing here?"

"Meeting Sebastian," he replies, glancing at his wristwatch. "He's late, of course."

"Has he spoken to you?" I ask, hoping I won't need to impart the bad news about Tony.

"About what?"

"Nothing. I'm sure he'll want to tell you himself. Then why are you meeting him?"

"Because he asked me to. He wants my advice but won't say why over the telephone, so I hot-footed it down here first thing this morning."

"Why did he want to meet you here instead of at the barracks?"

"I was wondering that myself."

"Perhaps he intends to see me afterwards," I reason. "Shouldn't you go back to the hotel and wait for him?"

"Probably," says Drake. "But it won't do any harm to make him wait for a while. He might be more careful about his timekeeping in future." Drake cocks his head and gives an unmistakable wink.

"Is it usually this empty?" he says, casting an eye at the deserted beach.

"Only out of season. But we get the occasional walker."

"That's a pity. I'd like to discuss something privately."

"Not a problem," I say. "Let me introduce you to my cave. I have chairs, blankets and all the books your heart could desire."

"Spot on," he says. "Lead the way."

I escort him to the cave, and Teddy comes bounding over to see us. But usually, he doesn't come inside, preferring instead to patrol the mouth of the cave. Drake and I sit down and pull blankets over our knees. He reaches into his coat pocket and produces a hip flask, which he places on the sand beneath his legs.

"What do you want to talk about?" I ask.

"The meaning of life," says Drake languidly.

"Very amusing."

"No, seriously. Have you ever been in love, Connie?"

"Well, yes, I think so." And suddenly, I know so. My heart flips, and an unashamed burn of desire leaves me craving Jim's touch. To hear his voice, feel his lips on mine. I did love him. How could I have forgotten? "Yes," I repeat firmly.

"It bloody hurts, doesn't it?"

"Yes."

"Especially when the love of your life throws you aside for a man who doesn't deserve her."

"Oh, dear. I'm sorry to hear it. But you never know. Perhaps she will see the error of her ways."

"No. It's done for good and as dead as a bloody dodo."

Drake reaches beneath the chair. "Here. I don't have a glass, but it's getting cold. Have a nip of this?"

I raise the bottle to my lips and swallow.

"What is it?" I ask, wiping moisture from my lips with the back of my hand. It's not very ladylike, but Drake's drink tastes as if it has gone off, and I cover a grimace beneath the gesture.

"Just a little concoction of my own. A cocktail if you like."

"I don't," I say, honestly. "You may want to revise your recipe."

"Funnily enough, that's what Ellen said."

"Ellen?"

"The cook."

"You've lost me."

"I do hope so."

I rub my eyes. Suddenly, I feel drained. Wiped of energy and desperate for sleep. And to cap it all, there is a strange, metallic taste in my mouth. I lean back and try to raise my hand, but it flops to the side and hangs limply from the chair.

"Shouldn't you find Sebastian?" I slur.

Drake Mallard pats my arm. "No point. He isn't coming."

Drake turns his head and smiles at me, a rictus grin bearing no affection or friendship. Only the satisfaction of a job well done. And at the top of his nose, where it meets his forehead, I see a smudge of black – a dirty fingerprint. I know how it got there and that knowledge is enough to send me hurtling back into the other world.

CHAPTER THIRTY-ONE

Flight

Keep your eyes shut, tightly shut, I mutter as I separate from my body and cross the astral realm. I know I shouldn't be here, but there is no choice. My body is already a distant memory. I left it collapsing, shutting down, my life leeching away – a barely controlled dream walk, my only chance of survival, but with the full knowledge of leaping from one danger to another. *Don't think about it, Connie. Don't think about him.*

Time slows, and I settle down until I am still, and daylight spreads a welcome glow through my closed eyelids. I risk it and open them, relieved that I have passed through the astral realm without falling prey to Crossley or his creatures. I wonder why I have passed through unscathed, and then I understand, for I have descended outside the bungalow where Hugh Chevis died. Ellen Yeomans is standing there, waiting for something. She is chatting to a woman I recognise as Frances Chevis. I have fallen through time. Hugh Chevis is still alive, the couple still residing in the bungalow at Deepcut. Can I stop death, or is it too late?

A painted van trundles by, inscribed with the word "Colebrook's." It slows and stops beside Ellen, and a young man hops out, carrying a wrapped parcel.

"Thank you, Mr Noyes," says Ellen.

"You can call me Bill," he replies, tipping her a wink.

"The cheek of it," says Ellen, scowling.

"He's being friendly," says Frances. "Now, put them straight into the meat safe and start on the menu."

"Yes, ma'am," says Ellen. I watch as they walk up the path side by side. Frances goes in, and Ellen squats by a concrete box attached to the wall. She opens it, places the package inside, and then follows her mistress through the door.

I make my way up the path and examine the safe, but it is a perfectly ordinary piece of masonry with no redeeming qualities. I am about to enter the house when I feel a quiver of uncertainty as a pall of gloom descends. The sky darkens without warning leaving me feeling exposed and vulnerable. I run towards the corner of the front garden and squat behind a broad tree, with an inexplicable urge to hide while knowing that no one can see me. It is a good decision. Within moments, a car pulls up and parks a few yards away from the house, neatly concealed by a row of shrubs. And a man dressed in a chauffeur's uniform emerges, his cap pulled low over his face. He briskly walks towards the front door, and I expect him to ring the bell, but he does not. Instead, he swiftly drops to his haunches and opens the meat safe. Then, quick as· a flash, he withdraws a syringe and jabs it into the packaging, squeezes and leaves as quickly as he came. I stand and crane my head through the hedge, desperate for a closer look. But just as he reaches the car, time stands still. A flock of birds, dark as a thunder cloud, swoop from the sky in a flailing black mass. They move towards the uniformed man, coming closer and closer, yet he doesn't see them. They travel quickly, but he barely moves. Then, with a burst of energy and a flurry of feathers, they are gone. And in their place is Felix Crossley, all six foot two of his towering jowly frame bearing down on the oblivious man. Crossley stops and rotates his head from side to side, nostrils aquiver. Then he stares into the eyes of the chauffeur, who, without knowing why, removes his hat. Crossley takes a slender index finger and marks the man's forehead with a dark fingerprint. "Good job, well done," he purrs. And the merest trace of a smile passes across Drake Mallard's lips.

#

I flail forwards in shock, dropping through the hedge and landing noiselessly on my knees about twenty yards from Crossley. He cannot hear me and is facing the other way. But he stops suddenly, and his head jerks from side to side. Then he turns, nostrils flaring as he sniffs the air like a giant snake. A slow grin spreads across his face.

"She is close. So close," he says. And I turn to run, and then logic stops me in my tracks. Hugh Chevis dies today, which means that I have fallen backwards in time to 1931. But when I left Pebble Cottage this morning, the year was 1932. Crossley cannot hurt me now, or I wouldn't have made it that far. Which means I escape. Running across the astral realm would put me in unnecessary danger. I must think of another way out of trouble. And I do.

I quietly pick my way towards the house and into the first quiet room I find. I wait for a moment to be sure that Crossley hasn't followed, and then I close my eyes and ride the wave of darkness back to my future again, not knowing what I will find.

It is a slow, torturous journey. I can't feel Crossley, and I don't stop to check if he's around. But I am crawling through the astral realm. Time has trickled to a grindingly slow pace. I am moving, but only just and then, to my horror, I stop. I'm far from home, and I know it – everything feels wrong, and my body must be a considerable distance away. The customary little breaths, heartbeats, and flashes of adrenalin are absent, and I am stranded in space, unsure where or even if I exist. Having no other choice, I open my eyes.

God help me, but it is dark. Not a solitary spark of anything resembling light. I raise my hand, but I cannot see it. If I closed my eyes again, it would make no difference. But I am not blind. I am stuck in limbo, existing, waiting, perhaps even dead. Please, no.

Then suddenly, an intense flash of light slices through the blackness, and I wake spluttering, my lungs screaming for air. Someone is thumping my back, and I have been violently sick. My mouth tastes of seawater, and my hand clutches the dregs of a glass of something resembling the contents of a rock pool. The unconscious body of Drake Mallard lies beside me, a pool of blood collecting from a deep head wound.

"You're alive. Thank God for that," says a feminine voice. And just as I slip into a welcome faint, the familiar face of Roxy Templeton looms towards me.

CHAPTER THIRTY-TWO

The Beginning of the End

Roxy bloody Templeton. Who knew that she would be my saviour? Her face was the last thing I saw before passing out, and she is the first visitor allowed into my room when I wake in Dr Arnold's sanatorium on Narrowcliff Road two days later. I had only been awake for an hour when she arrived, and I was trying to find out what had happened to me when I saw her loitering outside my ground floor bedroom window. Coralie and a pale looking Mrs Ponsonby were sitting by my bed, trying not to answer my many questions when Roxy turned up. "Oh, dear God. Tell her to go away," I had said as soon as I saw her. But Coralie had shushed me and let her inside.

We are now awkwardly waiting for someone to speak. I prop myself up, take a mouthful of water, and decide that it will be me.

"Well? Will somebody tell me what's been happening for the last few days? And why I am here rather than Pebble Cottage?"

Coralie looks at her watch. "Soon," she says.

"Not good enough."

"Well, you're clearly feeling better," says Roxy. "And in a good temper too. Oh, and you're welcome."

"What?" I snap.

"No need for excessive displays of gratitude," she says, smiling smugly.

"Thank you," I mutter, with all the enthusiasm of a marooned mollusc waiting to die on the sand.

"As I said, the pleasure is all mine."

Silence descends – a lot of silence. I sigh. "Please. I must know what happened?"

"There they are," says Mrs Ponsonby sounding relieved. She points outside the window, and my heart leaps at the sight of Peter, Elys, and Teddy. A moment later and they bowl through the door. Teddy hurls himself onto my bed, eagerly licking my face, while Peter disgraces himself by hugging Roxy. I swallow a queasy feeling of disgust and make room for Teddy to curl under my arm.

"Is that everyone?" asks Roxy.

"Not quite. But it will do for now." Coralie jumps to her feet and closes the door. "First things first. Let's get your Hampshire adventure out of the way, shall we?"

"How do you know I was in Hampshire?"

"You've been talking in your sleep. Not to mention the many questions we've had to field from the local constabulary after that blasted soldier tried to kill you. Thank goodness for Roxanne's swift actions."

"Which were?"

"Feeding you seawater. The little sewer rat tried to poison you, but luckily Roxanne was nearby and slugged him over the head with a plank of wood. You vomited the poison, and she called a passing tourist who alerted us, and the rest is history."

"What happened to Drake?"

"He's recovering from his wounds in Bodmin jail."

"Wounds?"

"I called Sebastian to tell him what happened, and he

254

intercepted Drake while they were transferring him to prison. Two swift punches later, Drake was sporting a cut lip and a broken nose. But it did the trick, and in the time it took for the local plod to break them up, he'd told Sebastian everything, which earned him another punch. I hope Sebastian doesn't get into trouble," says Peter ruefully.

"But how did you know what happened?" I say, thoroughly perplexed. I don't know the half of it, and Peter wasn't even there, yet they seem to know more than I do.

"I told him," says Roxy.

"How did you know?"

Roxy sighs. "I followed you and listened outside the cave. I could hear your conversation, although I couldn't see you. Otherwise, I might have realised he'd put something in that drink. But I'd no reason to suspect – he wasn't one of them."

"One of them?"

Mrs Ponsonby and Cora exchange glances, and then Cora nods imperceptibly.

"A Calicum Aureum agent," says Roxy.

"What here? In Porth Tregoryan?"

"I feared so."

"Why should you care?"

"She's one of us," says Mrs Ponsonby.

"Surely not? Then why are you so foul towards me? I thought you hated me?"

"I wanted to keep you out of the hotel," says Roxy. "But that can wait. Let's finish this business with which you've unwisely involved yourself. I've been around the block long enough to know when someone travels the astral plane. Where were you, and what were you doing?"

I stare around the room, realising that all my closest acquaintances are here with me now. They've just heard her mention dream walking, but how many of them know about it? Surely, not Elys?

"Now, don't be coy," says Roxy, taking command of the situation. "Speak up. You're among friends."

Her curt tone gives the opposite impression, but Elys raises an encouraging smile, and I assume that if she didn't know about my abilities before, she must do now. I quickly describe my encounter outside the Chevis bungalow, and Roxy nods her head.

"I'm not surprised about Crossley," she says. "Now, Peter. Given our earlier conversation and your chat with Sebastian, what do you conclude?"

"Well, Connie. You've certainly solved the Chevis murder," says Peter. "From what Drake told Sebastian, it went like this. Drake was posted to Woolwich barracks, where he saw a lot of Frances. At first, they met as friends, but it soon became more. Their encounter was just another in Frances' long line of affairs, but Drake was in love and wanted her to leave Hugh Chevis. Naturally, Frances refused and broke off the relationship. Frances had always been careful to keep the affair from Hugh as he valued his friendships, especially with the four musketeers. So, Drake had masqueraded as a chauffeur to keep things quiet. One day, he arrived at their bungalow out of the blue when Hugh was away from the barracks. At first, Frances was pleased to see him, but when he demanded that she leave Hugh or he would kill him, Frances sent him away, this time for good. That was several months before Hugh's death."

"He must have been watching their house," I say. "He knew the partridges were in the meat safe."

"He was," says Peter. "He planned the murder to the smallest detail, so furious with Frances by then, that he didn't care whether he killed her or Hugh. But on the way back to London, he clipped a cart with his car, and the horse bolted, causing a scene. The police pulled him over, and he'd changed back into his military uniform by then. He didn't want to risk drawing further attention to himself, so when they asked his name, he gave Tony's instead."

"Did Frances know?" I ask.

Peter nods. "Not about the name switch, but she must have guessed that Drake was the murderer. Frances accompanied her husband to Frimley hospital, where he died. She was also showing poisoning symptoms, but they were minor – she may have even been pretending. But she kept a cool head and sent her servants back to the bungalow to remove all traces of her affair and dispose of any evidence of poisoning."

"To protect Drake Mallard?" asks Coralie.

"No. To protect her reputation," says Peter. "That was very important to her. When she returned to London, she telephoned Drake and asked him if he had poisoned her husband. Drake denied it, but he had a few days' leave due and decamped to Ireland, where he decided to take steps to protect himself. Only Frances knew what he'd done, and she would not risk public ridicule. The police had pulled him over, but if they remembered the encounter at all, it would be with a soldier named Tony Harding. So, Drake decided to reinforce this by sending a couple of telegrams which, if properly decoded, would spell out Tony's name."

"How cunning," I say. "And how unexpected. More fool him that the anagram was too tricky for the police to crack. What a shame – I liked Drake. He was perfectly charming. I wonder why he changed?"

"Crossley's mark," says Roxy.

"On Drake's forehead? But he did it after he'd poisoned the partridge."

"Who knows how it works?"

"You're right, though," I say. "Crossley marked Annie Hearn and Grace Duff. But why?"

"Because he's wicked and getting worse. Crossley wants absolute power and believes it comes from death and destruction. He toys with people. Murder is a game." Roxy is pacing the room now, her face set with grim determination.

"That's enough," says Mrs Ponsonby through gritted teeth. She reaches for my hand. "Don't think too hard about it. You haven't fully recovered."

"She needs to know," says Roxy.

"Not now."

"Please tell me," I say. "It's worse not knowing."

"Don't..." Mrs Ponsonby looks pleadingly at Coralie.

"Oh, my dear," says Cora pityingly. "We will protect her. You know we will."

"And you will, as you always have," I say, smiling encouragingly at Mrs Ponsonby, hoping she will stop resisting their attempts to impart information. I need to know the truth; however hard it will be. But when she speaks, it floors me, and I immediately wish the words had remained unsaid.

"I won't be here to help you," says Mrs Ponsonby. "I am dying, Connie. My time is close."

"No. It can't be true."

"It is, my dear. But Coralie will protect you."

"We all will," says Peter, positioning himself on one side of the bed while Elys sits on the other. They reach for my hands, but I pull away, holding them over my face and covering my tears. I try to speak, but I can't. I want to tell Mrs Ponsonby that I'm sorry for all the worry I've caused, for my cold and selfish behaviour. But she smiles at me, love shining from her eyes. And she doesn't need to speak for me to understand that she forgives all my misdemeanours as she would if she were my real mother. I sob almost uncontrollably, and the room falls quiet as my friends watch over me. Then, a sudden sharp rap at the door interrupts us and my head jerks up.

"Who is it?" I whisper.

"Don't worry." Mrs Ponsonby squeezes my hand.

Roxy makes for the door, opens it a fraction, and then fully. And in steps Stella McGregor.

"Have you told her yet?" she asks without preamble.

"Not everything."

"Then I suggest you get on with it."

Coralie clears her throat. "I hoped for more time," she says.

"There is no more time. Tell her."

"Tell me," I echo.

"Connie. I haven't been honest or frank with you," says Coralie. "Not entirely and mainly because I hoped it wouldn't come to this. But things have moved quickly, and now there is no choice. Your father was a vicar, and his brother, your uncle, fell in with a bad crowd – particularly a young man who influenced him in terrible ways. He abandoned his family and all his principles for the sake of this man, who promised him power and worldly wealth. He joined a sect, an order not unlike ours but dedicated to evil and committed to sacrificing the one thing he cared about but had never met. A niece born of a man of God and a woman he had once known and loved. Unknown to her parents, he offered up this child, but they thwarted his plans at the eleventh hour. And the child, you, Connie, survived."

"And the man?" I ask the question, knowing the answer before it arrives.

"Felix Crossley," says Cora.

"How long have you known?"

"Does it matter?"

"Yes. You keep everything from me. I can't trust anyone."

"Yes, you can," says Peter. "Everyone in this room is here for you. We all know the risks."

"And now there's a new one," says Stella McGregor. "Crossley left this at our headquarters this morning, hence my telegram." She pulls out a folded purple cloth and shakes it free, and I stare at the unicursal hexagram on one side with the sun on the other and a dagger in between."

Coralie and Roxy gasp, riven with horror.

"What? What does it mean?" I cry.

Stella McGregor steels herself, her face a frozen mask of worry. "It's a formal declaration of war," she says grimly. "We're all in grave danger. Every one of us."

THE END

Thank you for reading The Poisoned Partridge. Unusually I have little comment to make on the true crime on which this book is based. My research has revealed nothing significant, though I found some of Frances Chevis actions suspicious. I hope you liked this story, and if you want to find out more about my books, here are some ways to stay updated:

Join my mailing list or visit my website for a **free** novella
https://jacquelinebeardwriter.com/

Like my Facebook page
https://www.facebook.com/LawrenceHarpham/

If you have a moment, I would be grateful if you could leave a quick review of The Poisoned Partridge online. Honest reviews are very much appreciated and are useful to other readers.

The Constance Maxwell Dreamwalker Mysteries

The Cornish Widow
The Croydon Enigma
The Poisoned Partridge

Also, by this author:

Lawrence Harpham Murder Mysteries:

The Fressingfield Witch
The Ripper Deception
The Scole Confession
The Felsham Affair
The Moving Stone
The Maleficent Maid

Short Stories featuring Lawrence Harpham:

The Montpellier Mystery

Box Set containing
The Fressingfield Witch, The Ripper Deception & The Scole
Confession

Novels:

Vote for Murder

Printed in Great Britain
by Amazon

10840899R00153